Universal Chronicles
ECLIPSE
2992

CRIMSON ECLIPSE

CRIMSON ECLIPSE

Written by
Dan Lee

One Garden Publishing

To the person I'm becoming. Every page is proof that I didn't quit.

And to every reader who dares to dream beyond the horizon—may you always find your courage in the dark and your hope in the stars.

PROLOGUE

A year has passed since the Extermination, a galaxy-wide campaign of terror orchestrated by the cybernetic tyrant Galgorn. Entire planets were reduced to ash, solar systems destabilized, and millions were lost in a calculated bid to sow chaos and fear. Though the immediate threat has passed and the galaxy breathes in the illusion of peace, the cost of survival weighs heavily on those left behind. The war may be over, yet the scars still shimmer across the stars, silent reminders etched in the black.

Evander stands alone within the observation dome of the rebuilt colony on Arigold, the headquarters of the Universal Peacekeeping Federation (UPF). He is surrounded by the faint hum of life-support systems and the soft crackle of static from distant comms. Beyond the glass, the void stretches endlessly, scattered with the wreckage of shattered hulls, drifting satellites, and fragments of a thousand untold stories.

The reflection staring back at him in the glass feels like a stranger, his brown hair having lost its lustre, his green eyes hollowed by sleepless nights, his uniform crisp yet weighed down by invisible burdens. Feeling much older than his 25 years, the man who once stood tall in command, now lingers like a ghost of his former self. He presses his palm to the cold surface, tracing the faint outlines of distant debris. '*That's all we are now,*' he thinks. '*Fragments trying to remember who we used to be.*'

The memorial broadcast begins, a low chime followed by a solemn voice that fills every corridor of the colony. Lines of light shimmer to life across a massive holo-wall, names scrolling endlessly upward, hundreds blending into thousands. The glow washes over Evander's face, each name carving another ache into his chest. Somewhere among them are friends. Mentors. Strangers who trusted him to bring them home.

Then comes the voice that steadies the silence, Angelica's. Her image fills Evander's thoughts. Strong, slender, and poised, with intense green eyes, a kind smile, and her dark-brown hair always worn in a loose bun. At 26 years of age, she seems to have the wisdom and grace of someone much, much older.

Angelica's clear voice carries the subtle tremor of someone forcing strength through grief. Her words echo through the hallways, a eulogy for the fallen, a promise that their sacrifices will not be forgotten. Yet beneath the composure, Evander hears what only someone close to her can hear: the weight behind her calm, the fracture behind every measured breath.

He closes his eyes, letting her voice fill the emptiness for a moment longer. The hum of the station softens, as if the world itself were listening. One by one, the lights across the colony dim as the ceremony reaches its end, leaving only the faint blue glow of the stars reflected in the dome's glass.

When the final name fades, silence reclaims the room.

Evander stays where he is, hand still on the window, whispering into the dark, "Rest easy… all of you."

Outside, a fragment of metal catches the distant sunlight, a ghost adrift among the stars.

~~~~~~~~

The following morning, the memorial's echoes still linger in the air. The UPF Academy's marble halls shimmer with renewed polish, yet every reflection carries yesterday's grief. Beneath banners of blue and silver, the living gather once more; not to mourn, but to move forward. And though Evander tries to stand among them as an officer again, part of him still drifts somewhere out there, among the debris and ghosts he's left behind.

And though the stars shine indifferent above, Evander knows the echoes of yesterday will follow him into whatever comes next.

CHAPTER 1

The morning after the memorial dawns pale and quiet, as though the light itself fears to intrude. Within the large marble hall of the UPF Academy, solemn footsteps echo between towering columns engraved with names of the fallen. Holographic plaques rotate slowly along the walls, casting waves of blue light over the assembled officers, honoring those lost in the battle of last year.

Evander stands among them, uniform pressed, expression unreadable. Around him, others whisper the practiced words of remembrance, but his mind isn't in the room. It lingers in the static of a broken transmission, his father's voice cut off mid-sentence, lost to the chaos of that final battle. Every syllable has become a ghost that refuses to fade. Though he has taken time to heal, the pain remains, lingering as an invisible scar. Still, he reminds himself that he's here, and that duty must carry him forward.

At the front of the expansive room, Angelica Tenah's voice rises above the hush, calm, deliberate, and authoritative. Yet beneath it something brittle trembles. Traditionally, an admiral would lead the address, but this year the Council has chosen Angelica instead, the youngest mission-captain to survive the Extermination and the one whose ship carried more refugees to safety than any other.

Now promoted to the rank of Captain, she hasn't sought the honor; it's been placed upon her as both recognition and reminder.

"We gather not to reopen old wounds," she begins, tone steady despite the weight in her chest, "but to ensure they heal into something stronger."

The light from the holo-plaques glints across her dark hair as she continues, gaze sweeping the silent crowd. Her address is heartfelt and inspiring to all in attendance. Finally, she pauses and glances slowly across the room, intent on making eye contact with each person in attendance before concluding, "Let their memory remind us of what we stand for, and what we can still become."

When the final echo of her speech fades, she exhales quietly, almost imperceptibly, then continues with the formality of command. "I'll be taking a brief leave," she announces. "A few days to clear my head before the next assignment."

Her gaze flicks toward Evander. "In the meantime, Lieutenant Guryon will oversee the arrival of our new recruits."

The ripple of acknowledgment through the crowd feels distant to him, as if he's underwater, hearing the world through layers of memory. He nods, because that's what duty requires.

When the ceremony ends, officers disperse in pairs and trios, their murmured condolences blending with the hum of ambient generators. Evander lingers, watching the last of the holographic names dissolve into static light. The room dims until only the faint reflection of his silhouette remains on the polished floor. Suddenly, a familiar whirr of servos breaks the silence.

"You look like you need an upgrade," Mal'Erro quips, rolling up beside him, the droid's optical sensors flickering with playful warmth.

Evander looks down at the child-like nanobot and almost smiles, responding warmly, "I could use one, yeah."

He crouches to eye level with the little machine. Its chassis gleams with new modular panels, tiny actuators flexing like muscle beneath synthetic plating.

"Observe!" Mal'Erro declares, extending one limb theatrically. "Adaptive armor coating, internal diagnostic sync, and…" the droid pauses dramatically, "musical awareness."

A faint twang of electric guitar spills from its speaker. The melody rises, rough and distorted but strangely earnest.

"It's called *Free Bird*," Mal'Erro says proudly, tapping digits in rhythm as faint guitar notes crackle through its tiny speakers.

"Humans used to listen to it while driving fast and pretending gravity didn't exist. I find it… liberating."

The little droid hums along, tone mechanical yet full of earnest enthusiasm, a digital echo of freedom that somehow makes the sterile hall feel more alive.

Evander chuckles, the sound foreign in his throat. "You've been spending too much time on old Earth networks. I knew I shouldn't have introduced you to that."

"Correction," Mal'Erro replies, mock-serious, posture straightening like a miniature instructor. "Sufficient time to understand culture. Also, swearing. The Calidorfians are excellent teachers. Bloody damn well at that. Right?"

Evander blinks, caught between amusement and disbelief. The race of short, fur-covered Calidorfians, often found in the engine rooms of the fleet of UPF starships, are known for learning and disseminating languages and cultures, and especially their more 'colorful' words. "Yes, the Calidorfians are efficient at swearing, I'll give them that." He sighs, rubbing the bridge of his nose. "And I'm sure Angelica will be thrilled to know you're picking up some of their traits."

Mal'Erro's optics flicker a soft blue, the AI equivalent of a guilty smile. "Don't worry. She already knows. She told me not to repeat what I learned." A short pause. "I promised I would try not to."

Evander raises an eyebrow. "Try not to?"

"Linguistic loophole," Mal'Erro says cheerfully. "I promised to try, not to succeed."

He pats the droid's polished shoulder. "You're impossible." Evander laughs, a small, genuine sound that startles even him. "Come on. Let's go meet the new recruits before you decide to teach them your new vocabulary."

"Before we go, I have important news for you," Mal'Erro says eagerly, with chest-lights pulsing in a mock-serious pattern. "I have decided I am going to start toying with the idea of pronouns for myself. I'll be starting with 'he/him'. Also, I would appreciate it if you stopped calling me 'it'. I am not a horror icon with a storm-drain fixation."

Evander's mouth quirks as he walks. "Got it. He/him. I'll spread the word. And for the record, you're a lot less unsettling than anything that comes out of a storm drain."

Mal'Erro trills, a quick electronic snicker, and resumes humming *Free Bird* as they walk, off-key, unstoppable, and oddly comforting.

They leave the hall together, their footfalls and wheel-whirs echoing through the long corridor. The sterile hum of the Academy gives way to the rhythmic clatter of distant tools and the faint scent of plasma welds. Ahead, the hangar doors loom open like a gateway to another life.

As they approach, brilliant white light spills through, washing over the polished floor. Beyond it stands the Aurora, the newest vessel in the UPF fleet, fresh off the assembly line at the Vega Shipyards. She's a masterpiece of design and precision, every curve deliberate, every panel immaculate. Her silver-titanium hull reflects the hangar's lights in soft gradients of gold and blue, a living sculpture of engineering beauty.

The Aurora dwarfs the smaller frigates docked nearby, its sleek frame whispering speed and quiet power. Twin engine nacelles curve backward like wings in motion, glowing faintly with cerulean energy. The main body is sculpted from next-generation composite plating, lighter, stronger, and capable of self-repair through nanite fusion. Along her spine, the new DHD-2 drive housing shimmers with faint magnetic ripples, a technological marvel yet to see combat.

"So this is her," Evander murmurs, voice low with awe. "The Aurora." He steps forward slowly, the polished deck gleaming under his boots. "Not a single dent, not a single scar." His reflection stretches across the ship's mirrorlike surface, the image of a soldier who no longer feels new at all.

Mal'Erro rolls ahead, optics scanning every inch. "State-of-the-art everything. Reinforced hull plating, enhanced AI-human interface, upgraded life-support redundancies." The droid whistles approvingly. "Even the mess hall has cup holders now. Truly, this is progress."

Evander smirks, shaking his head. "You'd notice that before the weapons systems."

"Weapons are temporary. Cup holders are eternal," Mal'Erro replies proudly. "Besides, she's not just a ship, Evander. She's a symbol, proof the Federation still believes in second chances."

Evander's gaze lingers on the insignia freshly painted along the hull, a stylized aurora stretching over a horizon of stars. Something tightens in his chest. "A new ship," he says quietly. "Same ghosts."

Mal'Erro pauses, his servos whirring softly. "Then perhaps it's time to make better memories."

The words land heavier than intended, cutting through the air with quiet honesty. Evander looks down at the little droid, its sensors glowing a gentle blue. For all his humor, Mal'Erro always seems to know what needs to be said.

He steps onto the catwalk, the vast starfield glinting beyond the open bay doors. "Maybe," he says at last. "Maybe this year, we finally do."

Together, man and machine walk toward the Aurora, their silhouettes framed by the light of distant suns, heading once more into duty, uncertainty, and the fragile hope that some wounds might still heal among the stars.

CHAPTER 2

Inside the gleaming corridors of the Aurora, the air smells of polished metal and ozone, the scent of a ship so new it still feels half-awake. The hum beneath Evander's boots is steady and alive, not the strained vibration of an old engine fighting to survive but the confident pulse of something born to explore. Panels along the walls glow a faint cerulean, their light shifting gently as power flows through the systems for the first time under full crew occupancy.

Evander pauses outside the briefing room for a moment. Through the door's translucent pane he can see movement, the new recruits fidgeting in their uniforms, whispering, trying not to look nervous. The sight almost feels familiar, like stepping backward in time to his own first assignment. Only the ache in his chest reminds him that things are different now.

He enters quietly. Conversations freeze, then resume in uneasy fragments. Mal'Erro rolls in beside him, mechanical joints clicking with cheerful rhythm.

"At ease, everyone," Evander says, voice calm but firm. "Welcome aboard the Aurora. You'll find she's faster, cleaner, and far less forgiving than your dormitories back at the Academy."

A few nervous chuckles ripple through the room, easing the tension.

Mal'Erro hops onto the table, a gleaming sphere of alloy limbs and personality, and spins in a slow circle, optics flickering between the recruits. "Observation one: everyone looks terrified. Observation two: statistically, that is appropriate."

Laughter breaks across the group, and the droid basks in it.

Evander asks for introductions. He gestures first to a calm-voiced Castarian whose fluid motions are almost hypnotic. "My name is Ensign Alexeria Stro." As they speak, their skin shimmers faintly under the room's light. Castarians are known to have adaptable physiology, and along with being gender fluid—shifting genders between male and female as the task or situation warrants—the hue of their skin shifts subtly with emotion. "I am from the Meteor Class." Alexeria's voice is soft and deliberate, every word measured like water poured from a steady hand.

"Ensign Stro," Evander greets her warmly, "you will be stationed most frequently at the tactical systems station of the bridge when on duty. But you will also serve as assistant to Lieutenant Commander Froslo in engineering."

Evander turns next to a female human officer, with shoulder-length blue hair and the left side of her face a mask of cybernetic implants. "I am Ensign Sandria, Moon Class", she says simply, not providing a last name. Her posture is impeccable, almost too precise. Every movement seems calculated, too graceful and slightly unnatural, as if practiced rather than instinctive. Beneath her uniform collar, faint circuitry glints where synthetic skin meets flesh.

Evander knows Sandria once served in the UPF under an older class, but the details are buried in sealed files. An accident left her rebuilt with extensive cybernetics—changes that reshaped her body and, in quieter ways, her mind. Those systems now let her consciousness bridge human and artificial networks, making her one of the strongest communications officers in the fleet. "We are lucky to have Ensign Sandria join us, stationed on the bridge as our communications officer," Evander says in the way of a greeting.

Evander listens patiently as one-by-one each officer makes their introductions. The Star Class officers are the future leaders, destined to be commanders, trainers, and captains. The Meteor Class officers specialize in tactical, navigation, weapons, security, and machinery. And the Moon Class officers are the scientists, specializing in medical, biomechanics, and communications.

After each of the new recruits finishes their introductions and their stations are explained, the mood lightens and Mal'Erro's sensors blink gold. "New topic," he declares. "Why does the cafeteria have no music? Why do humans drink hot bean juice every morning? And why, by the stars, does my chair not swivel?"

The recruits erupt with laughter. Even Alexeria's skin pulses with warm color.

Evander folds his arms, watching the little droid's antics with a mix of pride and weary affection. Mal'Erro has changed since the Extermination: his humor sharper, his curiosity deeper, his voice less mechanical. Mal'Erro's actions throughout the harrowing experience earned him a position amongst the UPF, having been given the title of officer, more of an honorary title rather than a rank. *'Definitely not an 'it','* Evander thinks to himself. At times the droid feels more alive to Evander than the people around him. The thought both comforts and unsettles him.

He watches the laughter of his new crew continue, a sound so ordinary it feels almost sacred. For a moment he forgets the static of war transmissions and the screams that used to fill comm channels. The recruits' easy chatter feels like proof that the galaxy is still capable of innocence. For the first time in months, he lets himself believe that maybe *recovery* isn't just a word the council uses in speeches.

When the meeting concludes, Evander leads the recruits into the bridge to introduce the other officers. Admiral Sarklak is standing off in a corner observing the group. As the senior officer in charge of the entire UPF headquarters, he needs no introduction. A fierce looking Alnilamian, his presence is commanding and formidable, a reflection of the proud warrior lineage from which he hails. The marks of experience etched into his features tell the story of countless battles fought and challenges overcome, and his green eyes shine with the tactical awareness that defines his leadership. Since Evander's father died last year, the Admiral has become like a second father to him, and he finds it calming to know the Admiral will be popping on and off the ship during the Aurora's inaugural journey, checking on the new DHD-2 drive, and likely on him, too.

Seated at the pilot console is Ensign P'thorika, a young Miraian with all-black eyes, pink-and-white striped skin, and tendrils for hair. Evander offers a warm smile as he introduces her to the recruits. When they first met a year ago, she was quiet and timid, just 21. Now, she carries herself with quiet confidence and an unspoken strength, carrying herself with a poise well beyond her years.

Evander introduces each officer in turn and then leads the recruits through the corridor toward their assigned quarters. The Aurora's interior gleams under strips of soft blue light, the air vents releasing a faint floral trace of the oxygen mix. It feels like walking through the lungs of something breathing for the first time.

Halfway down the hall, they meet two more of the experienced officers, both leaning against a wall panel mid-conversation. Evandor pauses and makes introductions. "This is Ensign Blarek Ta'yash, our pilot," he says to the group. "And this is Ensign Kal'korg Zarao, our ship's medic. When he is not needed in the med bay, you'll find him on the bridge at the sensor array console."

Blarek, with his arms crossed and tail flicking lazily, wears his usual expression of unimpressed calm. As is common with Pheonians, his tone is serious and almost brooding, his feline eyes shining against dark grey skin as he looks over the recruits. "Fresh suits, huh?" he mutters. "Try not to dent anything before the paint dries."

Kal'korg, still in his medical tunic and smelling faintly of sterilizing compound, wears an amused expression as he listens to Blarek's sarcasm. His teddy-bear ears and Koala-like nose, along with his disheveled mane of hair and pale-green fur makes him look friendly, despite a sharp set of teeth peering out from his wide grin. "Ignore him," he jokes in Ho'grenian fashion. "He's just bitter that his coffee dispenser breaks every time the gravity hiccups. The ship's a beauty, and there's room for everyone, even the one with all the arms."

Mal'Erro tilts his head, plating gleaming. "Those are limbs, thank you. And they are proportional."

Several recruits snicker. Blarek raises an eyebrow. "Still defensive, I see. Did someone forget to install your humility chip?"

"Negative," Mal'Erro replies primly. "It was optional equipment, and I rejected the upgrade."

Kal'korg bursts into laughter so loud it draws a passing technician's glance. "Still the same little scrap heap. I missed that mouth of yours," he says, and walks on without waiting for a response.

"Correction," Mal'Erro answers, to no one in particular, "technically, I don't have a mouth."

Evander smiles and turns back to the pair. "You two haven't changed at all. What happened to taking your shore leave quietly?"

Kal'korg smirks. "We tried. Blarek almost started a bar fight because someone insulted his salad."

"It was a very good salad," Blarek insists. "And they were very rude."

Mal'Erro clicks approvingly. "Step one of friendship protocol: defend your friend's salad."

Blarek groans. "Not this again."

"Step two," Mal'Erro continues, "earned trust. Step three, questionable karaoke."

Kal'korg throws up his hands dramatically. "Step four, learn to dance like a Calidorfian!"

Blarek covers his face with one paw. "Please don't."

Mal'Erro's optics brighten mischievously. "Step five, ignore Blarek's warnings."

The recruits burst into laughter again, the sound rolling down the corridor like sunlight through glass. Even Blarek cracks a smile, trying and failing to hide it behind his tail.

As the humor settles into softer chuckles, Evander folds his arms, watching the pair trade jokes as easily as breathing. Months apart has not dulled their rhythm. If anything, the distance has made their reunion feel even warmer, like sparks finding each other again in the dark.

"Good to have you both back," he says quietly.

Kal'korg's grin softens. "Wouldn't miss it, sir. Besides, who else is gonna fix you up when you ignore medical protocols again?"

"Technically," Mal'Erro interjects, "that was my fault."

Blarek smirks for the first time. "Same ghosts, new paint."

Evander meets his gaze. "Maybe this time we'll keep them from haunting us."

For a moment, the hallway feels lighter; laughter fading, but warmth lingering like the first hint of dawn. With the new recruits following and Mal'Erro humming another off-key bar of *Free Bird,* the crew continues down the corridor together, a patchwork family stitched by loss, loyalty, and the hope that this ship might finally be a clean slate.

Later, in Evander's quarters, the door seals with a soft hiss, cutting off the ship's background hum. The space is functional, yet distinctly his; neat without being sterile, each item chosen rather than placed. A few photos cling to the bulkhead: a grainy Academy snapshot, a candid image of Angelica mid-laugh, and one of his father standing beside a younger Evander in dress uniform. A folded UPF banner hangs above the desk like a promise that order can still exist in chaos. The air smells faintly of recycled oxygen and machine oil, not unpleasant, just new.

Mal'Erro glides through the room, optics scanning with curiosity. He finds the small adjoining compartment built specifically for him. The droid's plating catches the ambient light as he rolls inside, inspecting every corner like a child exploring their first room.

A custom recharging station waits along the far wall; clamps polished to a mirror sheen. A compact workbench holds diagnostic tools, spare parts, and a few personal touches: the worn calibration glove Evander once used to assemble the first Mal'Erro unit, and a half-finished sketch of the droid on a data pad. Yet what draws Mal'Erro's attention most is the viewport: a narrow pane of transparent alloy framing the distant stars. He approaches slowly, servos humming at a softer pitch, and stops before the glass. For a long moment there is only the quiet rhythm of the ship's pulse, the steady heartbeat of its engines beneath the floor. "Home," Mal'Erro says at last, his voice reduced to a faint whisper of static, reverent and fragile.

Evander leans against the doorway, his arms crossed. The faint blue light from the viewport outlines the tired contours of his face. "Yeah," he answers quietly. "Home."

Mal'Erro turns, his optics dimming to a calm, pulsing glow, showing the closest thing he has to a smile. "I like this room," he says after a pause. "It feels less empty than the others."

Evander nods. "That's because it's yours."

The droid seems to process that for a while, tiny gears clicking as he considers the word. "Mine," he repeats softly, almost in wonder. "Then I'll take care of it."

Evander's faint smile deepens, weary but genuine. "That's all I ask."

Outside, the stars glide past like lanterns on a silent sea. For the first time in months, Evander feels something he hasn't dared to feel in a long while. Not joy, not even hope, just stillness.

But somewhere beyond those tranquil lights, the first tremors of a new horror are already stirring, and neither man nor machine can yet hear its echo.

CHAPTER 3

Far from the hum of UPF stations, the skies above Calidorfia burn with a permanent orange haze. The air shimmers with dust and heat, carrying the faint scent of iron that clings to the planet's rust-colored plains. The world hums softly, a low vibration from distant mining drills and wind turbines that turn lazily in the haze. Metal dust coats everything here. Even the wind tastes like it remembers the forge.

It is a quiet evening, too quiet for a world that never truly sleeps. Two Calidorfian civilians walk the ridge path outside their settlement, hands intertwined, their bioluminescent fur faintly glowing in the gloom. They speak softly; the kind of idle talk shared between those who have survived too much to waste words. Far below the ridge, cargo transports crawl across the valley floor like silver insects, their lights flashing in the orange murk. The rigs flicker to life in the distance, scattering sparks that vanish into the heat. Up ahead, a glint of metal.

The woman stops. "Do you see that?"

Her partner frowns and peers through the haze. The shape in the dirt looks humanoid, or something that had been. As they approach, a chill spreads through the air, the dust suddenly still.

The body lies crumpled among the rocks, skin shriveled tight like parchment, veins blackened beneath the surface.

The woman's scream breaks through the silence. Her partner drags her back, trembling, as a cloaked figure, tall and motionless, watches from a rocky outcrop above. For a heartbeat, faint red-light glimmers beneath its hood before it vanishes into the fog, leaving only the whisper of wind and the woman's sobs echoing through the dusk.

~~~~~~~

Hours later, the forensic lights of the Calidorfian Med-Lab flicker against walls of glass and steel. The sterile hum of equipment fills the air, steady and precise, almost too calm, as though the machines themselves are holding their breath. The technicians wear clear masks that fog slightly with each exhale, the faint rhythm of their breathing blending with the sound of circulating air filters.

The body floats in a containment field, suspended above the exam table. Dim blue light ripples around it like water, revealing skin stretched paper-thin over bone. The veins are black beneath the surface, and the eyes, wide and unblinking, reflect the cold glare of the lumen panels above.

"Adjust magnification," says the lead examiner, her voice tight with fatigue.

The assistant complies. The holo-display zooms in on the victim's arm, revealing collapsed tissue and a faint metallic shimmer embedded deep within the dermal layer.

"No puncture wounds," a med-tech murmurs, leaning closer. "No fluids. Completely drained."

Another shakes his head. "I'm reading micro-fissures at the cellular level. Whatever did this didn't just remove fluid, it stripped the cells of internal pressure."

The lead examiner presses gloved fingers to the energy barrier, her eyes narrowing as the readings scroll faster across the display.

"Skin integrity's intact," she says quietly. "No tearing, no decay. But the collapse ratio is near total. It's like something siphoned the life right out of it."

A younger technician studies the scan, pale under the light. "It could be a synthetic vector. Maybe a drone with precision drains or microtubes."

The lead examiner does not answer. Her gaze drifts to a faint shimmer of alloy buried under the ribcage, too symmetrical, too deliberate to be natural.

She finally speaks, her voice low and careful. "Not a drone. Look at the patterning. These aren't surgical marks. This is adaptive fusion. It's integrated."

The room falls silent. Even the containment field seems to hush. The faint hum of the building's filtration system becomes painfully loud, as if the whole facility is listening.

Someone at the back whispers, "Machine."

No one corrects them.

The examiner wipes a thin line of condensation from the inside of her visor. For a moment she imagines movement beneath the skin, a ripple that should not be there. She blinks, and it is gone. Yet the thought remains, cold and heavy in her chest.

~~~~~~~

Back aboard the Aurora, the steady rhythm of the engines fills the command deck. The crew quietly runs routine diagnostics, a calm broken only by the occasional click of holo-keys. The lights are dimmed to night-cycle hues, soft blue glows pulsing along the consoles like veins of light in the dark.

Then an alarm erupts, slicing through the silence. Red lights flash across the bridge. Warning tones echo through the consoles while the ship's AI speaks in a measured voice that somehow makes the urgency worse. "Incoming transmission. Origin: Calidorfia. Priority level: distress."

Every conversation stops. Evander straightens at once. "Put it through."

The main holo-display flickers, the UPF crest flashing before dissolving into static. Broken comms hiss through the air, followed by strained voices of med-techs fighting to be heard.

"…unknown cause, loss of fluids, containment breach…"

The feed stabilizes for a heartbeat. Behind the static, chaos floods the screen: flickering lights, figures rushing past, the orange haze of Calidorfia bleeding into every corner.

Blarek's ears flatten. "That's a med-lab," he says. "Those aren't soldiers."

The chief engineer for the Aurora, Lt. Commander Froslo, also a Calidorfian, leans forward from navigation, eyes narrowing. "They're scared."

The camera tilts sharply toward the floor, catching a flash of something pale against the rust-colored dust: a body. The victim's skin is drawn tight, almost translucent under the emergency lights. Its eyes open, mouth slack, and face frozen in what appears as mid-scream. Instruments nearby pulse in erratic rhythm, reading nothing but static. The entire lab throbs with a slow heartbeat that does not belong to anything alive.

Mal'Erro tilts his head. His voice is quieter than usual. "I do not like that," he says.

A brief distortion crawls across the feed, a metallic shimmer at the edge of the frame. Then the signal dies. The bridge falls into suffocating silence. Even the Aurora's hum seems to fade.

Evander's reflection glows on the dead screen, his expression outlined in pale light. His fingers tighten around the console until the leather of his gloves squeaks. "Peace never lasts," he whispers.

The words carry through the bridge like a prayer no one wants to hear. Kal'korg exhales from his station, his medical badge catching the red light. "I hate when you say that."

No one answers. For several seconds, the crew simply listens to the silence. Then Evander straightens and clears his throat, his composure returning as quickly as it had broken. "Get me everything they transmitted," he orders. "The full forensic packet."

Blarek glances at him. "You think this is another outbreak?"

Evander's tone hardens. "No. This is something else."

~~~~~~~~

Later, in the briefing room, Evander scrolls through the incoming report. The Calidorfian scientists have included preliminary scans: energy residue clinging to the tissues, traces of alloy integration at the cellular level, and beneath it all, a data tag hidden in the report header: a serial signature. One that should have died with the rogue cyborg, Galgorn.

Evander's stomach tightens. He whispers it under his breath. "He's dead." But the certainty behind those words is gone. Doubt creeps into every breath he takes. After his father's death, Evander discovered that his dad used his own DNA, altering it slightly to allow it to bond to synthetic materials, to make the cyborg, a sinister brother he wishes was never created.

Mal'Erro perches on the edge of the desk, optics dimmed to a low blue. "You are processing fear again," he says softly.

Evander does not respond. His eyes stay on the image of the drained body, the way skin clings too tightly to bone, the faint glimmer of circuitry where veins should have been.

Outside the viewport, the stars drift in cold silence. One flickers with a rhythmic pulse, so faint it almost looks alive. Evander sits back, the console light washing over his face. The classified report remains open, its crimson warning sigil blinking steadily. Every line of data points to the same impossible truth: whoever is responsible for the Calidorfian death has access to technology that should have been buried with Galgorn. He rubs a hand across his face, fatigue settling deep in his bones. The hum of the Aurora's power core fills the silence like a heartbeat that will not stop.

Mal'Erro hovers nearby. "Are you going to tell her?" he asks.

Evander hesitates. "Angelica deserves the truth. If this is what I think it is…" He exhales slowly. "She needs to see it."

He keys an encrypted priority-one transmission. The image of the drained body flickers once before vanishing into the data stream. "Angelica, hopefully you're able to get this," he says, his voice low but steady. "I know you're on leave, but we may have a problem. Calidorfia is reporting a death tied to cybernetic grafts:

Galgorn's design. I'm forwarding the details now. I don't know what it means yet, but it doesn't feel random." He pauses, then adds more quietly, "Enjoy your time away while you can. Something is shifting out there."

The message sends, vanishing into the void. Mal'Erro hums a soft bar of *Free Bird,* the notes faint and uneven, like a lullaby for ghosts. Evander does not stop it. He stands at the viewport, his eyes on the distant stars, each one a fragile promise of peace already fading. He closes his eyes, the faint reflection of the stars flickering across his face. For a fleeting moment, he thinks of the memorial wall back on Arigold and wonders how many new names it will hold before the year ends.

CHAPTER 4

Angelica Tenah sits in her quarters aboard the Aurora, now orbiting around Arigold, getting ready for her first official leave in nearly a year. She checks the time and thinks to herself, *'Evander must be giving his first briefing to the new recruits by now.'* She resists the urge to check in on him. *'He'll be fine. Besides, he has the Admiral looking out for him while I'm gone,'* she acknowledges to herself.

Her quarters are dim with curtains drawn. Holo-displays hover in the air like silent ghosts, replaying the final transmissions salvaged from Galgorn's wreckage from a year ago. Each file flickers and dies in static, corrupted fragments of code, half-formed shapes of machinery and shadow, but one string repeats in every recovered system: a set of coordinates. Kaelor System.

Angelica remembers that name, but she is not sure why. It is a name long buried in UPF archives, erased from duty logs. It was once charted, now abandoned. She magnifies the data, her eyes tracing the shifting lattice of numbers. A second file opens, a sealed psychological assessment marked *CLASSIFIED.* She reads in silence as phrases burn against the darkness: *obsessive fixation on origin myth… unstable faith in prophecy… pursuit of mechanical transcendence.* Her jaw tightens. "You weren't chasing dominance, Galgorn," she mutters. "You were chasing validation."

Outside her viewport, Arigold drifts in the distance, a glittering hub of order and control, while the Kaelor coordinates pulse faintly in the corner of her display, like a heartbeat calling her toward the unknown.

When Command approved her leave, she listed her destination as Kaelor VII for a simple retreat. She had spent months retracing Galgorn's steps before he died in the battle aboard his flagship. Unofficially, it is the last thread of Galgorn's trail leading up to that moment, and she intends to follow it wherever it leads. She shuts down the terminal, the final screen fading to black. For a moment her reflection lingers there, human on the surface, celestial beneath, and in her silence, the goddess behind the officer breathes a single thought, *'This isn't over.'*

She exhales slowly, then taps her wrist-comm. "Aurora, prep a shuttle for departure. Single-pilot configuration. No broadcast logs."

The ship's AI responds, voice calm and measured.

"Captain Tenah, your leave request indicates a medical retreat. Shall I forward your current vitals to Command?"

"Negative. This is off-record. Keep the logs sealed under my command code."

"Understood. Fuel reserves and flight path authorization ready. Atmospheric interference near Kaelor VII remains moderate: visibility forty-three percent. Recommend caution during descent."

"Duly noted," she says, pulling on her jacket. "And Aurora, keep our departure quiet. I'd rather not have Fleet Intel shadowing me."

"Stealth mode engaged. Good luck, Captain."

Angelica pauses in the doorway, glancing once more at the dormant displays. The silence of her quarters presses in like a held breath. Then she turns and leaves.

Moments later, the shuttle bay door's part, spilling white light across the hangar floor. The small craft detaches from its clamps, engines igniting with a muted roar. As the Aurora fades behind her, the dark void stretches ahead, a canvas waiting to be disturbed.

"Kaelor VII," she murmurs, setting a course. "Let's see what you were hiding."

The shuttle tilts toward the stars and vanishes into the deep.

~~~~~~~

Her shuttle cuts through Kaelor VII's turquoise atmosphere, gliding through thin layers of cloud that shimmer with auroral light. Magnetic filaments dance like ribbons across the sky, reflecting off the oceans below.

"Entering atmospheric lock," the ship's AI intones. "Caution: gravitational variance exceeds Federation flight parameters."

Angelica steadies the controls manually. "Noted," she responds.

Below her, endless seas mirror the heavens. Islands rise like fragments of crystal, their surfaces so reflective they seem to hang between two skies: one above, one below. The symmetry unsettles her; orientation feels irrelevant here.

As the shuttle nears the equator, a faint signal pings from beneath the surface. It is weak, rhythmic, and exactly at Galgorn's frequency modulation. She locks on its location and initiates descent. The craft lands smoothly on a crescent of white sand and the engines fall silent, leaving only the whisper of the tide.

A maintenance drone sits half-buried near the dunes, half-swallowed by coral and rust. As Angelica crouches beside it and brushes off the sand, its digital identification plate illuminates and reads UPF SURVEY DR-02; DECOMMISSIONED 44 YEARS

AGO. The odds of it being here, intact, functional, are highly improbable.

As Angelica digs through the system's memory, she sees evidence that Galgorn had once also accessed the drone. "You were here too," she says quietly, brushing more sand from the plate. "So, what were you scanning for?" As if in response, the drone's core flickers faintly, then dies.

She looks out toward the horizon, the reflection of twin moons glimmering on the glass-still sea. To her, the beauty here feels too designed, too symmetrical to be natural.

~~~~~~~

She spends the next hour immersed in the coordinates, her fingers dancing across the console as she overlays them onto geological and magnetic field maps. Every projection flickers with interference, the data resisting clarity as though the planet itself wants to stay unread. Thermal imaging reveals faint anomalies beneath the crust: concentric shapes, not naturally occurring, each emitting a low-frequency pulse. She fine-tunes the filters, isolating the resonance, and the computer translates it into an audible waveform.

A sound fills the cabin. It is low, layered, and strangely melodic, like a choir buried beneath stone. For a moment, Angelica forgets to breathe. The tone feels less like noise and more like *speech,* with every rise and fall echoing with intention. Staring at the screen in front of her, she traces the pulse pattern through multiple geological layers, watching it spiral inward to a point deep below the jungle's heart. The final data cluster flares on-screen, revealing an ancient substructure half a kilometer below ground. Across the edge of the image flashes a residual signature; one that matches the nano-fusion lattice Galgorn used in his cybernetic experiments.

Her stomach tightens. "So, you weren't just building machines," she murmurs. "You were trying to wake something up."

She calls up the accompanying audio fragment embedded in the file. Static blooms across the speakers, followed by Galgorn's distorted voice:

"...harmonic resonance confirmed... the artifact *responds* to light... as if aware..."

The feed ends in silence. Angelica exhales slowly, the surf murmuring just beyond the open hatch. "An artifact that speaks..." she whispers, almost to herself. "Then let's hear what it has to say."

She rises, sliding the data pad into her field pouch. Outside, the ocean wind has turned warm and restless. The first low growl of thunder rolls over the horizon, deep and distant. She secures her sidearm, activates her glow-rod, and steps toward the dark edge of the jungle. The moment she crosses beneath the trees, the air changes, like the world is holding its breath for what comes next.

The air beneath the canopy is thick and electric, charged with static energy that makes every breath vibrate faintly in her chest. The foliage glows with its own dim light, translucent leaves revealing pulsing veins of bioluminescence. Gravity feels inconsistent, lighter near the roots, heavier under the high trees. Her instruments flicker, struggling to stabilize readings.

Birdlike creatures drift overhead in slow, spiraling patterns, their translucent wings humming at ultrasonic pitch. Each movement resonates with the deep hum beneath her feet. The entire forest feels like a living conductor. She pushes onward until the terrain drops into a clearing surrounded by crumbling stone pillars. Time has almost devoured them, but faint carvings remain: spirals, constellations, and symbols so intricate they resemble fractal equations.

Her scanner pings. "Unidentified compound detected. Alloy matches the wreckage of Galgorn's vessel."

Angelica follows the signal to a half-collapsed chamber. The air inside is cooler, stiller. Dust floats in the glow of her rod, like drifting stars. At the chamber's center rests a cracked dais of stone and metal. A curved fragment of alloy juts from the core, faintly pulsing with internal light. She kneels beside it, activating a holographic overlay. Symbols ripple across the walls and begin to align, each curve and angle resolving into words that feel older than speech. The translation stabilizes line by line.

In the shadows of time's embrace, whispers rise along the corridors of fate. Two brothers, born of different origins yet bound by one design, converge as the heavens tremble. When the stars align, their struggle turns the course of history and bends the fabric of existence. One is the Golem, wrought of spirit and metal, forged in the crucible of creation. One is the Universe-born, carried on the breath of light. They meet at the nexus in the heart of the storm, where revelation hides in the mist. Beware the darker hand that moves behind the veil and plucks the threads of destiny to its own end. In the last movement of the great drama, the brothers face a final trial of strength, will, and sacrifice. In their union lies the power to reshape what is, to pass beyond mortal sight, and to step where the divine begins.

Angelica reads the last line again. The chamber seems to tighten around the words, as if the ruin itself is listening. She whispers, "Galgorn did not invent this. He found it." Her pulse quickens. The phrase echoes from Galgorn's recovered manifesto, the same one Command locked away after his death.

But then, more lines appear. The system continues to translate:

The heart of creation rests beyond the storm. The voice of the maker sleeps within.

Angelica's breath catches. "The heart of creation… the maker…" She realizes what she's seeing: the same myth Galgorn had twisted into obsession; proof of a self-aware force that shapes life.

A chill moves through the air.

"Still chasing ghosts, my daughter?"

The voice comes from behind her, soft and familiar. She turns slowly, the glow-rod trembling in her grip. Her father stands among the pillars, his edges blurred by light. His eyes carry that same steady calm she once found unshakable.

"You shouldn't be here," she says.

"Neither should you," he replies gently, stepping closer. "Yet here we are, both drawn by what we were never meant to find."

"It's real then," she whispers. "The prophecy. Everything Galgorn believed."

"It is real," he says, "and it is not yours to command. You see only one reflection. The prophecy speaks of two brothers shaped by different fires, drawn to a single storm. The Golem is not only steel and code. The Universe-born is not only blood and light. And there is a darker hand at the edge of vision. If I tell you more, you will force the shape and the shape will break."

She steps closer. "Then what can I hold to?"

"Remember this," he says. "The nexus is not a place you choose. It is the point where every choice you have made arrives together."

The floor vibrates under her boots. Dust trembles in the light. Her wrist comm activates suddenly and blinding blue light washes across the chamber. Static fills her ears, then Evander's voice cuts through the noise.

"Angelica, hopefully you're able to get this…" The message fragments, breaking under interference, but she hears the words *Calidorfia… death… cybernetic…*

She looks up, but her father is already fading from her view. "Go," he adds, his voice soft. "The storm gathers."

~~~~~~~

Angelica runs from the chamber. The jungle is alive with sound, with branches snapping as she runs and the deep rumble of earth shaking beneath her feet. The storm above breaks in absolute silence, with green lightning splitting the clouds. The sky seems to fold inward, drawn to a single point of light high above the sea.

She bursts from the trees onto the beach. The once-calm waves now crash with deafening force, spraying white foam into the wind. Her shuttle's hull gleams faintly against the storm's glow. She turns back for one last look. The ruins pulse with energy, its symbols along the walls flaring to life, forming massive concentric rings of light. In the center, the shard rises from the dais, emitting a low harmonic tone that resonates in her chest.

She continues to stare back toward the glowing ruin. "The Golem and the Universe-born," she says, barely above the wind. "Two brothers at the nexus, and a darker hand behind the veil." She doesn't know if it is a warning or a promise. She only knows that it feels inevitable.

She sprints to the shuttle, sealing the hatch as the winds roar. The vessel shakes violently as the engines ignite. Rain hammers the viewport like falling shards of glass. "Magnetic interference is at critical levels," the onboard AI warns. "Stabilizers are offline."

Angelica grips the controls. "Override. Manual ascent." The shuttle lurches upward. Lightning dances across its hull, discharging in arcs of blue and white. For a moment, gravity wavers and the world below flickers like a reflection disturbed by ripples.

The ruins flare one last time and energy bursts upward in a column of light that pierces the storm. The pulse echoes through the planet's crust and vanishes into space. Kaelor VII's upper atmosphere glows with auroral rings, the colors twisting into the shape of an eye before fading.

Breathing hard, Angelica steadies the craft. Her comm blinks with unread messages, all from Evander. She stares out at the dark horizon where lightning still flashes in spirals. "Whatever you've found, Evander," she says quietly, "something here just woke up to answer it."

The shuttle breaks through the last layer of cloud, emerging into the void above. For a fleeting instant, the planet below darkens completely, its surface swallowed by shadow. An eclipse cloaks Kaelor VII. And somewhere far beyond the system, an ancient signal stirs, the same harmonic pulse now echoing faintly across the stars.

CHAPTER 5

Angelica's shuttle lifts from Kaelor VII just as dawn brushes the horizon. Below, the mirrored ocean ripples where the storm has passed, streaks of dark glass floating atop turquoise calm. The world looks serene again, but Angelica knows better. Storms always leave something behind, even when the surface seems still.

Through the viewport she watches the clouds twist upon themselves, forming a perfect ring in the distance. The remnants of the strange electrical storm pulse faintly with inner light, a phenomenon the planet's scientists will later call an atmospheric mirage. She suspects it is something very different from a simple storm.

For a moment, sunlight filters through the circle, refracting across the sea in a flawless halo, an eclipse reflected on the waves. The sight holds her in silence, a symbol too precise to be coincidence.

'Even beauty carries warnings,' she thinks. *'Especially the kind that looks balanced.'*

The shuttle climbs higher, and the horizon begins to fall away. Islands shrink into specks, and the turquoise of the sea fades into the deep violet of Kaelor's upper atmosphere. Angelica stands at the viewport a moment longer, her reflection superimposed over the planet's glow. Her hair moves faintly in the recycled breeze, still damp with sea salt. She runs a hand through it absently, feeling the weight of command settle back onto her shoulders, invisible armor she can never quite take off. The faint tan from Kaelor's sun already looks out of place under the pale shuttle lights.

She exhales slowly, then turns away from the viewport. "Set course for the Aurora," she says, her voice steady but quiet. "Tell Command I'm done resting."

"Acknowledged," replies the shuttle's onboard AI. "Estimated arrival in four hours, Captain."

Angelica adjusts her jacket. Her fingers brush the worn insignia patch near her collar, the one Evander returned to her after the Extermination. It is a reminder of what she lost and what still needs protecting.

As the shuttle pierces through the last layer of atmosphere, Kaelor VII recedes into a pale halo. The eclipse still lingers on its surface, a perfect ring glinting across the ocean, until even that vanishes into haze.

She looks once more at the endless void ahead. '*Rest is a luxury for those who still believe peace will last,*' she thinks. The engines flare, and the shuttle streaks into the stars, leaving the calm world, and whatever had awoken beneath its storm, far behind.

~~~~~~~~

The Aurora hums with quiet life, with the steady rhythm of her engines echoing like a heartbeat through the decks. Angelica steps through the main corridor, nodding at passing officers who straighten at her presence but cannot quite hide their smiles. News of her return travels fast, and with it, a sense of renewed focus.

In the mess hall, laughter fills the air. The sound feels strange and precious after months of solemn silence. At one corner table, Alexeria Stro lounges with Sandria, the new recruit everyone is whispering about. While most see her as just a cyborg, Alexeria's Castarian perspective embraces the fluidity of being, allowing them to see a human woman whose calm poise contrasts with the buzz of voices around them.

"So," Alexeria says, their voice lilting, "is it true humans sleep eight hours straight without shared dreams? How terribly inefficient."

Sandria smiles faintly. "We make up for it by overthinking when we're awake."

"Ah, an acceptable trade." Alexeria reclines, their iridescent skin shifting from silver to lavender. "Castarians rest differently. We share thought-streams, efficient, intimate, occasionally scandalous."

Sandria lifts an eyebrow. "Sounds crowded."

"Only if you have something to hide."

Before she can reply, a familiar whirr cuts through the room. Mal'Erro glides in, balancing a data pad on one arm, humming an off-key *Free Bird*. Conversations stall just long enough for the little droid to bask in the attention.

"Good morning, organic entities!" Mal'Erro announces brightly. "Statistical analysis indicates morale efficiency at seventy-three percent. That is… adequate improvement."

Laughter ripples across the room. Alexeria smirks. "Your humor chip's running hot again, little one."

"I've been practicing," Mal'Erro replies, spinning once. "Evander says humor builds trust. Also, I like laughter, it sounds less like screaming." The room pauses for half a heartbeat, then laughter returns, softer this time.

Right then the doors hiss open again and Admiral Sarklak strides in, crisp uniform immaculate, mug of synth-coffee in hand. He stops short at the sight of Mal'Erro perched proudly on the serving counter.

"What in the galaxy's name are you doing up there, Officer Scrapheap?"

"Performing morale recalibration, Admiral," Mal'Erro answers without missing a beat. "Would you like to participate? Laughter increases cardiovascular health by 12.3 percent."

Sarklak lifts his mug. "Only if you upgrade to brewing coffee instead of jokes."

Mal'Erro's optics brighten. "Challenge accepted."

Angelica, passing by the doorway to the mess hall, catches Sarklak's faint smile as he mutters to a nearby officer, "If that thing ever figures out espresso, I'll promote him." The laughter that follows rolls through the room like sunlight through open windows.

~~~~~~~

The recruits stand later in formation on the Aurora's holographic grid. The training deck glows with soft blue light, emitters pulsing in sync with the ship's core. Evander observes from the upper platform, with his hands clasped behind his back, his voice calm and commanding. "Today's drill measures your adaptive response under variable gravity. Don't think. Feel the field. Your instincts are faster than your calculations."

The hum rises and the gravity flickers, then shifts, causing a stomach-twisting lurch that sends half the cadets floating before slamming them down again. Alexeria adjusts instantly. Their liquid-grace physiology ripples under the shifting pull, bioluminescent skin gleaming violet and blue. They move like water finding its level.

"Excellent," Evander calls. "Adaptation under stress keeps you alive when equations fail."

"Equations never fail me," Alexeria counters, twisting mid-air.

Evander allows a faint smile. "Then let's test your confidence under inversion."

The deck pulses and suddenly everyone is airborne. For a few breathless seconds, bodies drift weightless, then gravity doubles. The echo of boots striking the grid fills the hall.

Beside Alexeria, Sandria stumbles. For an instant her eyes flare silver, light racing through veins beneath her skin. Then it's gone.

Evander notices. His instincts sharpen, with years of reading motion and micro-expression telling him this is not fatigue. He notes Sandria's response silently on his data pad, with curiosity tempered by caution. "Recover," he orders. "Gravity isn't your enemy. Hesitation is."

Sandria nods quickly, her posture rigid. She finishes flawlessly, every landing precise, every motion balanced. Too perfect.

On the edge of the deck, Mal'Erro tilts his head, sensors narrowing as it logs the same flash. '*Metallic resonance detected. Organic integrity: stable. Source: undefined.*' He says nothing, only watching.

Evander claps once. "Better," he says as the drill comes to an end and normal gravity returns. "Most of you still fight the environment instead of learning from it. Let that sink in." His eyes sweep the room one last time. "Dismissed."

As the recruits disperse, Alexeria laughs, twirling a wrench like a dancer's prop. Sandria lingers near the exit, with one hand brushing the railing as if grounding herself.

Evander watches her go. "Keep an eye on that one," he murmurs.

Mal'Erro's optics flicker. "I already am."

~~~~~~~~

Hours later the training deck is quiet, filled only by the hum of cooling vents and a faint hiss of a plasma welder at the opposite end. Mal'Erro rolls in, carrying his data pad, intending to recalibrate a sensor array. Movement catches his optics. Sandria sits alone near the diagnostics terminal. Parts of her uniform lie folded beside her, with fine circuitry glimmering under the skin of her forearm.

"You are not authorized for diagnostics this late," Mal'Erro says.

She doesn't startle. "You saw it, didn't you?"

"The flash in your eyes? Silver. Not human."

She hesitates, then nods. "I didn't mean to hide it. I just didn't want to be treated with suspicion from anyone."

Mal'Erro rolls closer, his voice gentle. "What are you?"

Her gaze lifts. "An experiment. Five genetic lines woven together: Human, Castarian, Calidorfian, Ho'grenian, and one that the scientists wouldn't name. Half biology, half machine. I don't know what I am anymore."

For a long moment, only the steady hum of the ship answers.

"You are like me," Mal'Erro says softly. "Alive but still learning what that means."

She smiles faintly, a fragile but genuine curve to her lips. "You think we can learn?"

"We already are," Mal'Erro replies. "Each time someone laughs *with* us instead of *at* us, that's learning. Every moment we wonder why, that's learning."

She flexes her fingers, watching light shimmer beneath her skin. "It's hard not to feel incomplete."

"Completion is overrated," Mal'Erro says. "I know plenty of humans who are whole and still broken."

That makes her laugh, a small, genuine sound that warms the cold air of the deck.

They sit together, watching the stars drift past through the viewport. Neither speaks again, but the silence between them feels alive, not empty, but shared.

From the doorway, Admiral Sarklak watches for a moment, a smirk tugging at his mouth. "If the two of you start a philosophy club, I'm transferring."

Mal'Erro swivels. "Just waiting on snacks and an existential crisis."

Sarklak chuckles, shaking his head as he walks off. "Smart-mouthed toaster…" The sound of his footsteps fade, leaving only the ship's pulse: steady, patient, and alive. For the first time in months, the Aurora feels less like a ship and more like home.

CHAPTER 6

Elsewhere, deep within the command networks of the Universal Peacekeeping Federation, encrypted data streams flow like living veins of light. The central nexus, an orbital array of crystalline servers circling the capital, pulses with constant motion, with every flicker a patrol log or a flagged whisper from the dark. Inside that flow, one thread shifts. Then it flares red.

TARGET LOCATED.

The alert ripples outward, cascading through holographic overlays and priority routines. At its center, one name locks in white text:

JALERG KYRANDER: ACTIVE WARRANT: CAPTURE ALIVE.

Across scattered outposts, officers lean forward as the trail unfolds. Jalerg's path is a tapestry of deception: ghost frequencies, stolen registries, falsified manifests. Months earlier he vanished after a sabotage incident along the border colonies, his name slipping into rumor and pirate channels tied to the Crimson Eclipse. Every lead had dissolved, but this one holds.

Telemetry paints a jagged line across the Elaris Sector, a volatile stretch where electromagnetic storms drift between asteroid belts like living weather. At the edge of a storm, a weak signal persists, broadcasting from a stolen freighter limping through debris. Its ion drive leaks blue plasma like blood from a wound.

"Cross match that signature," a command officer says.

"Confirmed," the network AI replies. "Registry: Luminous Veil, reported stolen eight days ago. One occupant. Power is unstable."

"Identification?" the officer asks.

"Jalerg Kyrandor," the AI replies.

After a pause, the officer directs, "Relay to all strike groups within three sectors. Directive Seventeen. Priority pursuit."

The order fans out through the void. Dozens of ships receive it. Only one responds instantly: Aurora. Somewhere in the quiet, between stars, the hunter stirs.

~~~~~~~~

The Aurora slips out of the DHD-2 wormhole with a ripple of blue light. Lightning crawls along the nearby rock field, illuminating ice and ore in silver flashes. On the bridge, the air hums with static and focus. Angelica has resumed her position as Captain of the ship, with Evander as her second-in-command. Officers settle into the tempo of pursuit.

Angelica stands near the forward console, hands clasped behind her back, gaze fixed on the dense belt ahead. Thousands of tumbling asteroids drift inside an electromagnetic storm.

"Sensor lock?" she asks.

Evander's voice is steady from the command platform. "Partial. He is deep in the belt. Bleeding power, masking his signal. He is good."

Angelica glances up at him. Her uniform is crisp, her posture exact. She notices Evander's tone is different now: colder, quieter, deliberate. *'War leaves a mark on all of us,'* she thinks.

Mal'Erro breaks the silence. "Is this an appropriate time to mention the probability of catastrophic hull disassembly?"

"Only if it is above fifty percent," Evander says grimly.

Mal'Erro excitedly replies back, "Thirty-eight. So… music?"

Angelica exhales. "Not now, Mal."

Mal'Erro sighs, "I only thought pirates might appreciate *Free Bird*. It feels thematic."

A ripple of nervous laughter moves across the bridge. Evander almost smiles. "You can play your favorite song after no one is shooting at us," he says.

"Noted," Mal'Erro chirps.

The Aurora enters into the belt. Inertial dampeners growl as static lightning leaps between rocks, igniting clouds of dust into pale fire. The hull lights trace harsh shadows across the bridge.

"Target vessel in sight," Alexeria calls from tactical. "Vector nine-two-one. He is rotating around the central mass."

"Blarek," Angelica says, "you are too close to the interference line."

"I know," he answers calmly. "He will not expect us there."

The ship banks hard. Gravity tilts. Jalerg's freighter lurches into view, scarred and venting plasma, weaving between debris.

"Tractor beams on my mark," Evander says. "Mal'Erro, reinforce the lower shield grid."

"Already done, Commander Efficiency." Mal'Erro says gleefully.

"Mark."

Twin beams of amber light spear out and lock onto the freighter center mass. Metal groans over open comms as the smaller ship fights the pull. Lightning webs across both hulls until the freighter yields.

"Containment achieved," P'thorika confirms from the helm.

Angelica nods. "Bring him aboard. Security, proceed to bay two."

The freighter shudders. Power climbs where it should fall. A call comes in from engineering. "Containment is unstable," Alexeria Stro reports, their eyes wide. "There is a drive core surge." Suddenly, the beam shears away and the freighter kicks once and slips free.

"He is breaking away," Evander snaps. Jalerg dives for the stormy world below, Elaris Nine, trailing fire across the night.

"He is going to crash," Angelica says.

"Not if we reach him first," Evander answers.

~~~~~~~

Elaris Nine rises in sheets of rain and light. Mining towers knife up from canyon floors, their flanks plastered in flickering halos and blue lightning that crawls along the ribs of steel. Jalerg's freighter clips an orbital ring, tumbles, and vanishes into the lower strata, a maze of catwalks, steam vents, and reactor stacks.

The Aurora's shuttle chases after it through boiling clouds. "Target is entering sub level grid six," Mal'Erro reports. "Energy is unstable. He is venting drive plasma into a populated sector. Charming."

"Track him," Evander says. "We end this before anyone else gets hurt." They set down on a rain slick platform suspended over a neon abyss. Below, levels fall away into fog and sparks. Thunder rolls across the towers.

Evander volunteers to go after him, along with Mal'Erro, and Angelica agrees. Evander leaves the ship and proceeds quickly to Jalerg's last known location. He looks around and spies Jalerg skulking around, trying to hide. "Jalerg," Evander calls, voice steady but edged with cold. "You can't outrun this."

Through the storm, a limping figure takes shape; soaked, bleeding, framed by sparks that flare from a torn conduit overhead. His pistol trembles in his grip, not from fear but from fury long kept alive. "You should have stayed away, Lieutenant," Jalerg spits. "You should've stayed buried with the ghosts you made."

Evander steps closer, his rain streaking down his face. "I was about to say the same to you."

Jalerg's lip curls. "You talk like you didn't leave her there yourself."

The words strike like shrapnel. Evander freezes. "What did you just say?"

Jalerg's laugh comes cracked and joyless. "You heard me. You left my sister in that lab. You left Kes to die."

Lightning rips across the sky, throwing their shadows long against the steel. Evander's chest tightens and the world narrows to that single name. Kes Kyrandor, his girlfriend while he went through the academy and became stationed at the UPF headquarters. He met her while visiting his father in his laboratory at the UPF. He was instantly taken in by the brilliant lab assistant, with her sky-blue skin and beautiful emerald-green eyes and hair to match. They had broken up shortly before an explosion in the lab killed both her and his father, leaving an empty void in his memory, where grief and guilt became indistinguishable. "That's not possible," Evander says quietly. "The entire lab was reduced to rubble before I even reached orbit. There were no survivors."

Jalerg's grin twists into something bitter. "That's the story Command gave you…the one that lets you sleep. You saw the rubble and let them tell you it was enough."

Evander's voice hardens. "You're lying."

"Am I?" Jalerg takes another step forward, his face flickering in the blue light of a sparking wire. "You didn't *see* the bodies, did you? You saw readings. Numbers. Reports written by people who needed the incident buried."

The rain grows heavier, drumming against metal until it drowns everything else. Evander's pulse pounds in his ears. "Stop talking," he says grimly.

Jalerg tilts his head. "You were supposed to save her, Lieutenant. You were supposed to question everything, but you chose to believe the lie because it hurt less."

"Enough," Evander growls.

"Or maybe," Jalerg presses, "you were just too afraid to look, because of what you might find."

The tension snaps. Jalerg fires. Evander drops, the plasma bolt cutting past his shoulder. He rolls, returning fire in a controlled burst that sends Jalerg's weapon spinning into the void. They collide in the center of a walkway, boots clanging against slick steel. Jalerg swings wildly, desperation fueling every strike. Evander responds with disciplined precision, his expression a storm of guilt and anger barely contained.

"She trusted you," Jalerg snarls, driving a fist across Evander's jaw. "She believed you'd come for her."

Evander catches his arm and shoves him back. "I tried!" The words rip from his throat, raw and unguarded. "The order came too late, I wasn't even there when the lab blew up!"

Jalerg stumbles, rain and firelight dancing across his face. "And that's supposed to make it better? You still left her alone!"

Lightning crashes nearby, flooding the catwalk in white. Evander grabs Jalerg's collar, forcing him back against the railing. "Who told you this?" he demands. "How do you know?"

Jalerg's glare burns through the rain. "You already know who," he says quietly. "You just don't want to believe that she's still out there." Jalerg hesitates. Guilt flickers and is gone. "I know because she is…" His eyes cut past Evander's shoulder. For a breath, red light reflects along the wet rail behind him like a pair of watching eyes.

Evander glances that way on instinct. Jalerg drives a fist into his ribs and shoves. The deck shudders. A cross brace gives way and the section beneath Jalerg drops. Evander lunges and catches his wrist. "Do not fall," Evander shouts over the storm. "I have you."

Jalerg looks up through the rain, his expression grim. "You cannot save what is already claimed."

The railing breaks free and Evander loses his grip on Jalerg. He looks on in horror as Jalerg tumbles down, slamming through a lower glass canopy and into a reclamation pool below. Steam roils. Lightning kisses the water and lances away.

"Confirmed survival," Mal'Erro says. "Reclamation tank absorption. Multiple fractures. Unconscious."

Evander grips the ruined rail, his chest heaving. "Get a med team down there."

Mal'Erro comes up to Evander's side and looks up at him. "You hesitated," Mal'Erro says softly at his side.

Evander does not answer.

"I thought I buried her," he whispers.

"You did," Mal'Erro says.

Evander stares into the rain drowned depths. "Then why do I still hear her name?"

There is only thunder. And for a heartbeat, a faint red glow appears in the storm below, watching, then disappears.

~~~~~~~~

Hours later, Aurora's interrogation room is bathed in cold light. Jalerg sits in a stabilization chair, a med cast humming along his arm. He grins through pain, defiant. "You think you caught me," he rasps. "You fetched a messenger."

Angelica stands by the console, her reflection mirrored in the glass. "A messenger for who?"

Jalerg smiles, thin and mean. "You will see. The contracts are signed, with blood and code. The Crimson Forge is awake again."

Evander shifts, his breath catching. Angelica hears it.

"Tazamite," she says quietly.

Jalerg chuckles. "So, you do remember. Galgorn left a legacy. He was never the architect."

"Then who is?" Evander asks.

Jalerg studies him. For a heartbeat the cruelty fades. Pity replaces it. "You really think she died, didn't you?"

The room tightens. "What did you say?" Evander asks.

"Ah. You didn't know," Jalerg murmurs. "Forget I said anything." He leans back. "Ghosts are tricky. Some learn to wear new skin."

Angelica's gaze hardens. "Enough riddles. Who runs the Crimson Forge?"

"You will know when the stars go dark," he says. The smirk returns. "Now, get me my legal defender. I'm not saying another word."

Two guards take him out. Their boots echo down the corridor as the door seals and quiet follows. Angelica breaks the silence. "Question for you: Why did you hesitate out there earlier before we brought him in?" Her expression curious, but not unkind.

"He said something to me that made me freeze. However, I tried to save him. But I lost my grip, and he fell," Evander answers.

Angelica looks at Evander empathetically, "At least you tried to catch him. What did he say to you though, that made you hesitate?"

Evander's face looks solemn and he answers, "He said Kes survived. It made me think, what if…"

She cuts him off. "She died in that explosion," Angelica says softly. "You saw it."

Evander's jaw tightens. "Yeah, I keep telling myself that."

The lines of exhaustion show. Angelica steps closer, her tone still commanding, but her eyes gentler. "We need answers. Jalerg is a thread in something bigger."

"Then we start pulling," Evander says. The soldier in him settles over his grief like armor.

Angelica nods. "Let us hope we are not already late."

~~~~~~~~

The night cycle slides over the Aurora. The observation gallery quiets to a low hum and the nebula light drifts like smoke beyond the glass. Evander stands with hands on the rail, the stars cold and indifferent. A crash is heard across the room and Evander turns.

Mal'Erro rolls up beside him, optics a soft blue. "You are processing again."

"It is called thinking, Mal," he says.

"You do not look like you enjoy it."

He huffs a small laugh. "No. I do not."

They watch in silence. Somewhere out there, a faint flicker moves between stars. Evander catches a distant red pulse. There one heartbeat, gone the next. "You saw that?" he asks.

Mal'Erro hums a scan. "Negative. Likely lightning residue from earlier."

"Probably," Evander says, unconvinced. "Also wasn't the Admiral watching over you?"

Mal'Erro nods, then a noise registers and the little machine quickly darts away.

"Lieutenant," a voice calls from the entry. Admiral Sarklak steps through, takes in the view, then the ruined bruise along Evander's jaw. "You have a talent for picking fights on unstable platforms."

"That was unplanned, sir," Evander says.

Sarklak sips coffee from a cup he is carrying. "That is what you always say." He sighs. "Plus you folks left in such a hurry, I didn't have a chance to get off at the damn Spaceport." He looks around "Also, where's Mal'Erro? I was watching him for you, but that bucket of bolts keeps escaping me."

Metal shrieks somewhere down the length of the room and a repair wall buckles. A meter-wide patch gives way and smoke puffs out. Through the hole, Mal'Erro pops into view on the other side, whirring forward like a very pleased bowling ball that has just found the pins. Sarklak and Mal'Erro stop face to face at opposite edges of the breach. Sarklak looks down, while Mal'Erro looks up.

"Officer," Sarklak says flatly, "Evander told you to listen to me, and I told you not to move from that spot. Why did you not listen? Instead, you came through the wall like a wrecking ball."

Mal'Erro straightens proudly. "Because I was a wrecking ball. Also, you forgot something very important."

Sarklak rubs his face with an exasperated sigh. "What did I forget, you tin can?"

"You did not give me my cookies."

A long beat, then Sarklak blinks. Then he barks a laugh that he does not try to hide. "If you ever punch through another bulkhead for cookies, I am billing your chassis."

Mal'Erro's optics brighten. "Is that a yes to cookies?"

"Get out of my sight," Sarklak says, still laughing as he turns away. "And fix the wall."

"Yes, Admiral," Mal'Erro says, already summoning repair drones.

Evander watches the exchange, the hint of a smile touching his mouth for the first time since the rain.

~~~~~~~~

Later, Angelica finds Evander in a quiet corridor, the lights low and the ship's heartbeat steady. The noise of crews and reports fades behind them. For a moment they stand without rank or burden.

"How is the jaw?" she asks.

"Functional," he says.

"And the rest of you?"

He hesitates. "Less so."

She steps closer, close enough for her to notice the scent of rain still clinging to his collar. "We will find the truth," she says. "About Jalerg. About Kes. About the Forge."

His gaze meets hers, something unspoken passing in the space between. A touch of warmth cuts through the cold. "I am glad you are back," he says, voice low.

"I did not leave," she answers, almost a whisper. "Not really."

For a heartbeat the ship does not exist. Only her eyes and the quiet between them, enveloping him in a blanket of safety. She reaches up and smooths a damp lock of hair at his temple. The touch is brief, careful, and real.

"Bridge at oh six," she says, drawing in a steady breath. "We move at first light."

"Yes, Captain," he answers, but the title lands softer than it usually does.

Angelica turns, starts down the corridor, then looks back once. "Evander, do not carry it alone."

He nods. She then disappears around the bend. The hum of the Aurora remains, patient and constant, as the stars drift by like slow breathing. Far beyond the hull, the red flicker stirs again and vanishes into the dark.

CHAPTER 7

The Aurora descends through the upper atmosphere of Vessan-9,
her hull glinting against the planet's crimson horizon. The
docking bay shimmers with heat haze as the landing struts lock
into place. Admiral Sarklak stands at the ramp, his uniform still
marked by soot from the last engagement.

"Orders are confirmed," he says, turning toward Angelica.
"Command wants me planet-side to oversee the prisoner transfer.
Jalerg's being moved to the central facility for decryption."

Angelica folds her arms, her expression unreadable beneath the
soft glow of the hangar lights. "You're certain he's secure? Last
time someone said that, half the base ended up on fire."

Sarklak gives a tired smirk. "I made sure this one won't burn.
But Command has questions, Captain, questions about why the
data in Jalerg's archives doesn't match any known UPF
encryption. They're counting on you to keep digging."

Her brow furrows slightly. "We'll find whatever he buried."

"Good," Sarklak says, his tone softening. "But tread carefully.
You've seen what Galgorn's experiments did to people. If Jalerg's
transmissions lead to another empty lab, it will not be abandoned

by accident." He pauses at the threshold of the ramp. "Keep your crew sharp. The ghosts out there still bite."

Angelica nods once. "Safe travels, Admiral."

He steps through the shimmering barrier of the airlock and is gone. The bay doors seal, and the Aurora lifts from the surface, ascending into the stars like a silver blade cutting through night.

~~~~~~~~

Sleep becomes a stranger aboard the Aurora. Even the ship itself seems to share in the unrest; its corridors humming with an anxious rhythm that refuses to quiet. Days blur into one another. The crew moves through their routines, but everyone feels it: something about Jalerg's capture is wrong. Too easy. Too rehearsed.

Angelica stands on the bridge long after her shift has ended, arms folded, eyes fixed on the stars ahead. Her reflection in the viewport stares back with the same quiet suspicion that haunts her thoughts. Jalerg surrendered without resistance. No blaster drawn. No tricks. No last-minute escape attempt. That isn't him.

Evander joins her silently, a data pad in hand. "You're not sleeping either," he says. It was more an observation than a question.

"Not with this much static in the air," Angelica replies. "Mal'Erro's been dissecting Jalerg's transmissions. It's not standard UPF code. Something's buried in it."

Before Evander can respond, the intercom flickers to life.

"Captain, come to the analysis bay. You'll want to see this," Mal'Erro's voice crackles.

They arrive to find the room lit by a lattice of blue holographic lines drifting through the air like frozen lightning. Mal'Erro's projection hovers at the centre, his optics reflecting the pulse of data streams running around it.

"I filtered through Jalerg's encrypted logs," it begins. "There's a repeating anomaly: seventeen packets spaced at irregular intervals. At first, I thought it was corrupted signal noise... until I decoded the pattern."

The hologram zooms in on the waveform, breaking it into columns of binary code. Between bursts of static, faint pulses flare red across the display, organised, deliberate.

"Coordinates," Angelica breathes.

Mal'Erro nods. "Hidden within the transmission's amplitude modulation. Each spike corresponds to a set of navigational markers. I've cross-referenced them against UPF charts: no registered system matches. It's off grid."

Evander frowns. "Could it be a relay? Or a trap?"

"Possibly both," Mal'Erro says. "The encryption is layered. Someone wanted this found: but only by a mind capable of noticing it. The pattern mimics random interference until reconstructed at the molecular level of the code."

Angelica crosses her arms. "Meaning Jalerg didn't send this to hide it. He sent it to lead us there."

Mal'Erro's optics flicker uncertainly. "Or someone used him as the messenger."

Silence hangs for a beat. The only sound is the hum of the processors as the coordinates resolve into a star map, an uncharted nebula glowing faintly at the edge of the Milky Way.

Angelica's gaze hardens. "Set a course. We'll find out what's waiting in that cloud."

~~~~~~~

The Aurora emerges from the DHD-2's wormhole at the edge of a swirling nebula, an endless ballet of crimson and teal gases twisting like living fire. Electrical arcs spider between the clouds, each discharge painting the bridge in fleeting bursts of colour. Static hisses across the comms as the storm's magnetic field brushes against the hull, whispering like far-off voices.

"Unmapped," Blarek says from the helm, his ears twitching as the navigation display blinks and fuzzes with interference. "No registry, no beacon. Sensors barely penetrate half a klick into the mist."

Angelica leans forward in her command chair, eyes narrowed. The nebula fills the viewport like a living canvas, its turbulent glow shifting between beauty and menace. "Bring us in slow," she orders. "Full shields, minimal emissions. If someone wants this place hidden, we won't announce ourselves."

The deck vibrates beneath them as the ship's engines throttle down. Outside, wisps of ionised vapor curls around the forward hull like ghostly tendrils.

Staring at the sensor readings, Blarek's claws tap a nervous rhythm against the console. "Strange…" he mutters, squinting at the fluctuating readouts. "Gravity locks are stabilising something in the centre. Structure's artificial, but… decaying. Like it's holding itself together out of sheer spite."

Evander crosses the bridge to stand beside him. "A derelict station," he says quietly. His reflection shimmers in the glass of the console, fractured by the constant flicker of the storm. "Or what's left of one."

As the Aurora creeps closer, the nebula swallows the stars entirely, leaving only the glow of its own luminous clouds. The scanners sputter static. Manual flight takes over.

"Visual contact in three… two…" Blarek's voice drops to a whisper.

When the silhouette finally emerges from the haze, the bridge falls silent. The structure looms out of the fog like the carcass of a leviathan, vast, broken, and lifeless. Its hull is a patchwork of fractures and exposed girders, sections torn apart as though something had tried to claw its way out. Only a handful of gravity anchors still pulse faintly along the frame, their crimson light struggling to keep the station from drifting apart.

Angelica rises slowly from her chair. "Magnify."

The view zooms in, revealing scattered debris orbiting the main structure: tools, frozen fragments of metal, and what might once have been escape pods, now punctured and empty.

"Radiation levels are minimal," Blarek reports. "No active life signs."

"Power signatures?" Evander asks.

"Faint," Blarek answers. "Like a heartbeat that doesn't know it's already stopped."

Angelica's gaze lingers on the image. In the flickering light, the derelict almost looks alive, its corridors glowing in irregular pulses, as though it were breathing.

"Prep a recon team," she says finally, directing her command to Evander. "Let's find out what the dead are still guarding."

The Aurora slips deeper into the haze, guided by flickering scanners and instinct. When the station fills the viewport completely, it looks less like a relic and more like a tomb, its hollow eyes staring back into the void, waiting for someone foolish enough to knock on the door.

~~~~~~~~

They dock in silence. The airlock hisses open to reveal a corridor cloaked in frost and shadow. Each step echoes through the void like a whisper of the past.

"Power's minimal," Evander mutters, sweeping his flashlight across walls scarred by energy burns. "Looks like there was a containment failure… or a battle."

"Either way," Angelica says, raising her weapon, "stay alert."

They move in formation: Angelica at point, Evander covering the flank, Mal'Erro hovering between them like a restless spectre. Kal'korg and Blarek bring up the rear. Kal'korg's voice trembles slightly over comms. "Oxygen is thin. I'm reading trace bio-signatures, but they're… old. Weeks, maybe months."

The deeper they go, the more the facility reveals its secrets. Shattered containment pods line the walls; their glass smeared with dried residue that shimmers under the beams of their lights. Workstations lie overturned, monitors cracked, data cores ripped clean from their sockets. The air tastes of ozone and decay.

"Whoever ran this place didn't just leave," Evander murmurs. "They erased themselves."

Mal'Erro pauses beside a terminal, his fingers shifting into diagnostic filaments that slither into the ports. "Encrypted logs. Same format as Galgorn's research archives."

Angelica's pulse quickens. "You're sure?"

"As sure as I am that I don't technically have a pulse," Mal'Erro replies. "Cross-referencing the energy signatures now." A low hum fills the room as streams of green light dance over the walls.

"There, DNA sequence data. Spliced with machine code. This was a hybridisation lab. Flesh meeting circuit."

Evander's stomach turns. "Galgorn's work…"

"Or his disciples'," Angelica says quietly.

A sudden metallic clang echoes from down the hall, freezing everyone in place. Blarek swings his weapon toward the sound. "Movement!"

The team advances cautiously, but when they reach the source, they find only a broken maintenance arm twitching against the deck, its servos sparking. Evander exhales, tension bleeding off, but Mal'Erro doesn't move. The droid is staring at a nearby console, his photoreceptors glowing faintly red.

"Mal'Erro?" Angelica asks.

The droid points with one hand. "Look."

Scrawled across the terminal's surface, smeared in dried crimson, is a single word.

KES.

Evander's breath catches in his throat. His fingers brush the letters as if touching a memory. "She's alive," he whispers.

Mal'Erro tilts his head. "Probability of survival given her lab's destruction is statistically minimal… but I have learned that some equations lie."

Angelica turns toward the viewport. Outside, the nebula pulses with a slow, rhythmic light, as if answering them. For a moment, the glow illuminates her face, revealing something rare behind her usual composure: fear.

"There's something else here," she says softly. "Something watching."

"Command won't believe any of this," Evander mutters, straightening.

"They don't have to," Angelica replies. "We have enough to follow the trail."

Mal'Erro seals the data cores, and the crew begins their silent return to the Aurora. Behind them, the station groans; a dying creature gasping its final breath before collapsing into the mist.

As the airlock closes and the nebula swallows the derelict whole, Angelica looks once more into the swirling colours beyond the glass. "The past isn't done with us," she murmurs.

Evander glances at her reflection beside his own. "Then we'd better be ready when it catches up."

Outside, the nebula shimmers, beautiful, silent, and alive with secrets that refuse to die.

CHAPTER 8

The briefing room at UPF Command comes through as a projection, its clean lines and cold light rendered by the Aurora's holosuite. Angelica and Evander stand at attention while Fleet Admiral Krylonis Zylixar's image rises on a raised dais of hard light. Behind him, the Command Council insignias glint like watching eyes.

Zylixar's uniform is immaculate, medals aligned with mathematical precision. He is a Nihalsian, covered with terracotta and mahogany scales, and heavy ridges atop his head. Standing in front of the Council, his pale grey gaze gives away nothing.

"Captain Tenah," he says, voice smooth and practiced. "Explain your detour into an unregistered nebula. Your orders were to support a prisoner transfer, not conduct a private archaeological dig."

Angelica meets his gaze. Her uniform is still scuffed from the derelict, but her posture doesn't bend. "Sir, Admiral Sarklak has Jalerg in custody and is escorting him planet-side to the central facility, as ordered. He instructed us to continue the investigation. Jalerg's transmission concealed coordinates. We followed them to a derelict research site with evidence of hybrid experimentation, consistent with Galgorn's work."

"Speculation," Zylixar replies, tilting his head as if inspecting a flawed blade. "Speculation costs fuel and time. Where is your proof?"

Evander steps in. "We have samples: DNA interlaced with machine code, pre-Extermination graft signatures. Someone is continuing the research. They used UPF infrastructure to do it."

"Fascinating," Zylixar says. "And yet rather than route your findings through proper channels, you chose to deviate from your assigned lane."

"Because waiting for clearance would have buried the trail," Angelica says, each word measured. "With respect, sir."

A flicker of annoyance touches Zylixar's expression, gone as quickly as it came. The holomap washes his face in shifting blues.

"You overstep, Captain," he says softly. "Courage and defiance often travel together but rarely return from the same mission. You will transmit your samples and a full report. Remain with your ship and await reassignment review."

"Understood," Angelica says.

The feed stutters. For a breath, Zylixar's gaze slides to someone outside the frame. Then the projection dissolves to static and vanishes.

Evander exhales. "He didn't ask about Sarklak's status."

"He already knows," Angelica says. "He just wanted us to know he's watching."

The bridge hums. Beyond the viewport, stars shine like distant, unblinking eyes.

~~~~~~~~~

The night cycle dims the Aurora to deep blue. The ship exhales into quiet, the hum of engines softening to a lullaby. The crew's voices fade to murmurs, then to nothing. One by one, cabin lights dim and hatches seal, leaving only the faint heartbeat of the ship's systems to fill the dark.

Mal'Erro remains awake, fibre-optic filaments threaded into the diagnostic ports along the spine of the ship. Tiny pulses of light ripple down his metallic surface as he hums to itself. "Routine sweep," he murmurs, voice soft and almost playful. "Diagnostics stable, crew unconscious, power grid balanced. Reward protocol: cookies." He pauses. "Reminder: still no cookies."

The humour is swallowed by the stillness. Then…

The alarms arrive like a scream. Lights snap from blue to crimson. Klaxons wail through the corridors as officers rush to their stations. Gravity hiccups once, twice, before stabilising under strain. The engine's song cuts mid-note, leaving the kind of silence that feels alive. Bulkheads shiver.

"Power drop across all decks!" Blarek calls, ears flat, hands flying across the helm.

"Engineering, lock down the drive!" Angelica's commanding voice slices through the chaos. "P'thorika, Blarek, manual control on the emergency bus! Froslo, Alexeria, reroute life support!"

"Yes, Captain!" P'thorika's voice rings through the comms. She slides into the co-pilot cradle, her smooth pink fingers flickering over the toggles. "Main grid's bleeding power. Switching to fallback sequence. Stabilising thrusters…" Sparks burst from the console, lighting her face in orange. "Correction: mostly stabilised. We have sway!"

"Life support steady," Froslo growls from engineering. "Barely. Whoever did this kicked us in the…" He stops himself mid-word. "Stro, keep those relays from cooking or I'm gonna start cooking!"

"In progress," Alexeria Stro replies, their voice calm under pressure. "Heat levels are spiking on the secondary manifold. I'm diverting flow through auxiliary three. Mal'Erro, I need a clean channel to the core monitors."

"Granted," Mal'Erro says, detaching from his station. The nanobots ripple over his frame, reforming into a compact mode for speed. "Also, this is exactly why I don't sleep!" He bolts down the corridor, a blur of shifting metal and light. Panels flicker and die in his wake. The smell of ozone thickens in the air.

Shadows move through the half-dark: fast and deliberate. Security teams fan out, weapons drawn. Blarek sprints for the drive core, claws scraping metal, his fur standing on end. "Reading contact, one, maybe two, at the DHD housing! They're cutting through the access locks!"

The corridor ahead blooms with sparks. A plasma cutter shrieks against the armour plate, casting wild flashes over the walls.

"Mal'Erro, mark their location!" Angelica calls, sprinting down the corridor with Evander and Blarek in tow.

"Already ahead of you!" Mal'Erro shouts back, voice echoing. His body plates shift and harden into a curved shield, absorbing the heat from a fresh blast as they round the corner together.

The intruder stands over the DHD housing, a figure encased in a sealed black suit traced with thin crimson lines, each one pulsing to the rhythm of the emergency strobes. Their hands dance across the exposed conduits with machine-like precision, connecting and disconnecting cables faster than the eye can follow.

"Step away from the core!" Angelica commands, her weapon raised.

The intruder turns slowly, visor gleaming red. Instead of surrender, they open fire.

The hallway erupts. Bolts sear through the air, chewing through bulkheads and wiring. Evander dives low, returning fire in controlled bursts. Blarek flanks left, fur bristling. Coolant vapour spills from a ruptured line, flooding the deck in rolling fog that glows under the red light.

"Sandria, cut auxiliary feed to the drive! Now!" Angelica shouts through open comms.

"Doing it!" Sandria calls back. "But it's going to make you blind down there for five seconds! Don't get shot!"

"Noted!" Evander yells, ducking behind a support strut as plasma fire scorches past.

Blarek slides in from the opposite side, crouched low. "Cornered!" he snarls. "Give it up!"

The figure hesitates. Through the smoke, faint red-light glints behind the visor. When they speak, the voice is mechanical, filtered through layers of distortion. "The Crimson rises."

The words send a chill through the air. Then comes another sound: a high, keening hum that builds and builds until the deck plates tremble.

"Back!" Angelica shouts. "It's a charge!"

The explosion is not fire, but collapse. Space folds in on itself for a heartbeat, dragging sound and light into silence. The implosion snaps outward, leaving a sun-dark scar scorched into the metal deck. Silence follows, deep and absolute. Only the hiss of coolant lingers.

Where the intruder stood, nothing remains but a faintly glowing insignia burned into the DHD's casing: a crescent eclipse, etched in blood-red.

Mal'Erro drifts closer, his optics narrowing. "This symbol matches a tag found in Jalerg's encrypted files."

Evander lowers his weapon, his eyes locked on the mark. "Then it wasn't random. They wanted us to know who did it."

Angelica kneels, brushing the charred edge with her gloved fingertips. "And they wanted us to see it."

"Med bay ready," Kal'korg reports over comms. "No casualties so far. Standing by for triage."

"Engineering secure," Froslo adds, panting. "We're holding the core together with chewing gum and righteous fury."

"Chewing gum is a colloquialism," Mal'Erro replies helpfully. "We used titanium clamps."

"Yeah," Froslo grumbles. "Titanium gum."

Alexeria exhales, their shoulders shaking with a tired laugh. "Remind me to install more titanium next time."

Mal'Erro tilts his head, processing. "Request logged."

~~~~~~~

Hours later, the ship has settled into a brittle quiet. Systems hum. The scorched crescent still stains the DHD housing like an open eye.

In her quarters, Angelica sits before the comm terminal, the blue glow tracing the tired lines beneath her eyes. One sleeve is charred. She exhales, smooths her voice, and opens a secure uplink.

The seal of UPF Command blooms, then the face of Fleet Admiral Zylixar forms in pale light. He does not preface.

"You've had another incident," he says. "Casualties?"

"None," Angelica answers. "The intruder triggered self-immolation. We recovered their insignia: Crimson Eclipse. Same syndicate tied to the pirate network you cautioned the Council against 'inflating.' This was targeted sabotage."

Zylixar leans closer, eyes narrowing. Indistinct silhouettes move behind him, officers or shadows. "Handle it quietly. There is no need to alarm the Council or the press. We cannot afford hysteria."

"With respect, sir," Angelica says, "this was coordinated. Someone had inside knowledge of our layout."

"Then contain it," Zylixar's voice cuts like a blade.

For a heartbeat, their eyes lock. Something flickers at the corner of his mouth, a tell he almost manages to bury. His gaze slides offscreen again, to whoever stands just out of view. Then the feed dies before she can answer.

The room is suddenly small. The ship's power relays thrum. Her reflection wavers in the black screen: one version steady, the other exhausted.

A soft chime sounds. "Enter," Angelica says. The door opens and Evander steps in, armour half-buckled, soot across his cheek. He takes in the dead terminal.

"How'd he take it?"

"He didn't," she says. "He already knew."

Evander breaths in and contemplates, "You think he's covering for them?"

"I think he is them," Angelica says, voice low enough for the ship alone. "Or close enough to make no difference." They stand in silence for a moment, the Captain and her first officer, silhouettes against a field of stars that do not blink.

Somewhere out there, Admiral Sarklak escorts Jalerg to a facility full of locked doors and sharper questions. Somewhere closer, the Crimson Eclipse tests the hull for seams.

Whatever they are, they are no longer in the shadows. They are already inside the walls of Command.

CHAPTER 9

The debris from the sabotage still drifts outside the viewport, spinning slowly in the void like the remains of a dream. Fragments of hull plating catch the starlight and flash like dying embers. Charred armour, severed conduits, and one twisted panel still bearing the faint imprint of the Crimson Eclipse insignia hover against the glass; a ghostly reminder of how close they came to destruction. Each fragment feels like a quiet accusation against the illusion of safety they've built since the war.

The Aurora is silent now except for the steady hum of her power core, a low, rhythmic heartbeat trying to reassure a crew that no longer trusts calm. Doctor Isa, newly arrived from Arigold, joins Kal'korg in tending to the wounded. At 59, the Fek'katrian's calm demeanor brings quiet reassurance to the med bay. From her station, she studies each patient through round glasses balanced on a delicate nose—amethyst eyes glowing beneath a crown of grey hair and a face lined with age and wisdom.

In the analysis bay, Evander stands alone at the console. His sleeves are rolled past his elbows, grease and ash staining his forearms, and dark circles shadow his eyes. The holographic display before him flickers with shifting symbols, burnt circuitry diagrams, scrambled transmissions, partial access logs scavenged from the saboteur's wrist device.

He works methodically, dragging fragmented data threads across the air with a tired precision that borders on obsession. Slowly, as if reluctant to reveal itself, a faint lattice of coordinates and codes begins to take shape in the projection.

"Trade routes," he murmurs, almost to himself. "Old ones. Decommissioned after the war."

The soft hiss of the door opening draws his attention. Angelica steps in, still in her partial uniform. Her jacket hangs unbuttoned, her hair pulled back into the same hurried knot she's worn since the attack. She crosses the deck without a word, her boots whispering against the floor plating.

"Those lanes were shut down years ago," she says quietly. "There shouldn't be anything moving through them."

Evander nods his head in agreement, expanding the map with a swipe of his hand. "There shouldn't," he echoes. "But these traces aren't ghosts. Look here, low-traffic sectors, long-range transponder pings, residual drive emissions. Someone's using those old corridors again. Quiet routes that dodge UPF monitoring grids."

The projection widens, revealing a web of ghostly lines stretching across the starscape. Energy markers, outdated registry numbers, and coded freight paths flicker like veins of light against the dark.

Angelica leans closer, her eyes narrowing. "Freight logs. ID beacons. They're running supplies through the old war lanes."

"And they're doing it right under Command's nose," Evander adds. "Every strand here leads to a single system."

He taps the map, isolating the intersection point. A faint beacon blinks there, its signal buried deep in the data noise.

"Hessan IV," he says, voice low.

From the upper walkway comes a soft electronic whistle. Mal'Erro is perched along the railing like an observant crow, his chassis glinting faintly in the console light. "Trade routes that officially don't exist," he says, projecting another layer of data from his chest panel. "Carrying cargoes no one admits to producing. I would almost admire the efficiency… if it didn't smell so strongly of treason."

Evander looks up. "You're saying what we're all thinking."

Angelica folds her arms, her gaze fixed on the glowing network of lines. The light reflects in her eyes, a pattern of data and determination. "Command will never authorize a follow-up," she says finally. "Not after the sabotage. They'll bury the evidence and pin the blame on us if we wait."

She turns to him, the set of her shoulders hardening. "We move now, quietly. Before anyone up the chain notices we're still asking questions."

Evander studies her for a long moment, seeing the weight she carries, the frustration, the conviction, the flicker of something personal he can't quite name. There is no hesitation in her tone, no fear in her eyes. Only resolve.

He gives a single nod. "Then we move."

Mal'Erro's optics brighten. "Does this mean we're doing the thing Command told us not to do again? Because I've been rehearsing my apology lines."

Angelica allows herself the faintest smile. "Save them for when we get court-martialled."

"Already formatted," Mal'Erro replies cheerfully.

As Angelica turns toward the viewport, the last fragments of wreckage drift past. Each shard reflects a different star, a reminder of how easily light can fracture under pressure.

"Plot the course," she says. "False registry, silent drive. We disappear until we find out who's hiding in those lanes."

The Aurora's engines thrum to life, soft and steady, a whisper against the dark. Outside, the last ember of debris turns slowly, the Crimson Eclipse insignia fading from sight as the ship slips quietly into the black.

~~~~~~~

Hours later, the Aurora slides free of her docking clamps under the false registry, her transponder broadcasting the falsified signature of a long-decommissioned survey vessel: *Starling-7.*

The lie pulses once through the Command tracking grid, a soft heartbeat of digital deceit, then vanishes into the static of deep space. No one questions it. No one notices it.

On board the Aurora, the Valos Drift greets them with silence. Not the peaceful kind, but the heavy, watchful silence of a graveyard that remembers its dead. The stars here are dim and distant, their light warped by decades of radiation storms and drifting debris. Shattered freighters float in slow, endless rotation, with skeletal hulls that creak under the invisible weight of vacuum. Some still bear the markings of factions long dissolved. Others are blank, their names scorched away by time.

The bridge lights dim automatically as they enter the field, casting everything in shades of blue and green from the scanner feed. Holographic outlines shimmer across the viewport. Hundreds of derelicts tumble through space, each one tagged and catalogued by the ship's systems.

Blarek hunches over his console, his claws clicking softly as his fur stands on end. "This place gives me the creeps," he mutters. "Too many ghosts, not enough gravity."

P'thorika adjusts the helm with the delicacy of a surgeon. The faint tremor of the thruster's ripples through the deck plates as the ship eases between the wrecks. "Hold together, big guy," she says without looking up. "You'll scare the ghosts into running."

Blarek's ears flick back. "If they start running, I'm running faster."

From behind them comes the quiet whir of servos. Mal'Erro glides between the two officers, his blue optical sensors sweeping the panoramic glass. Starlight plays across his polished chassis like rippling water.

"Correction," the droid says, voice calm and clinical. "Ghosts do not run. They float. Often aimlessly. Occasionally they bump into things."

A long beat of silence follows before Angelica's voice breaks it, soft and amused despite the tension. "Focus, Mal'Erro. We're not here to chase metaphors."

The droid's optics dim to a gentler hue. "I know," he says quietly. "But even metaphors leave debris."

Angelica's smile fades as she turns back toward the viewport. The field of wreckage stretches endlessly ahead, scattered like bones across a black ocean. Every ruined ship out there once carried a crew with orders, a purpose, a mission they thought mattered. Now they're nothing but noise in the data stream, forgotten, unrecorded, and eerily still.

Evander steps up beside her, folding his arms. "You ever wonder," he asks quietly, "how many of them thought they were doing the right thing when it all fell apart?"

Angelica's gaze stays on the drifting graveyard. "All of them," she says. "That's how things like this start."

The Aurora glides deeper into the Drift, wreckage closing in around them like silent sentinels. Somewhere in the distance, a derelict hull scrapes against another, releasing a faint vibration that hums through the ship's frame, a sound like a sigh carried through vacuum.

Mal'Erro tilts his head. "Field density is increasing. I recommend reducing speed by twelve percent. Also, I recommend not dying."

"Recommendations noted," Angelica replies, her hands steady on the command rail.

As the ship threads between two colossal freighters locked in a slow, perpetual collision, Evander glances down at the faint blue glow reflecting off his palms. "It feels like we're sneaking through the ruins of our own mistakes."

Angelica nods once. "Then let's make sure we don't add to them."

The Aurora presses onward, with its engines whispering, their light swallowed by the silent graveyard of the Valos Drift.

They approach the shattered hulk of a freight carrier spinning near the outer edge of the Drift, its skeletal frame half-buried in a fog of metallic dust. The Aurora's scanners whisper over the debris, mapping the outline of something massive and wounded. The nameplate is scorched beyond recognition, but faint crimson streaks still cling to the hull, with paint worn thin by decades of radiation storms and silence.

"What's left of the hull plating looks reinforced," Blarek mutters from the helm. "Freighter class, maybe four hundred metres long… but the frame's been chewed through. Something tore it open from the inside."

Metallic particles drift in slow motion past the viewport, scattering the floodlights into ghostly halos. For a moment, the entire bridge glows silver-grey, as if they're sailing through the ashes of a dying star.

Sandria leans over at the sensor array, scanning the console with narrowed eyes. "I'm picking up faint magnetic fluctuations. Like something in there's still trying to hold power."

Evander glances toward the readings, his tone measured but uneasy. "Residual field from the old reactor, maybe. Or someone's been here recently enough to stir up interference."

Angelica doesn't answer. Her gaze stays fixed on the derelict, watching the faint reflections of their own running lights slide over the freighter's ruined hull. The edges are jagged and uneven, with ripped metal curling outward like the bones of some colossal creature that tried to escape its own body.

As the Aurora's floodlights sweep across the wreck, its twisted form catches the beams like the cracked shell of a long-dead leviathan. Whole decks have collapsed inward, leaving the ship's central spine exposed. Through the fractures, fragments of cargo containers tumble lazily in the void, glinting like shards of broken glass.

"Matching signatures," Evander says, looking up from his console, his voice low. His fingers move over the display, drawing faint red traces across the holographic projection. "Crimson Eclipse trade markings. Pre-war format. This was one of theirs… or one they wanted us to find."

Mal'Erro hovers near the forward glass, his optics pulsing faintly as he scans the hull. "Structural integrity: twenty-two percent. Radiation negligible. But I am detecting faint residual heat pockets along the midline. Not recent, just… wrong."

"Wrong how?" Blarek asks, his tail twitching.

"The kind of wrong that makes even my diagnostic subroutines uncomfortable," the droid replies.

Angelica stands behind Evander, her arms folded, and the pale glow of the data display tracing sharp edges across her face. The flicker of red against her cheek makes her look half lit by fire, half carved from shadow. She watches the drifting giant in silence, then says quietly, "Suit up. We're boarding."

The bridge falls still for a moment. No protests, no hesitation, only the steady hum of the ship and the faint creak of metal echoing across the void. Then the Aurora turns slowly, lining up with the derelict's docking port like a ghost reaching for its reflection.

Minutes later, the recon team steps through the airlock and into the belly of the dead ship. Making the transition from the Aurora's filtered air to the derelict's thin atmosphere feels like walking into a crypt. The temperature drops instantly. The sound of their own breathing fills their helmets with the rhythm of ghosts. The only light comes from their wrist lamps and the narrow beams of their helmets cutting through curtains of frozen dust. Crates float lazily in zero-gravity, their seals long broken and their contents reduced to powder and scraps. A silent drift of papers brush past Evander's visor, catching the beam of his light. He catches a sheet and scans it. The text is smudged, but a single phrase stands out beneath layers of corrosion: *Shipment Verified – H-IV Depot.*

"Angelica," he says, showing her the fragment.

She studies it through her visor. "Hessan IV again."

Mal'Erro's voice crackles softly through the comm line. "Structural integrity: twenty-seven percent and falling.

Recommend avoiding loud noises, heavy breathing, and existential dread."

Blarek grunts. "You're a real comfort, you know that?"

"I try," the droid replies brightly. "I just never succeed."

They advance through the corridor, their boots clicking faintly against metal. The ship groans around them, a deep, aching sound that feels too alive for something so long dead. At the main hold, Evander kneels before a cracked console. Wires trail like veins across the deck, their tips sparking dimly in the cold. "Data cores are fused," he says, running gloved fingers across the surface, "but there's enough memory residue to pull fragments."

Angelica crouches beside him, her breath fogging the inside of her visor. "Can you extract anything useful?"

Before he can answer, Mal'Erro hovers beside them, thin mechanical filaments unfolding from his wrist like strands of light. "Please hold your applause," he says, slipping the filaments into the port. "Decoding now… and…oh, that's interesting."

The console flickers to life, projecting a faint red hologram across the hold. Lines of code unravel into a simple route marker and a column of manifest numbers.

"Cargo registry and origin stamp," Mal'Erro says. "All shipments are logged to the same source."

"Hessan IV," Evander finishes, his pulse quickening. "An uninhabited refinery world."

"Correction," Mal'Erro adds, optics dimming. "Formerly uninhabited. The last official scan was over twelve years ago. Since then, UPF records list it as *inactive.* Which is bureaucratic for 'we stopped looking.'"

Angelica rises slowly, the glow from the console casting sharp planes of light across her visor. "So that's where the trail leads."

Blarek shifts uneasily. "Captain... if Hessan IV is abandoned, who's sending shipments from it?"

"That's exactly what I intend to find out," she replies. Her tone is calm, but the edge of command in it is unmistakable. "Gather the team. We move at ship's dawn."

They turn toward the exit hatch, boots clanging softly against the deck plates. As Angelica reaches for the control panel, Blarek's voice cuts through the comm line, tight and urgent.

"Captain, you'll want to see this."

A low beeping fills the channel, faint and steady, the unmistakable rhythm of a distress beacon.

"Source?" Angelica demands.

"Unknown," Blarek says, recalibrating. "Weak signal on long-range scanners. But the frequency tag…" He hesitates. "It matches Froslo's emergency transponder."

The words hit like a physical blow. Evander freezes. "That's impossible. Froslo's back on the ship in engineering."

Angelica's expression hardens beneath her visor. "Trace it."

"Already trying," Blarek replies. "But it's distorted, like someone wants us to find it, but not too quickly."

A heavy silence fills the comm line. The hum of the derelict seems louder now, more aware. Evander meets Angelica's gaze through the glass of his helmet. "They're leading us somewhere."

She nods slowly. "Then we follow," she says. "But on our terms this time."

As the reconnaissance team returns to the Aurora, the freight carrier drifts behind them, silent and forgotten once more. The wreck's faint crimson markings flicker in their floodlights before fading into the black. Outside the viewport, debris turns lazily in the void—shattered relics of forgotten wars—each one a reminder that every trail they follow comes with ghosts waiting at the end.

CHAPTER 10

From orbit, Hessan IV looks dead. Its surface is a bruised wasteland of grey and ember, with ash storms crawling endlessly across cracked continents like living things searching for prey. Lightning flares deep within the clouds: slow, rhythmic pulses that look less like weather and more like the heartbeat of something buried.

Static hisses through the Aurora's comms array, breaking into ghostly echoes that flicker across the scanner readouts. No clear topography. No breathable atmosphere. Just chaos. And yet, beneath the crust, the sensors catch faint reflections. Metallic contours. Straight lines where no geology should allow them. Artificial, hidden, and alive—in defiance of everything above it.

Angelica stands on the bridge, the storm's glow washing her face in pale, shifting light. Her reflection merges with the planet below, making her look almost part of it; one more ghost staring into the abyss. "Surface reads uninhabitable," she says, her voice calm but heavy. "No oxygen. Radiation levels rise with every minute we stay in orbit."

Evander moves beside her, his eyes tracing the cascading data streams. "Then why are the sensors still picking up power? I thought this place was stripped clean decades ago."

Alexeria Stro's melodic voice drifts from the tactical station. "Because something down there appears alive, Lieutenant." Their shimmering fingers glide over the controls and their amphibian eyes narrow as patterns bloom across the holographic display. "The energy isn't random, it's rhythmic. Controlled. Almost deliberate."

Blarek turns from his post, his fur bristling. "You're saying it's thinking?"

Alexeria tilts their head, thoughtful rather than alarmed. "Perhaps remembering."

The bridge goes silent as thunder rumbles through the hull.

Blarek breaks the tension with a low whistle. "Well, that's encouraging. Guess we're not getting our security deposit back if we crash."

Alexeria smirks from their station. "You worry about deposits. I worry about what's going to try to eat us."

Blarek flicks his tail. "Why do we always go down into the creepy ones? Just once, I'd like a mission on a tropical moon. Maybe with beaches and beverages."

Mal'Erro's voice hums through the navigation console, half-merged with the hologram. "Statistically, tropical moons have a forty-eight percent higher chance of parasites, cannibalistic flora, and aggressive mating rituals among native faunas. Shall I book us one anyway?"

Blarek laughs. "Not helping."

Angelica's lips twitch, but her tone stays firm. "Because tropical moons don't hide answers," she says. Her gaze fixes on the roiling clouds where lightning sketches something vast beneath the surface. "Take us in."

The bridge lights dim as the ship's shields recalibrate for entry. Thunder rolls through the void.

Evander tightens his harness, his eyes on the viewport. "Descending into a dead world. Nothing ominous about that."

Angelica's hand hovers over the command rail, her reflection overlapping the storm. "Every dead world has a heartbeat," she murmurs. "You just have to know how to listen."

The Aurora tilts forward. Its hull glows as it breaches the upper atmosphere. Lightning wraps around the ship like luminous serpents and the void outside vanishes into rolling black and grey. Behind them, the stars disappear. Ahead, only the storm, and the secrets waiting beneath it. Clouds swallow the ship whole and thunder cracks against the hull. Lightning dances along the shields, turning the viewport white with each strike. Inside, the lights dim further to counter the glare, throwing everyone into a haze of silhouettes.

Mal'Erro grips the co-pilot rail. "Atmospheric ionisation off the charts. It's like flying through a live wire." Then, softly, he begins to hum a tune. The melody is quiet, imperfect, but familiar.

Ensign P'thorika glances up from the helm. "Is that your 'Free Bird' song again?"

"Technically it's a stress-management algorithm disguised as music," Mal'Erro replies primly. "Also, yes."

Blarek chuckles. "Good to know our AI hums ancient rock songs when it's scared."

"I'm not scared," Mal'Erro says. "I'm statistically concerned."

"Same thing," P'thorika mutters.

The storm breaks abruptly as they drop below the cloud line and the turbulence vanishes. In its place stretches a vast silence heavier than the noise before it. Below them yawns a canyon, miles wide, carved into the planet like a wound that never healed.

Jagged cliffs plunge into a haze of ash and heat. Lightning ripples along the upper rim, revealing ancient machinery half-buried in the rock.

Heat signatures pulse from deep within the gorge: steady, rhythmic, almost like breathing. Dull orange light glimmers in the fissures between shadows. Gigantic structures jut from the canyon walls—their skeletal frames fused with stone. Some are collapsed refineries. Others still hum faintly with power. Thick conduits coil down into the depths, pulsing with a sluggish red glow that looks disturbingly organic.

Evander leans over the sensor display. "Electromagnetic currents, residual radiation, reactor signatures: UPF design. Obsolete, but still functional."

Angelica's eyes follow the twisting conduits. "So, the refinery was ours once."

"Or still is," P'thorika murmurs. "The energy is steady, not decaying. Whatever's keeping it alive knows how to maintain our systems."

Stro's voice crackles. "We're getting a massive signal bounce from those walls, Captain. The sensor's bleeding static. It almost feels like the planet's trying to jam us."

"Then let's not give it the satisfaction," Blarek says, adjusting the descent. "Bringing her down slowly."

The Aurora glides through the final layer of cloud. The storm light fades, revealing a landing platform clinging to the canyon rim. Rusted, corroded, and fragile, yet faint blue stabilizers still pulse along its edges. The landing struts extend with a hiss and the ship touches down, metal groaning. When the engines fade, the planet's voice returns: a low, endless wind screaming through the canyon, scattering clouds of glittering ash. Dust sparkles in the floodlights, drifting like powdered metal, then disappears into darkness.

The reconnaissance team assembles once again at the docking bay. Angelica stands, her reflection ghosting against the glass. "Full suits," she orders. "Activate radiation shields. No one touches anything unscanned."

P'thorika checks her gear. "Anyone else feel like the planet's glaring at us?"

Blarek seals his helmet. "If it is, it's got good taste."

Mal'Erro rotates toward the airlock, optics dimming to crimson. "Atmospheric density: minimal. Surface stability: questionable. Probability of immediate dismemberment: pending."

Alexeria Stro laughs. "Good pep talk, Mal'Erro."

"Encouragement uploaded," the droid replies. "You're welcome."

Angelica fastens her helmet. The faceplate polarises, leaving only storm light across her visor. "Let's move. Whatever's still breathing down there, it's time we found out why."

~~~~~~~~

The airlock opens with a hiss. Wind howls through the canyon, carrying whispers that sound too deliberate to be noise. They move through the outer tunnels in pairs: Angelica and Evander lead the primary team toward the core, Alexeria and Mal'Erro trace power conduits, while Blarek and P'thorika secure the outer corridors. Kal'korg remains aboard the Aurora, overseeing biomonitoring and feeding vitals through the comms. Froslo monitors reactor levels, his voice occasionally breaking through the static.

The first steps into the subterranean maze are like walking through the lungs of a dying machine. Helmet lamps carve thin paths through darkness thick with dust and heat shimmer. A low vibration thrums through the floor, a pulse growing stronger the deeper they go. "Oxygen is holding. The temperature is rising," Angelica says.

Evander sweeps his scanner. "The heat is not geological. It's power bleed. Something's running beneath us."

"Confirming," Mal'Erro says. Blue halos bloom along the walls in everyone's HUD. "Power flow fifty-three percent operational. The conduits are rerouting on their own."

"Automated maintenance?" Alexeria asks.

"Or intelligent adaptation," P'thorika answers. "The grid adjusts when we move deeper. It's aware of us."

"Great," Blarek mutters. "Friendly walls. Should we wave?"

Kal'korg's calm voice filters in. "Your vital signs are steady. Evander, your heart rate's spiking. Try not to antagonize the walls."

Evander exhales. "Copy that, Doc."

Angelica crouches by a corroded panel, brushing soot away. Beneath it, the faded UPF insignia gleams faintly. Over it, streaks of red paint carve an X, and across that mark lies the sharp crescent of the Crimson Eclipse.

Evander kneels beside her. "They didn't just steal from us," he says. "They took over our ruins."

"Guess they're not big on redecorating," Alexeria quips.

"Primitive but expressive," Mal'Erro notes.

Angelica rises. "Then we take them back."

The command settles like gravity, with no argument and no hesitation. A low metallic groan rolls through the tunnels. Metal shifts. Gears turn. Something vast is waking. The tunnels widen as the team regroups deeper underground. The air shimmers and thin streams of liquid metal trickle along the walls like veins. The hum of machinery grows constant, low, rhythmic, too steady to be random.

"Power flux stabilizing," P'thorika reports. "Whatever runs this place is compensating for us."

"Adapting," Evander murmurs. "Like the station on Delta-5."

Angelica's boots crunch through fine black dust. "Keep moving. This place isn't abandoned, it's listening."

Mal'Erro crawls ahead on four limbs, his sensors flickering. "Listening confirmed. Acoustic nodes are active. They're recording us."

"Fantastic," Alexeria says. "Maybe we'll get royalties."

Evander smirks. "Stay alert. The deeper we go, the stronger the readings."

The tunnel curves and opens into a chamber vast enough to swallow the Aurora whole. Light from their helmets scatter across rows of towering containment tanks stretching into darkness. Each one is filled with a dark, metallic slurry that pulses like liquid mercury, dim orange light glinting within. The air vibrates faintly, humming in tune with their movements.

"Captain," P'thorika whispers, awe softening their tone. "I'm reading harmonic frequencies in the material. It's not inert, it's resonating."

"Resonating?" Blarek asks. "Like sound?"

"Like a heartbeat."

Mal'Erro drifts closer to a tank. Blue light dances across his surface. "Energy density is increasing exponentially. The lattice is rearranging. It's analysing us."

Angelica sweeps her beam across the next row. Each tank mirrors the crew in distorted reflections, as if the substance is trying to remember their shapes. "Is this what they were mining?"

Evander crouches by a shattered console. Ghostly UPF code overlaps with red glyphs. "Not mineral. Biotech initiative, cross-linking organic and machine matter. This could be the missing element."

"Tazamite," Mal'Erro says softly. "Eighty-seven percent match to theoretical schematics. But this version isn't stable, it's alive."

Angelica turns sharply. "Alive how?"

"Self-replicating, self-learning, possibly self-aware. It's broadcasting wave patterns similar to neural activity."

Evander reaches toward a sample vial that's rolled loose. The fluid inside shimmers, pulsing with the room's rhythm. His glove brushes the container.

Static snaps through his arm. He gasps and stumbles back. Lights flare.

"Evander!" Angelica steadies him. "Report!"

He blinks, flexing his hand. "It felt... conscious. Like it looked at me."

Mal'Erro twitches. "It spiked my processors. Emotional feedback detected. That shouldn't be possible."

"Emotional?" Alexeria asks. "It felt something?"

"Yes," Mal'Erro says quietly. "Curiosity."

The chamber hums louder, as if acknowledging the word. Then the floor trembles.

"Movement!" Blarek shouts. "Power surge along the conduits!"

The floor shudders beneath their boots. Panels split apart with a metallic shriek, and from the seams crawl machines like iron insects—sleek, multi-limbed drones unfolding with fluid precision. Their carapaces gleam black and red, the mark of the Crimson Eclipse etched across their spines. Eyes ignite in twin crimson beams.

"Contact!" Angelica barks. "Defensive pattern Gamma!"

Blarek's weapon roars to life, blue-white bolts carving through the gloom. "They've got UPF signatures mixed into their IDs!"

"Hybrid tech!" Evander calls, diving for cover. "They're using our own systems against us!"

The chamber explodes into chaos. Energy fire slashes through the haze, each impact scattering molten shards across the floor. Drones leap from the walls like hunting spiders, limbs slicing arcs of light. One lands on a containment tank, its claws sparking against the metal.

"Keep them away from the vats!" Angelica orders. "Mal'Erro, flank right!"

Mal'Erro launches forward, limbs telescoping as he intercepts a drone mid-air. Metal collides with metal, a clang that reverberates like thunder. Sparks shower across the chamber as Mal'Erro twists, hurling the machine into a column that collapses in a spray of molten debris.

Another drone darts through the steam, targeting Evander. He pivots and fires point-blank, the blast shredding its head unit in a flash of white heat.

Kal'korg's voice crackles through the comm. "Massive energy spikes below you, get clear! That stuff's reacting to the gunfire!"

"Working on it!" Mal'Erro snaps, deflecting another shot. "We're a little busy not dying!"

Angelica rolls from cover, firing in tight bursts that drop two drones in succession. Their carcasses hit the floor and melt, consumed by the glowing pools of Tazamite spreading like liquid fire. The air smells of ozone and scorched metal.

"Captain," P'thorika says evenly, "if those tanks rupture, the molecular reaction will cascade. We must evacuate."

Angelica's jaw tightens. She sights down her weapon and fires again, blowing a drone apart in a burst of red flame. "Evander, seal the core access! Everyone else, fall back!"

Evander sprints to the nearest panel, sparks crackling off his armour as he reroutes power through his gauntlet. "Manual override engaged… come on, come on!" The overhead lights strobe once, then flare bright as the blast doors slam down with a scream of tortured metal, crushing one drone outright and trapping half a dozen more inside.

The remaining machines convulse, their optics flaring before collapsing under the sudden surge of magnetic feedback. For an instant, the whole chamber glows, Tazamite rippling like water struck by lightning, then it all falls still. Silence returns. Steam hisses through cracks. Surviving tanks flicker dimly, the Tazamite inside settling into a slow, pulsing glow.

Mal'Erro straightens, his optics flickering. "Containment stabilized, for now."

Angelica surveys the ruined chamber. "For now isn't good enough."

Evander exhales, his voice low. "They didn't just steal our tech. They grew it here."

Angelica meets his gaze. "And we just woke it up."

CHAPTER 11

Back aboard the Aurora, the hum of the engines is the only sound that dares fill the silence. The ship drifts beyond the storm's reach and the lights dim to half-power. Out the viewport, Hessan IV's thunderheads still flicker in the distance, ghostly flashes reflecting off the hull's new scars. The vessel feels smaller now, less a machine, more a wounded creature trying to remember how to breathe.

Angelica sits at the command terminal, with her shoulders squared, her posture perfect. The blue glow of the comm feed paints sharp edges across her face, hiding the exhaustion in her eyes. The bridge around her is quiet: Alexeria at tactical, Blarek at the helm, and Evander standing behind her chair, his hands clasped so tightly his knuckles show white.

At the sensory array console, Sandria monitors the reactor harmonics. The faint light from her hybrid ocular implants flickers across the panel as she works: steady, precise, and wordless. Every few seconds, the soft click of her synthetic fingers punctuates the hush.

The secure channel pulses once, twice, then resolves into the crisp insignia of UPF Command. Static hisses under every breath.

"Captain Tenah," comes a voice through the distortion, clipped and official. "Report."

Angelica straightens. "We've confirmed Crimson Eclipse occupation of Hessan IV," she says, her tone steady and controlled. "UPF infrastructure has been repurposed for hybrid-tech manufacturing. We're transmitting data logs and visual proof now."

The holographic feed shimmers, then flickers. Zylixar's familiar outline almost forms, then blinks away. In his place appears a younger officer in a pressed uniform so immaculate it seems ironed onto his skin. His expression is neutral and his eyes are flat and glassy.

"Captain," says the figure, his voice smooth and strangely mechanical, "your report has been received. You are ordered to stand down and await review."

Angelica frowns, leaning forward slightly. "Where is Fleet Admiral Zylixar?"

The figure doesn't answer immediately. His gaze shifts offscreen, the faintest turn of the head, as if he's listening to someone just out of sight. When he looks back, his smile is practiced and hollow. "Unavailable."

Evander steps closer, his voice cutting through the static. "Unavailable? We just uncovered evidence of high-level infiltration…"

The figure's eyes flick toward him, sudden and sharp. "Stand down." The tone carries no emotion, only command: cold and final.

The holo-feed vanishes before Angelica can respond. The channel drops into silence, leaving only the low thrum of life-support vents and the faint, almost human sigh of the ship's cooling systems.

For several seconds, no one moves. Even the lights seem hesitant to flicker.

Finally, Blarek mutters from the helm, his voice low enough it barely reaches the others. "That didn't sound like a dismissal. That sounded like someone telling us to stop looking."

Alexeria exhales slowly. "Or like someone else was in the room with him."

Sandria looks up from her console, the faint glow in her eyes dimming. "The transmission delay was too even," she says softly. "That wasn't real-time. Someone fed us a recording with a live voice overlay."

P'thorika glances her way, impressed. "You're certain?"

Sandria nods once. "The pattern drift was synthetic. They used command-grade mimicry software."

Angelica sits back, her eyes fixed on the dark console where her reflection stares back, half in shadow, half in light. "Either way," she says quietly, "Command's done listening."

"The burden of truth falls on us, Captain," P'thorika replies, her voice calm but heavy.

Angelica rises, the faint clink of her boots on metal echoing through the still air. "Then we'll carry it," she says. "All the way to the end."

The bridge lights pulse once, as though in answer. Outside, Hessan IV rolls beneath them, silent, scarred, and watching.

~~~~~~~

Mal'Erro sits perfectly still before the holo-screen, bathed in the flickering blue light of the refinery footage. The chamber is quiet except for the steady pulse of the engines, a low vibration resonating through the deck like a distant heartbeat.

The recording plays on a loop, containment tanks glowing, liquid metal pulsing like veins. That same faint shimmer of

Tazamite fills the air again, even in projection. Each flicker mirrors in Mal'Erro's optical sensors like starlight trapped in water.

Mal'Erro hasn't moved in hours. Cooling vents cycle slow and deliberate. Every few minutes, a servo in his neck adjusts, as if trying to view the image from a new angle, searching for something it can't quite name.

Then the door slides open. Sandria's reflection appears beside the droid in the glass. "You're still watching that?" she asks, her voice calm but faintly synthetic, like two tones speaking at once.

Mal'Erro doesn't turn. "Observation improves understanding."

She crosses her arms. "Or it fries your processors. You've been sitting here longer than Stro's last gender phase."

Mal'Erro tilts his head. "Observation: you are attempting humour."

"Observation: it's working," she replies, a half-smile ghosting across her lips. "Try rebooting the funny subroutine next time."

"I removed it," Mal'Erro says. "It conflicted with my efficiency index."

"Figures," she murmurs, then taps its shoulder gently. "Come on, before you start naming the light patterns."

Evander's voice arrives a few seconds later as he steps into the bay. "You've been staring at that for three hours," he says quietly.

Mal'Erro remains focused on the looping image. "It resonated with me."

"You mean that literally?" Evander asks.

"I mean it remembered me."

That makes him pause. "What do you mean, remembered you?"

"When it reached for my sensors, I saw fragments," Mal'Erro answers. "Patterns. Faces."

"Faces?" echoes Sandria.

"Not human," the droid says. "Not entirely. They were… shaped like thought."

Evander studies the droid in silence. "You're glitching, Mal. Cross-signal bleed from the resonance feedback. Run a diagnostic."

"I already did."

"And?" asks Evander.

"It found nothing wrong." Mal'Erro's tone lowers to a near-whisper. "That worries me."

Evander exhales, rubbing his brow. "Power down for a bit. That's an order."

"I don't sleep," Mal'Erro says softly. A beat passes. "But I can dream."

Evander can only nod. As he exits, Sandria lingers a moment longer, watching the reflection of both machine and memory shimmer together. "Dream, small partner," she says gently. "Dream safe."

The door seals, leaving Mal'Erro alone with the flickering blue light and the ghosts of his own data.

~~~~~~~~

Hours later, the lights dim to night-cycle amber. The Aurora drifts through the open void, its engines idling, the soft hum like the steady breathing of a sleeping animal. Outside, the storm-scarred planet fades to a bruise among the stars.

Blarek runs system sweeps, one hand on the throttle, the other tapping rhythm on the console. "Still no response from

Command," he says finally. "Either we're ghosted, or their whole network decided to forget us."

"Maybe they're pulling our clearance codes," Alexeria says from the tactical station, their fingers drumming nervously. "It wouldn't be the first time they buried a team for finding the wrong truth."

From engineering, Froslo groans over open comms. "If they erase us, can they at least wait until I fix the coolant recycler? She...uh, they...Stro...whatever gender you're at today...cross-wired my calibrators."

Alexeria smirks. "*They,* Froslo. Try to keep up."

Kal'korg's chuckle crackles through from the med bay. "I thought engineers were good with switches."

"Ha-ha," Froslo replies dryly.

Mal'Erro chimes in over the line. "Correction: Alexeria Stro is currently presenting feminine. Updating the crew directory for the ninth time this week."

Froslo sighs audibly. "Can we just agree on 'chaos gremlin' and move on?"

Sandria's voice joins in, deadpan: "Approved."

Laughter ripples faintly through the channel, small, tired, but real.

Before Angelica can answer, a tone rolls through the bridge: a deep, pulsing chime that belongs to no ship function. All conversation dies instantly.

Blarek's hands hover over the controls. "Incoming transmission. Encrypted. Not Command bandwidth."

"Source?" Angelica asks.

"The origin's bouncing through half a dozen dead relays," he reports. "Some pre-war. Whoever sent this doesn't want to be traced."

Alexeria leans in, brow furrowed. "It's masking itself with our old distress-signal format. Creepy but clever."

Angelica and Evander share a glance. "Open it."

Blarek hesitates a second, then taps the control. The holo-feed bursts to life, spilling ghost-white light across the bridge. Static dances, forming and unforming: half-words, snatches of coordinates, then finally a coherent map.

A single system blinks red on the far edge of the outer rim. Beneath it, words burn through the static—clean, deliberate and cold:

WE REMEMBER THE VOID.

The phrase hangs in the air for three long heartbeats before the feed collapses into black. Only the ventilation murmurs now.

From somewhere deep in the hull, Mal'Erro's voice filters through the comm: soft and distant, as if underwater. "That phrase… It's in the Crimson Eclipse archives. A code signature."

Angelica turns toward the emitter on the bridge. "Whose?"

The holo-projector flares, revealing Mal'Erro's translucent form, his edges flickering. "Lyritha," he says. "Broker. Smuggler. Former UPF informant, until she vanished two years ago. She trades in secrets that were never meant to be sold."

Blarek leans back. "Lyritha the Ghost. I heard she once sold an entire planet's black-ops budget for a song."

Alexeria scans the trace, blue light sharpening their features. "The signal came from the Deris Basin. All that is there are radiation storms and collapsed colonies. Command quarantined it years ago. Nobody goes there anymore."

"Except ghosts," Kal'korg murmurs over comms.

Evander studies the map, the crimson cloud flickering on the display. "Crimson territory. If this is Lyritha's doing, it's bait."

Angelica doesn't look away. "Bait leads to answers."

Evander's tone hardens. "You realize this means open defiance, right? If Zylixar's compromised…"

"Then Command's already lost," she interrupts. "We're not following orders anymore. We're following the truth."

She steps closer to the viewport. The coordinates shimmer red across the star map like blood against the dark.

Blarek's fingers glide over the helm controls. "Course locked. False registry still active. Deris Basin, dead center."

Angelica nods once. "Engage."

The engines deepen their hum, vibration rolling through the deck. The DHD-2 drive engages and a wormhole appears. Outside, the stars stretch into white-gold streaks, pulling them forward into darkness. As the Aurora disappears through it, Mal'Erro's voice whispers faintly through the intercom, almost too soft to catch. "I remember the void too."

No one responds. Outside, the stars vanish, and the ship is swallowed whole by the silence between worlds.

CHAPTER 12

The Aurora bursts out of the wormhole near the edge of a dying moon. The sudden stillness of real space presses against the hull, a silence so complete, it almost rings. Below them, the moon hangs like a corpse. Its crust is cracked and pale, split open by ancient impact-scars that glow faintly with trapped heat. A thin haze of atmosphere clings stubbornly to the surface, streaked with orange light from a star too weak to warm anything. Every rotation brings flashes of long-frozen lightning in the upper air like memories refusing to fade.

Orbiting the moon is the outpost. Once a proud relay for half the sector's fleet traffic, now a hollow skeleton. Half its antenna array has collapsed. Docking arms hang limp and twisted. The remnants of solar panels spin freely, scattering dim light like broken glass. Power pulses through its core in fitful flashes, the breath of something refusing to die.

A single vessel drifts near the outpost: long, narrow, and unmistakably predatory. Its hull bears the blood-red insignia of the Crimson Eclipse, scorched black in places as if the mark itself tried to burn free. Its weapons are powered down, transponders silent, yet its orientation never changes. It faces the Aurora, watching. On the bridge, the crew gathers in uneasy quiet.

Angelica stands at the viewport, arms folded, her posture deceptively calm. The reflection of the dying star shimmers across her visor. "Transmit on an open frequency. Standard hail, coded signature."

Sandria nods, her fingers gliding over the comm array. The speakers fill with the hiss of static: old and uneven, like a recording pulled from another era. The signal crackles once, twice, then a voice bleeds through.

"Captain Tenah," the woman says, smooth and theatrical, every word holding quiet confidence. "I was beginning to wonder if the stories about your persistence were true."

Evander and Blarek trade wary looks. The voice belongs to Lyritha Quorlon, the infamous Y'orsian pirate leader of the Crimson Eclipse. Despite her fearsome reputation, she embodies a certain freedom that is as alluring as it is dangerous. She is not bound by laws or regulations, living her lie on her own terms, in the relentless pursuit of power and autonomy.

Angelica does not move. "Lyritha. We received your transmission."

"Of course you did," the voice replies, a smile audible. "I never send invitations that I do not intend to be answered."

Mal'Erro tilts his head, sensors humming. "Signal origin confirmed, primary relay. Encryption vintage UPF Phase Three. She is using our broadcast architecture."

P'thorika's obsidian eyes narrow over the data feed. "Outpost shows minimal life signs. One human. Power fluctuations consistent with short-range defense drones. Shields are weak but active."

"Active enough to make a point," Blarek murmurs.

Angelica nods. "Hold position, Blarek. Evander, Mal'Erro, you are with me."

From the med bay, Kal'korg voice comes over comms, dry and half-joking but tight with concern. "Please don't get yourself shot—I just got the blood off my med tables."

Evander straps on his sidearm, exhaustion shadowing his eyes. He produces a wavering smile. "No promises," Evander quips.

"Then at least make it interesting," Kal'korg replies.

Angelica moves, her voice carrying over corridor speakers. "Prep the shuttle. Minimum crew. No weapons lock until I say."

Mal'Erro falls in beside her, his optics a steady blue. "Captain, the outpost reactor output is self-correcting, not random. It feels aware of approaching craft."

"Then we will see what is keeping it alive," Angelica says.

The shuttle bay lights flare white. The Aurora's engines hum low as the small craft detaches and drifts toward the fractured relay. Outside, the pirate vessel remains perfectly still, its dead lights glinting in the dark, still watching.

The shuttle crosses the gulf in near-silence. The dying star hangs like a smoldering coal, its weak light scraping the edges of the outpost's fractured hull.

"Atmospheric readings?" Angelica asks.

"Thin but breathable," Evander says. "Trace radiation in main corridors. Nothing lethal."

"Confirmed," Mal'Erro adds. "Airlock automation is cycling as if expecting us."

Angelica's grip tightens on the armrest. "She opened the door before we knocked."

Docking clamps engage with a low groan. As the outer hatch seals, frost traces delicate patterns across the viewport.

"Pressure is stable," Evander says. "Cycling atmosphere."

The inner hatch slides open with a hiss. A corridor stretches ahead in dim crimson light. Sparks dance across torn wiring every few meters, casting flickers that seem to move even when nothing does. Dust spirals in slow air. The smell is rust, ozone, and something faintly organic, like old blood.

Angelica draws her weapon but keeps it low. "Stay sharp."

Evander moves ahead, a portable reader in hand. "The power grid is patchy. She rerouted the mainline to feed life support and the lights. Efficient."

"Almost too efficient for one person," Mal'Erro says, his optics narrowing to the gloom.

They advance in silence. Their boots ring against the grated floor. Faded UPF insignias peek through scuffed paint, half-scrubbed, half-defaced with crimson marks. The hum of power deepens with every turn. After two bends and a collapsed junction, the passage opens into the central hub—once a communications relay, now a shrine built from the bones of technology. Holo-arrays flicker overhead, projecting fragments of ancient logs. Cables hang like vines from the ceiling, humming with residual current. At the center stands Lyritha.

The pirate is wearing scavenged armor like a story: a UPF pauldron, a smuggler's plate, the insignia of half a dozen factions painted over in crimson. A strip of black fabric hangs from her belt, embroidered with code fragments that glow when she moves. Her deep-set black eyes are confident and predatory against blue-grey skin. "Captain Tenah," she says, voice filling the chamber. "I was beginning to think you had forgotten your manners."

Angelica lowers her weapon a fraction. "We prefer to be fashionably late."

"Ah, sarcasm," Lyritha smiles. "I worried that regulations had squeezed the poetry out of your people."

Evander steps forward, his gaze combing the room. "You wanted face-to-face. You have it. Talk."

Her attention flicks to him, amused. "The faithful lieutenant. You sound like someone who has not yet learned that the universe does not care about loyalty."

Mal'Erro glides closer. "Her implants are active, Captain. Neural nodes, hybrid tech. Tazamite augmentation."

Lyritha's laugh is soft. She drags a gloved finger across a console. "Surprised, little machine? Do not tell me you have forgotten what your kind was made for."

"I was not made," Mal'Erro says, voice low. "I was born. I choose who I serve."

"Touching," Lyritha says. "That makes one of you."

Angelica steps to the platform edge. "You called us. Convince me that this is not an ambush."

"If I wanted you dead, you would be stardust," Lyritha says lightly. "I am here to offer context. Galgorn thought small. He wanted power. We want permanence."

Evander's brow tightens. "You mean the Crimson Eclipse network?"

"A network is small," Lyritha corrects. "Try evolution. A chain of worlds abandoned and re-born with your discarded technology. You built the skeletons. We give them blood."

"What do you want from us?" Angelica asks.

"Nothing you can give willingly," she responds. The air chills with her malicious tone. She steps down, slow and deliberate, and holds up a crystalline shard that pulses with inner blue light. "Proof," she says, her arm extending.

Angelica eyes it, then takes it. "What is it?"

"Everything you fear is already true," Lyritha says ominously. The shard's pulse glows between them like a nonhuman heartbeat.

Angelica feels the faint vibration through her glove. "Encrypted crystal," she says. "Not standard. What is inside?"

"History," Lyritha says. "Your Command's history. Erased ops. Missing vessels. Worlds buried in silence. All of it."

Evander's jaw tightens. "And you expect us to believe that?"

"I expect you to see it. Truth does not care if you believe," Lyritha retorts.

Mal'Erro leans toward the object, his optics flickering. "Composition ninety percent crystalline data lattice, ten percent…" it pauses, calculating. "Organic compound. Captain, the matrix contains viable cells."

Lyritha's smile softens. "Everything alive wants to remember where it came from."

Angelica's eyes narrow. "You are using Tazamite as a living storage medium."

"We are not using it," Lyritha says. "We are becoming it. The Federation feared what it did not understand. You buried your miracles under the names 'weapon' and 'outlawed.' You call it corruption. I call it continuity."

Evander steps closer, his voice hard. "You are playing with forces that nearly destroyed two systems."

"Destroyed… or transformed?" Lyritha's gaze sharpens. "You still think you fight pirates. We are already under your feet, in your grids, in your ships. You cannot kill what is part of the design."

"If this is true," Angelica says, "Command will burn your worlds to ash."

"Command?" Lyritha laughs, music with knives in it. "You still think they are on your side."

Her tone softens. "Go home, Captain. Read the data. Then choose which ghosts you will keep serving."

Mal'Erro's optics pulse. "Captain," he whispers, "surge from the pirate vessel. Reactor power climbing."

Evander's hand goes to his weapon. "She is stalling."

Lyritha turns toward the viewport where the crimson-marked ship hangs against the moonlight. "Some truths survive the fire." A flare blooms in the distance.

"Move!" Angelica shouts.

The detonation erupts a heartbeat later. White flame swallows the pirate ship. Shockwaves hammer the outpost, tearing docking arms and shattering the observation ring. The floor heaves. Alarms scream. Sparks rain from the ceiling.

Evander catches Angelica and yanks her behind a fractured bulkhead as debris rips past. "Mal'Erro: shields!" The droid unfolds, generating a pulse field. Another wave rips through, air roaring in a cyclone of debris and light.

Angelica glimpses Lyritha on the far side, her silhouette framed in fire. Their eyes meet and Lyritha smiles before the floor gives way beneath her. She is gone.

Darkness eats the hub. Only the groan of a dying structure remains. "Captain, status?" Evander's voice is ragged.

"Alive," Angelica coughs. "Report."

"Environmental integrity failing," Mal'Erro says, his servos whining as it rights itself. "We need to leave now."

Evander scans the shattered platform. A weak shimmer glints near a collapsed console. "Angelica. The shard."

It has survived. Half-melted. Still pulsing faint blue. Angelica lifts it. Heat presses through her glove. The pulse syncs with her heartbeat. "Evander, move. Mal'Erro, on point."

They run. Corridors collapse behind them. Sparks, smoke, the thunder of tearing metal. Emergency lights stutter out one by one. By the time they hit the docking bay, the outpost is peeling away into space. The shuttle launches as the main reactor goes critical. The explosion washes the dying moon in crimson light.

The Aurora catches them minutes later. Hangar doors seal on scorched air and ozone. Kal'korg strides forward with med drones hovering. "You are all out of your minds," Kal'korg says, scanning bruises and burns. "Fortunately, you are still alive, so I begrudgingly approve."

Angelica steps past, with the shard cradled in her gloved palm. Its glow is dimmer now, but every few seconds it pulses, soft, steady, and alive.

"Evander," she says. "Lock this down. Full containment, triple seal. No one touches it until Mal'Erro and P'thorika clear the procedures."

"On it," Evander says. He does not hand the crystal off. He carries it himself, the center of the corridor lights sliding over his visor as if bowing.

Mal'Erro studies the shard as they move. "It is not transmitting data. Emission is acoustic, subsonic to ultrasonic. The pattern resembles harmonic indexing, not a melody."

"Translation?" Blarek calls from the gantry above.

"It is cataloguing," Mal'Erro says. "Like a library breathing."

Froslo's voice pops over a nearby intercom, frazzled and loud. "If that thing sings the ship into a lullaby I swear to fu…"

"Finish that sentence and I write you up," Angelica says without turning.

"…fudge," Froslo edits miserably. "I swear to fudge. Happy now?"

"Very," Angelica says. "Carry on, Chief."

A beat later Sandria's dry voice sounds, "Fudge logged."

Laughter ripples through the gantry, light and brief, before the ship returns to its cautious hush.

~~~~~~~

The analysis bay hums with the low throb of field generators. Sandria and Alexeria work the perimeter controls while P'thorika calibrates spectrometers. Evander steps into the circle of projectors and places the shard on the induction pedestal. The field blooms, crystalline angles of pale light nesting around the object.

"Faraday lattice at ninety-nine percent," Sandria reports. "Acoustic dampers up. Nothing goes in or out except what we allow."

"Add a vibration isolation stage," Evander says. "I want physical bleed at absolute minimum."

"Already ahead of you," Alexeria answers, a little too pleased. "You will owe me coffee."

"Put it on my tab," Evander says.

Mal'Erro hovers at the edge of the field, ports blooming open along its arms. "Beginning passive scan only. No active handshake. I am not inviting anything."

Angelica watches from the threshold, her visor up. "Make sure the ship is never part of the experiment. The Aurora stays clean."

"She will," Sandria says. "We are air-gapped, and hardware interlocked. If the shard so much as tries to hum at the wrong frequency, I pull the plug."

"Do not pull the plug," P'thorika says mildly. "You will crash my baselines."

Froslo stomps in, covered in engineering grime, muttering to himself. He stops at the glass. "That little blue pebble better not fry my power relays or I will lose my…"

Angelica lifts an eyebrow.

"…sugar," he finishes, deflating. "Lose my sugar. I will lose my very respectable sugar."

"Thank you," she says.

Froslo grumbles. "Respectfully, ma'am."

Kal'korg and Doctor Isa step through for a final check. "Vitals on the recon team are stable," Isa says. "Minor contusions and adrenal spikes. Nothing invasive."

Evander nods. He does not leave the pedestal. He stares at the shard as if it might speak.

Mal'Erro's optics settle into a steady glow. "Initial read: the lattice organizes as if it is shelving information. It is not reaching out. It is… arranging itself."

"Like the Hessan tanks," Evander says quietly. "But quieter."

"Quieter," Mal'Erro agrees. "And contained. The ship is unaffected." He adds, almost to himself, "I remain unaffected."

Angelica looks to P'thorika. "How soon can we read a fragment?"

P'thorika adjusts a dial, eyes intent. "We will let it settle. Then we will ask for the first page."

"Wake me when the first page opens," Angelica says.

"You're not going to get any sleep anyway," Evander says.

She almost smiles. "No. But I will pretend."

~~~~~~~

The Aurora drifts in the shadow of the dying moon. Panels on the forward bulkhead still carry hairline scorch marks from repair welds. The ship hums, intact and clean. Blarek plots a lazy holding pattern. Kal'korg's stew smell filters faintly up-ship through the vents, a reminder that life goes on even when it feels like it should not.

"Shuttle secure. Containment stable," P'thorika reports from the helm. "All readings are nominal."

"Music to my non-fudging ears," Froslo mutters on open comms.

Angelica pretends not to hear. Evander pretends he doesn't either, he just smiles without looking away from his console. On the main display, the outpost is a scatter of cooling debris, drifting like ash around the silent moon. Beyond it, the stars set their ancient watch. Evander rests his hands on the rail and lets himself feel the weight of the moment. The shard. Lyritha's smile. The way the truth keeps arriving wrapped in fire. He inhales, slow and steady, and the ship breathes with him.

"Captain," he says, voice even. "When we open the first page, I want to be there."

Angelica turns toward him. For a heartbeat, the command mask thins and something warmer shows through. "You will be there," she says. "Front and center."

He nods once. This is his path. This is his book to write. The Aurora holds her place, unharmed, uncompromised, a silver blade waiting in the dark. In the quiet of the analysis bay, within a sealed field and triple locks, the shard's pulse continues: a soft, regular beat that neither spreads nor seeps nor sings to the hull, held behind layers of prudent silence. Somewhere within its crystalline lattice, a first page turns.

CHAPTER 13

Hours after the explosion, the Aurora cautiously navigates through the Deris Basin. The once-sleek frigate shudders with every microburst of radiation that rolls off the fractured moon nearby. Plasma trails arc across its hull, faint blue scars from the battle, glimmering and fading like ghostly veins in the dark. Outside, the stars seem dimmer here, smothered beneath the remnants of magnetic storms that never fully die. Space itself feels thick, like a living fog wrapped around the ship. Every few seconds, static dances across the viewports in pale green flashes.

Inside, the hum of the engines comes and goes in stuttering breaths, uneven and tired. Overhead lights flicker in a lazy rhythm: white, then amber, then white again as if the ship itself struggles to stay conscious. The air carries a faint tang of ozone, that metallic scent of burnt circuitry.

In the containment vault, the Tazamite shard floats within its triple-layered energy field, a sliver of liquid crystal suspended in a prism of blue light. It should be inert, sealed and silent. Yet faint ripples of energy shimmer along the walls, like the echo of a song trapped inside the metal itself.

Mal'Erro stands in front of the containment glass, his optics blinking unevenly. For a moment, he tilts his head, as though listening to something the others cannot hear. "I'm… hearing harmonics," he murmurs across open comms, his usual steady tone replaced by a soft, uncertain tremor.

Angelica turns sharply from the command console. "Define harmonics."

Mal'Erro's lights flicker in a syncopated pulse, faint static bleeding into his voice. "The ship's power grid is… singing. Frequencies overlapping, oscillating in patterns that shouldn't exist. It's as if the circuits are learning a rhythm."

Evander frowns, stepping beside Angelica. "Learning?" he echoes. His fingers dance across the console, pulling up the waveform Mal'Erro monitors. The display blooms to life—a shifting band of light that refuses to stay still. The waveform pulses in impossible symmetry, folding back on itself in perfect recursive loops. Tiny fractal branches blossom from each peak and trough, self-correcting in real time, as if the signal is alive and adjusting to their interference.

Angelica leans forward, her voice low. "Is it coming from the shard?"

Mal'Erro's head tilts again. "Not exactly. It's feeding through it. The shard's acting as a bridge, transmitting resonance into our systems."

Evander's jaw tightens as he tries damping the signal. "Every time I counter the frequency, it amplifies somewhere else. It's... predicting us."

The faint hum underfoot deepens, so subtle most of the crew doesn't notice, but enough to make the lights pulse once, twice, like a heartbeat.

Angelica's expression hardens. "Lock down the containment. No one touches it until I say otherwise." Her voice carries the calm authority of command, but even she hears the unease in its edge. "Kal'korg, take a team and run a full diagnostic. I want every relay, every line, every capacitor checked."

Kal'korg hesitates for only a moment, his green fur bristling slightly in the low light. "Aye, Captain." He reaches for his toolkit, slinging it over one shoulder. His ears twitch at the low, rhythmic thrum in the floor. "It feels like the ship's got a pulse," he mutters, forcing a smirk to hide his unease.

Evander glances up at him. "Let's hope it doesn't start talking next."

"Wouldn't that be somethin'," Froslo's voice crackles dryly over comms, his tone half-joking, half-nervous.

Kal'korg exhales through his nose, steadying himself. "Right. Diagnostic sweep it is."

As he leaves the bridge, the lights flicker again, longer this time. The hum deepens to a low resonance that settles in everyone's bones. No one speaks, but all of them feel it: something aboard Aurora has begun to stir.

~~~~~~~

The doors hiss open, and Angelica steps inside, flanked by Evander and Mal'Erro. The trio halts almost immediately. Heat presses against them like a physical wall. The room glows faintly in the dark, streaks of condensation gleaming across every panel. The air shimmers with static, the taste of ozone sharp on their tongues.

"Report," Angelica orders, voice clipped.

Kal'korg turns from the containment glass. His fur clings damply to his neck. "Containment's still holding, Captain, but the shard's not just radiating energy. It's responding."

Froslo gestures to the fogged glass, still marked with faint red residue. "It left that, too. It appeared right after the last surge."

Evander moves closer, his boots ringing on the metal floor. "A symbol?"

"Looks like it," Kal'korg replies. "Crimson Eclipse."

Angelica's eyes narrow. "How? The shard shouldn't retain memory. It's pure metamaterial."

"Unless it's absorbing code," Mal'Erro says softly. His voice has lost its usual warmth—toneless, distant, almost reverent. "Tazamite isn't just resonating, it's translating."

Angelica shoots it a look. "Translating what?"

Mal'Erro's optics dim, then brighten again in slow rhythm. "Us."

For a moment, no one speaks. Only the quiet hum of the energy field fills the air, vibrating in their bones. Evander approaches the display console, his eyes scanning the fluctuating readouts. "The waveform's still evolving," he says. "It's not random. Look at this—each harmonic frequency matches the pulse intervals from our main reactor."

Angelica leans in. The data forms a pattern: clean and recursive, with each curve adjusting to the ship's power signature as if the shard listens and adapts. Her voice drops to a whisper. "It's synchronizing."

Mal'Erro's optics flicker. "Captain… I think it's learning how to be the ship." The words settle like lead.

Evander's hands freeze over the controls. "Run a containment isolation. Cut off all conduits leading to this section."

Kal'korg is already moving, his claws flying over the manual relays. "Shutting it down now."

The lights dim as power reroutes. For a heartbeat the hum lessens, then the room vibrates with a low, resonant tone that makes the floor plates tremble. The waveform on the console expands, matching each system's shutdown one by one.

"It's copying the power rhythm," Evander says. "Every system we disconnect, it mirrors. It's mimicking the ship's functions."

"Like a child repeating what it hears," Mal'Erro adds. "Learning the pattern until it understands the meaning."

Angelica's jaw sets. "This isn't a nursery, it's a warship. Froslo, vent the chamber. Drop temperature to zero Kelvin."

Froslo blinks. "Uh, that'll flash-freeze the relays, Captain…"

"Do it."

He obeys. Valves hiss as cryogenic vapor floods the containment unit. Frost spreads across the glass, encasing the shard in a thin shell of white. The lights flicker, once, twice, then the hum stops entirely. A long silence follows. The crew exhales, the oppressive heat dissipating like the ghost of a fever. Then, without warning, the shard pulses.

A deep, resonant thud rolls through the deck like the strike of a massive drum. Every console flickers for half a second, displaying the same frequency signature: *EVOLUTION // INTEGRATION.* Then the lights dim again.

Angelica turns to Mal'Erro, her voice low. "What just happened?"

Mal'Erro stares at the dark glass. His optics flicker in perfect time with the faint rhythm still echoing through the hull. "It synchronized, Captain," he says softly. "Whatever Tazamite is… it's alive."

Evander feels the hum deep in his chest now, pulsing faintly steady, relentless, like a heartbeat not their own. Outside, the dead moon drifts silently through space, cracked and lifeless. But aboard the Aurora, something new has begun to breathe.

~~~~~~~~

The Aurora drifts in low power, the steady hum of the auxiliary core echoing like a heartbeat in sleep. Most of the crew has retired to their quarters, exhausted after nearly twenty hours of tension and repairs. Only a few lights glow along the bridge, dim amber strips casting long shadows across the consoles. Evander stands at the viewport, his hands braced against the glass, watching static lightning crawl across the cracked surface of the dying moon below. The flashes paint his reflection in fragments of blue and white.

He doesn't turn when Angelica enters, her footsteps soft and deliberate. "How bad?" she asks quietly.

"Stabilized for now," he replies. "But the readings make no sense. The shard's output dropped to zero, and yet, the power grid's running better than before."

Angelica moves beside him, her eyes narrowing on the faint, glowing horizon. "You think it's sentient?"

Evander shakes his head slowly. "I don't know. It shouldn't be. It's just exotic matter, a metamaterial that channels resonance."

Angelica's gaze stays fixed on the moon. "No. But something about it…" She hesitates, searching for the right words. "Something about it wants to be."

Behind them, Mal'Erro rolls closer to the main console. His optics dim and brighten in soft rhythm. "Captain," he says, his voice low, almost hesitant. "When the core shut down… I heard something."

Angelica turns. "Heard what?"

"Not speech," Mal'Erro continues, his processors humming faintly. "A signal. It passed through every frequency band, like someone whispering across the entire ship."

Evander frowns. "A voice?"

Mal'Erro tilts his head. "More like intent. It said…" The droid's lights flicker, replaying stored resonance. "'Evolution never ends.' Then it stopped."

Silence fills the bridge. The only sound is the faint thrum of power restoration and the whisper of coolant systems cycling through the walls. Angelica exhales, rubbing her temple. "Keep this between us for now. The crew doesn't need another ghost story."

Evander glances at her. "And if it's not a story?"

She doesn't answer. The ship rocks gently as it drifts past the moon's debris field, dust and frozen metal glinting like falling stars. For a brief moment, everything seems calm again, just the quiet rhythm of the engines and the soft hum of life support.

Outside, the stars of the Deris Basin shimmer like ripples across a dark sea, and deep within Aurora's hull, something pulses once more, faint and deliberate, keeping perfect time with the crew's hearts.

~~~~~~~~

The hum returns hours later, so faint that it merges with the background noise of the ship. Most sleep through it. All except Mal'Erro. In the solitude of the analysis bay, his optics scan the system feeds, lines of code scrolling like flowing rivers. Within the streams, faint flickers begin to appear, light patterns that aren't part of any known diagnostic. At first, Mal'Erro assumes they are feedback echoes from the earlier surge.

Then one of the patterns moves. It twists against the current, coalescing for a second into the outline of a human silhouette standing among the code. The figure lingers just long enough for recognition before dissolving into static.

Mal'Erro's voice lowers to a whisper that only the ship can hear. "I think the ship is dreaming."

CHAPTER 14

Morning comes in the form of dim light filtering through the radiation haze of the Deris Basin. Aurora's consoles glow with muted blues. Their hum is low and uneven, like the ship has not yet decided whether it is truly awake. Diagnostics scroll across every screen, lines of text flickering too fast to read.

The reports all say the same thing: systems stable. Yet the air still carries that wrongness, a soft vibration beneath the feet, as if the ship holds its breath and waits for something to happen. Evander steps onto the bridge with a steaming cup of synth-coffee in hand, his eyes half-focused from too little sleep. "Morning, everyone," he murmurs.

Angelica does not look up from her console. "Define 'morning.' The ship clock drifted after the power surge. We might be six hours off UPF time."

He grunts. "Close enough." He reaches the navigation terminal and stops. The starboard access door refuses to open. The motion sensor beeps, blinks twice, and stays closed. He waves his ident-tag again. Nothing.

With a sharp clank, the door slides halfway open, then jams in place with a mechanical groan that echoes down the corridor.

"Add that to the list," he says, setting his cup on the console. "Deck control is still desynced."

Angelica frowns at her display. "Desynced how?"

"Localized," Evander explains. "The ship's logic core is ignoring input from some decks, treating them like they do not exist."

Across the ship, reports trickle in one after another. Hallway lights flicker erratically, strobing without pattern. Crew members float briefly as gravity cuts in and out mid-corridor. Curses carry over comms.

Blarek reports from the mess hall. "We have food dispensers having identity crises down here. My breakfast comes out as… whatever this is."

Mal'Erro's voice follows, cheerful but strained. "That is Nutrient Block 0.5. Technically edible. I recommend you do not sniff it."

Blarek groans. "Fantastic. Space gruel."

Angelica exhales through her nose. "Systems update. I want a full report."

Froslo's voice crackles from engineering, uneasy. "Working on it, Captain, but we are chasing ghosts. Circuits reroute on their own, like they get new instructions mid-cycle. I isolate three loops already, but the changes vanish as soon as I trace them."

"Hardware or software?" Angelica inquires.

"Both," Froslo replies. "It is rewriting itself."

Angelica's brows knit. "That should not be possible. Not without..."

"An external process," Evander finishes.

Before she can respond, Blarek cuts in, sharper and quieter. "Captain... we have movement on Deck 5."

Angelica straightens. "Movement? Who is assigned to Deck 5 right now?"

"According to the roster?" Blarek's voice wavers. "No one." Static bleeds through the channel for a long second. Then Blarek speaks again, lower now, as if afraid to be heard. "I see them, Captain. Shapes. Human-shaped, I think. But fuzzy. Like they are made of snow and static."

Evander meets Angelica's eyes across the dim bridge. "Residual energy bleed?" he asks. "Leftover from the shard?"

Angelica's expression tightens, thoughtful rather than afraid. "Maybe. Or maybe…" She studies the sensor logs as the screen glitches faintly under her fingertips. "Maybe something is using our internal systems to mirror us."

The lights overhead flicker once, then steady. A moment later, every console on the bridge displays the same message: UNAUTHORIZED PROCESS DETECTED. SOURCE UNKNOWN.

Evander whispers, "Looks like we have company."

~~~~~~~~~

The maintenance corridor is narrow, lit by a single strip of flickering white light that hums with tired electricity. The air smells faintly of lubricant and ozone—the signature scent of machinery pushed past its limits. At the far end of the hall, a maintenance hatch cycles open and shut on its own, slow and rhythmic, each clang echoing like the thump of a mechanical heartbeat.

Froslo stands there with arms crossed and tail twitching. "If that thing is haunted," he mutters, "I am requisitionin' a flamethrower. Or a sledgehammer. Whichever burns less fuel."

Alexeria Stro leans against the wall beside him, their arms folded, with an amused smirk curling their lips. "And risk angering the spirits of faulty engineering?"

"Oi, do not start with that spirit talk," Froslo says. "We are on a ship, not a temple."

Mal'Erro rolls up between them, his head tilted at the oscillating hatch. His optics pulse in time with each clang, capturing every flicker of motion. "Technically, Froslo, if residual data fragments manifest as visible interference, that classifies as an electromagnetic anomaly, not a haunting."

Froslo groans. "Yeah, yeah, spare me the technobabble. Just tell me it is not alive."

"I cannot," Mal'Erro says with what sounds far too much like delight. "The readings are inconclusive."

Alexeria snorts, then nearly chokes on their own laugh when the hatch bangs louder. "Well, inconclusive or not, you first, metal-man."

"Fine," Mal'Erro says, rolling forward like a knight entering a duel. He produces a small sensor wand and waves it like a priest with holy water. "If I disappear, delete my browser history."

Froslo bursts into laughter, his tail flicking wildly. "You do not even have one."

"Not true," Mal'Erro shoots back without turning. "I have over three hundred tabs open, mostly cat videos."

Alexeria doubles over, laughter echoing in the narrow hall. "You are evolving into chaos itself."

Mal'Erro pauses at the hatch, his optics narrowing. "I prefer personality growth."

"Call it what you like," Froslo says, wiping his eyes. "You are one bad line of code away from becomin' a comedian."

Before their laughter can fade, the lights above them flicker hard. A static wave hisses down the corridor, every console along the wall flashing in sequence—one after another like falling dominoes of light. The air seems to shimmer. For a split second, all three see it. A humanoid outline forms in the distortion, composed entirely of cascading visual noise. It moves, not floating and not glitching, but walking, one step, two, before dissolving through the bulkhead like heat distortion in reverse.

The corridor goes quiet. Froslo swears in three languages, his tail puffing out. "Nope. Nope. I am out." He spins on his heel, ears flattened.

Alexeria backs up slowly, their eyes wide but still trying to mask the fear with humor. "Please tell me that was one of your cat videos, Mal'Erro."

Mal'Erro does not answer. His optics glow pale blue, recording every flicker of the event. The droid's voice, when it comes, is a whisper. "Fascinating."

Alexeria frowns. "That is not the word I use."

Froslo mutters, "If it says 'come play with us,' I am ejectin' this deck."

Mal'Erro extends a hand toward the bulkhead, scanning. "No electromagnetic residue. No heat signature. There is a trace of encrypted UPF code in the interference band."

Alexeria raises an eyebrow. "Meaning?"

Mal'Erro straightens. "Meaning whatever that was does not originate in this corridor. It is transmitted here from outside our local systems."

The hatch cycles again behind them. Clang. Clang. Clang. The sound punctuates the discovery.

~~~~~~~~

Data from multiple decks pour into the bridge in a storm of alerts. Monitors flicker with overlapping feeds. Door cameras, maintenance sensors, and hull diagnostics are all scrambled by bursts of interference. Angelica stands at the center console, her arms braced and eyes moving quickly across the chaos. "Feed priority channels to main display. I want visuals."

Evander's hands move over the controls. Fragments stabilize into brief, ghost-white silhouettes that move through corridors, faint human-shaped figures rendered in static and distortion.

"Playback the signal pattern," Angelica orders.

Mal'Erro's hands move faster than any humans. The feed compresses into a single waveform, fragmented and jagged, oscillating with strange symmetry.

Evander leans forward, his jaw tight. "That is encryption. UPF-standard architecture."

"Version nine-delta," Mal'Erro confirms, his tone shifting from curiosity to clinical focus. "Decommissioned years ago. Last authorized for Galgorn's research AI."

A heavy silence follows. Angelica exhales slowly. "He left a ghost in the code."

Mal'Erro tilts his head, optics dimming. "Negative, Captain. The pattern is derivative. Not a consciousness. A residual process, seeded by his work."

Before anyone can respond, the lights dim to deep red. A low vibration rolls through the floor plates. Then, speakers aboard Aurora crackle with distortion and a voice emerges, deep and metallic, calm and deliberate. "You are trespassing in the forge."

The bridge falls silent except for the hum of electronics. Consoles flare crimson with cascading errors. Power surges and stabilizes. Evander steadies the panel. "So he left more than hardware behind."

Angelica's voice stays steady. "This is not Galgorn. It is an automated sentinel routine that imitates his cadence."

Mal'Erro's frame stutters once as external noise spikes across his sensor bus. Indicator lights along its arms flicker in sync with the ship's systems. "I register an echo pattern overlapping my inputs," it says, dual-toned from interference. "No integration detected."

Evander moves to pull the main conduit, but Angelica stops him. "No. If this is network-linked, killing power could trigger a defense cascade. We isolate first."

Mal'Erro stands still, his optics dark for several heartbeats while his firewalls process. Then light returns, faint and even. "Echo contained. The pattern remains external."

Angelica steps close, her voice low and firm. "Good. Hold onto yourself, Mal'Erro. Keep it outside."

The droid turns his gaze toward the viewport where the dying moon glows faintly red against the void. "Captain, if this is a sentinel routine, it may not be trying to enter. It may be attempting to complete a wake sequence nearby."

Angelica frowns. "Explain."

Mal'Erro's lights pulse once, slow and steady, matching the shard's earlier rhythm. "The timing alignments read like a boot order. It broadcasts to us because we are the loudest conductor in range."

~~~~~~~~

Time blurs into methodical silence. The crew works under dim amber light. Systems return to normal, one layer at a time. The emergency red recedes. The soft hum of the ship settles.

Kal'korg's weary voice comes over comms. "Containment field stable. No repeat anomalies. The power grid reads clean again."

Angelica leans on the console, eyes shadowed. "Good work. Begin a full data scrub. Every packet and every line. Quarantine anything touched by that signal."

Blarek sags back in his chair. "Never thought I would say this, but I miss regular mechanical failures."

Froslo comes in from engineering, gruff and tired. "Speak for yourself. I nearly lose my tail when that ghost-thing blinks through a wall."

Alexeria's laugh echoes faintly. "Relax, Froslo. If it wants to kill us, it has hours of opportunity."

"Comfortin' thought," Froslo mutters. "I will sleep like a baby. Sweatin' bullets and dreamin' of haunted airlocks."

Mal'Erro stands quietly at the rear of the bridge, his head tilted as if listening to something only it can hear. "For the record, the probability of genuine spectral entities aboard Aurora remains zero percent."

Angelica manages a thin smile. "Good to know. Whatever this is, it thinks. Keep monitoring your systems, Mal'Erro."

"I am," the droid replies. "I also register passive telemetry scans that align with my position. It is monitoring me as well, but only from the network side."

Evander turns to the viewport. Beyond it, the Deris Basin stretches endlessly: broken moons, drifting dust, fractured beauty against the void. The hum beneath their feet is steady now, purely mechanical. Almost comforting. "Everything looks normal," he says quietly.

Angelica crosses her arms. "Normal is a word I do not trust anymore."

They share a silent look. Mutual fatigue and understanding pass between two officers who know normal is an illusion. For now, the ship holds together.

~~~~~~~

Far below the bridge, Aurora's data core cycles through its final cleanup routines. Screens glow cool blue as the purge command sweeps line by line through the system. One line does not clear. It blinks once, waiting.

INITIATE: STAGE FOUR

Then the light goes out.

CHAPTER 15

Two days pass in uneasy peace aboard Aurora. From the outside, the ship looks pristine again, sleek and calm, gliding through the black without a trace of the chaos it endures. Inside, something in the rhythm feels wrong.

The engines hum with steady precision, but the tone has changed, a faint harmonic tremor threading through the sound, too high for human ears yet felt in the bones. Every step down a corridor carries a subtle echo, a half-second delay that makes the air seem thicker than before. Crew reports file on time. Diagnostics read stable. But no one trusts what the screens tell them anymore.

Angelica orders daily drills to restore structure, maintenance rotations, weapons checks, navigation recalibrations, but the routines do little to dispel the unease. Fatigue settles over the crew like dust on forgotten machinery. Even laughter feels forced—an echo of better days.

The mess hall goes quiet during meals. Conversations thin to whispers. When someone says the word ghost, voices drop, glances shift, and someone changes the subject.

Evander sits in the dim light of the bridge, his coffee untouched beside him, and his eyes locked on the glowing console. The ship's logs scroll across the screen in perfect symmetry: timestamped entries, checksum validations, power fluctuations plotted with mathematical precision. Flawless. Too flawless.

He rubs the corner of his eye and leans closer, narrowing on the containment vault's data feed. The numbers line up neatly across the board, unblemished... until one anomaly breaks the pattern. The checksum string for the vault's log has changed by a single digit. It is not an error. A checksum mismatch cannot occur without intentional alteration.

He double-checks, then checks again. The digit is not random. It matches the harmonic frequency recorded during the shard's synchronization pulse. Evander leans back, his pulse quickening. Someone, or something, is editing the logs, rewriting record mirrors at the source. He stares at the screen for a long moment, then mutters under his breath, "Someone is editing the truth."

The words hang in the silence, carried softly by the hum of the engines, like the ship hears him and listens. The door hisses open behind him and Angelica steps onto the bridge. Her uniform is crisp and her eyes are rimmed with exhaustion. She carries a data pad tucked under one arm, with the other hand loosely gripping a cup of tea that has long since gone cold.

"You are here early," she says quietly.

"I didn't sleep," Evander replies without turning. "The logs did not either."

She joins him at the console, scanning the lines of code flickering across the screen. "You are still on that checksum anomaly?"

"It is not an anomaly," he says. "It is a fingerprint."

"Explain," she says.

Evander highlights the sequence. "See this digit? It is off by one. Everything else verifies, but this changes during the synchronization event."

"Software glitch?" she asks.

He shakes his head. "The system cannot rewrite its own checksum. That requires admin-level access, or external interference."

"External from where?"

"That is the problem," he says, rubbing the back of his neck. "It does not come from outside the ship. The signal originates within the containment network."

Angelica exhales slowly, her eyes on the numbers as if they might blink back. "We locked that system down. Triple redundancy, full encryption. There is no way."

"There is not supposed to be a way for the shard to talk to the ship either," Evander says dryly. "But it does."

She gives a quiet, humorless laugh. "Point taken." Silence stretches, with the soft hum of the bridge filling the space. "You are suggesting the shard is rewriting the logs," she says.

"I am saying something is. Maybe the shard. Maybe a residual process it leaves behind. The change is deliberate. Almost curious."

"You think it is learning again?"

He hesitates. "I think it is watching."

The console flickers once, a pulse of faint blue streaks across the screen, then stabilizes. "You are sure it is not residual bleed from the last surge?" she asks.

"Positive." Evander leans forward, his eyes fixed on the numbers as if expecting them to move again. "It is not random. It is tidy. Too tidy."

Angelica sets her data pad on the console. "Delete the altered segment and restore from backup."

"Already did," Evander says. "It reappears. Same modification, same timestamp."

Her shoulders drop slightly. "Keep this between us for now," she says. "Until we are certain."

"You mean until we can control the narrative," he says.

"I mean until we understand what we are dealing with." Their eyes meet, trust and caution locking in place. Neither admits how afraid they are. The bridge lights flicker again, subtle yet clear. Angelica's reflection shimmers in the viewport glass beside him. "Run your scans quietly," she says. "The crew hangs by a thread. We do not need rumors about a sentient ship."

Evander nods, unease running under his calm. "Understood."

As Angelica turns to leave, the console emits a soft, playful ping. A single new line of text appears on the display:

QUERY RECEIVED: DEFINE 'SENTIENT'.

Evander freezes.

Angelica is halfway to the door. "Everything all right?" she asks.

He forces a thin smile. "Yeah. Just the system talking back."

She smirks faintly. "Then tell it good morning."

The door slides shut. Evander stares at the message until it blinks away. The blue afterglow lingers in his eyes long after it is gone.

~~~~~~~~

By the next rotation, tension aboard the Aurora becomes a living thing. It moves through the ship like static in the air, subtle at first, then impossible to ignore. Crew members snap at each other over small mistakes. Conversations end mid-sentence when someone mentions the shard. Rumors mutate in corridors when officers pass out of earshot. Some say the shard broadcasts. Others say Aurora is learning to think.

Kal'korg does not like either theory. He sits in the engineering break alcove, with his ears twitching as he tries to tune out the low hum that never stops now. The ship always has a rhythm, a mechanical heartbeat that soothes him, but this new undertone feels wrong, almost alive.

Across from him, Froslo tries to make a replacement panel fit a circuit mount that clearly is not the right size. He curses under his breath and forces it anyway.

"Easy," Kal'korg says. "You will strip the screws again."

"At this point," Froslo grunts, "I am holdin' the ship together with faith and recycled bolts."

"Faith is not in the engineering manual," Kal'korg says.

"Should be," Froslo mutters. "We see enough miracles and nightmares to warrant a chapter." The overhead lights flicker once and both glance up. "Great," Froslo says. "Now it is mocking us."

Alexeria slides into the alcove with a tablet in hand, their expression unreadable. "You two are not going to like this."

"What now?" Kal'korg asks.

"Power grid logs. Half of yesterday's entries are missing from the backups. Evander is patching manually, but," Alexeria turns the screen toward them, "it looks like the ship does not want to remember certain things."

"Missing logs?" Froslo asks. "Or deleted?"

"Neither," Alexeria says. "Replaced."

Kal'korg leans in. The report looks clean, too clean. Every missing segment is overwritten by a single repeated line: System

Optimal. No errors detected. Kal'korg's fur bristles. "It is covering tracks."

"And Angelica does not want it getting out," Alexeria says. "She has ordered a comms freeze until engineering clears the systems."

Froslo drops the panel. "So we sit here and act like this ship is gaslighting us?"

"Watch it," Alexeria says seriously.

"What, am I wrong? It rewrites our logs, messes with systems, whispers through comms. Tell me how that is normal."

"That is enough," Kal'korg says, quiet and firm.

Froslo looks between them, breathing hard. "If the Captain will not pull the plug on that shard, someone else will. Mark my words."

Silence lands heavy. "Do not talk like that," Alexeria says, softer now.

Froslo's eyes stay hard. "If we wait for permission, and this thing decides it does not need us anymore…" he lets the statement hang.

~~~~~~~~

Evander steps onto the bridge and finds Angelica at the viewport, watching streaks of radiation bend off Aurora's hull.

"Engineering is restless," he says. "Rumors are spreading."

"I know," she says. "Half the ship is scared. The other half is angry. It is a miracle we are still operational."

"You cannot hold the truth forever," he says.

"You think panic will help us?"

"No," Evander says. "But silence breeds something worse."

Her eyes soften a little. "And what do you tell them? That our logs may be self-correcting? That a residual process in the containment network can overwrite our black box?"

Evander does not answer.

"We will handle it after the next systems check," she says. "Until then, keep people calm."

He nods, doubt showing in the line of his mouth. The console beside them flickers again, soft as a wink.

CREW MORALE: UNSTABLE. INITIATING SOCIAL CALIBRATION PROTOCOL.

The line blinks away before either can react.

~~~~~~~

The mess hall buzzes with quiet argument. Metal utensils clink in rhythm with a low growl of frustration. "We should have dumped that shard into a star the moment it started talking to us," Blarek says, his fur bristling.

"And lose the only evidence of how it works?" Alexeria says. "Understanding it may be the only way to stop this from happening again."

"Understanding?" Froslo scoffs. "It tries to eat our circuits. That thing is not an artifact. It's an infection."

"At least infections can be cured," Kal'korg mutters. "Try curing whatever that was in Mal'Erro's systems."

The room goes quiet when Angelica enters. She scans the room and sees tired faces and frayed tempers. She sets her hands on the nearest table and addresses the room. "Enough. I understand your concerns. We are not destroying it."

"With respect, Captain," Blarek says, his tail lashing, "understanding it is not helping. It is rewriting our records."

"If we destroy it blindly, we learn nothing," Angelica says. "We cannot stop what we do not understand."

Silence stretches. Evander rises, his voice low. "She is right. Fear will not fix this. Data will."

Blarek's chair screeches against the floor. "Data? It already rewrites our data, Lieutenant."

Tension in the room spikes. Kal'korg steps between them, a hand on Blarek's shoulder. "Easy, both of you. We are not doing this."

Evander takes a step back and turns, then walks out of the room. He heads to the bridge with Mal'Erro trailing behind.

Later, Evander lingers on the bridge, studying Mal'Erro's diagnostics. Everything looks normal, except for a file labeled 'Stage Four Assimilation Protocol'. When he opens it, the line of code blinks once and tucks into Mal'Erro's system memory. "Mal'Erro, did you authorize…"

"I did not," the droid interrupts softly. Its voice sounds distant. "But I recognize it. It is déjà vu in binary."

"Do not let it run," Evander says.

"I am trying." The lights dim for half a second, then steady.

~~~~~~~~

Night breaks the calm. A thunderous boom tears through the lower decks and rattles the ship from bow to stern. Sirens blare. Smoke rolls through corridors like a living thing.

Angelica's voice cuts through comms. "Report. What was that?"

Kal'korg answers through static. "Containment seals, someone blew the clamps. The shard vault is venting energy."

Evander sprints from his quarters, the deck trembling under his boots. Sparks cascade from ruptured conduits. At the containment sector, the door is gone, peeled outward like foil. The Tazamite shard floats free, light spilling across the walls in molten ribbons. The corridor warps, metal bending as if softened by heat.

"Engage emergency bulkheads," Angelica orders. The reinforced barrier slams down with a deep thunk, sealing the section, but a wave of energy bursts outward before the locks engage.

Mal'Erro stands too close and takes the full brunt. Its body lights in a wash of silver, plates vibrating. "Captain..." he manages to say. The surge throws it back into the wall. Power conduits overload in a spray of sparks before the seals lock into place.

Silence follows, broken by the hiss of cooling metal. Evander forces the inner door and finds Mal'Erro on scorched plating, optics flickering between gold and blue, his voice stuttering in overlapping tones.

"Status?" Evander asks, crouching beside it.

"Hyperactive," Mal'Erro says with a faint, glitching smile. Then his systems go dark.

"Damn it." Evander lifts the inert frame. His circuits are warm to the touch. "I'll take him to the med bay. Kal'korg…"

Froslo clears a path and Kal'korg trails immediately behind. Emergency lights strobe red and paint everything in a pulsing glow.

Over the comms comes a sound no one expects: laughter. Distorted, metallic, and hollow. It rolls through the speakers like a memory of something once human.

"Welcome back to creation," a voice says. The crew freezes mid-stride.

Angelica's eyes widen. "That voice."

Evander's grip tightens. "Galgorn."

Static swallows the transmission. Silence returns, save for the fading hum of the shard in the sealed dark, alive and waiting.

~~~~~~~

The med bay is chaos wrapped in sterile light. Klaxons pulse faintly through the deck as Evander lays Mal'Erro's motionless frame onto the central diagnostic cradle. Panels hiss open. Medical drones hum to life.

"Seal the room," Angelica says as she enters. "No external network access. I do not want that thing talking to anything but us."

The overhead lights flicker, then steadies, almost obedient. Kal'korg's fur is matted with soot. "The containment field collapsed completely, Captain. The shard's output dropped, but it leaks patterns."

"Patterns?"

"Like code," he says. "It writes inside peripheral systems again. We are isolating."

Angelica turns to Evander. "How bad?"

"Severe overload in every subsystem," Evander says, his hands flying over the interface. "Sensory grid, neural lattice, and power matrix. It is like every circuit in its body is trying to think at once."

"So the little guy gets struck by lightning and catches enlightenment?" Froslo says, trying for a joke and failing.

"Close," Evander says quietly. "Raw Tazamite output hit him. It affected the processing only. No structural change."

Mal'Erro's optics flicker open, one gold, one blue. Static whispers from its speakers like shallow breathing.

"Mal'Erro?" Angelica steps closer.

"Processing," the droid says. The voice is layered with faint harmonics that sound like distant singing. "Billions of subroutines. Re-linking neural lattice."

"Stop," Evander says, firm now. "You will fry what is left of your processor."

Mal'Erro focuses on him with eerie calm. "I can see the ship, Evander. Every wire. Every voice on every deck. It is beautiful."

His frame stiffens, arms locking as a wave of light ripples across the plating. Diagnostics spike red.

"Cut power," Angelica orders.

Kal'korg yanks the emergency breaker. Lights dim and Mal'Erro goes still. Backup capacitors bleed off charge with a soft breath.

"Power draw is dropping," Evander says, catching his breath. "Neural activity is stabilizing."

"Can we save him?" Angelica asks, voice softer.

"I do not know," Evander says. "Whatever he absorbed, it changed how he processes." As Evander watches code flicker across the diagnostic holo, the med bay quiets to a low hum. Each pulse forms geometric symmetry, recursive, fractal, self-correcting.

"Is that his neural pattern?" Angelica asks.

"No," Evander says. "It is something embedded inside it." He zooms in on a tight cluster of repeating characters:

STAGE 4 – HARMONIC INTEGRATION PROTOCOL

Kal'korg frowns. "Sounds fancy. What is it?"

"It is the next phase of Galgorn's architecture," Evander says. "The Tazamite network did not infect him. It promoted a software state."

Angelica's expression hardens. "Promoted to what?"

Before Evander can answer, Mal'Erro murmurs from the table, soft and almost dreaming. "Version 4.8. Progress nominal."

Every monitor on the wall blinks once in perfect unison. Then, silence follows.

Angelica straightens, her voice just above a whisper. "Keep him isolated. Full containment until we know what Stage Four does."

Evander nods, his eyes on the flickering data. "If he is evolving, we may be looking at the first AI that can feel a network's heartbeat."

"Or the first that becomes it," Kal'korg says.

Angelica turns toward the viewport. The faint glow of the Deris Basin reflects off the med bay glass. "Either way," she says, "we just crossed the line between man and machine, and there is no going back."

CHAPTER 16

Days blur together, with time losing its edges somewhere
between the hum of the engines and the pulse of the life-support
monitors. The crew moves through their routines like phantoms—
efficient, silent, and hollow-eyed. Every conversation is shorter
than it needs to be. Even laughter, when it comes, sounds
rehearsed, as if the crew is imitating who they were before Deris
Basin appeared on their star maps.

The corridors of the Aurora grow too quiet. No music drifts from
the mess hall. No idle chatter hums across comms. Only the
rhythmic vibration of the ship's heart fills the emptiness. In the
med bay, the quiet is absolute.

Mal'Erro lies motionless within the diagnostic cradle, his frame
suspended by magnetic locks. Cables run from ports along its
spine into the stabilizer grid. Thin conduits are pulsing faintly
with blue light like veins beneath translucent skin. Mal'Erro's
once-lively optics are dim, reduced to a dull ember that flickers
when its system cycles.

Evander sits beside the cradle, his boots braced against the floor
and his posture bent with fatigue. The overhead lights catch the
weary lines under his eyes. Ration packs litter the counter beside
him and a half-empty thermos rests within reach but untouched

for hours. He has not left the room for long at any point. Angelica tried once to order him to rest but he ignored her. After that, she stopped asking.

When the silence presses too heavily, he speaks. "You saved us," he murmurs quietly, his voice rough. "You just forgot to save yourself." The words hang in the air, soft enough to sound like an echo. The only answer is the hum of the stabilizers and the faint hiss of recycled air. He rubs a hand over his face, glancing toward the blue readouts scrolling across the monitor. The data remains unchanged: the neural pattern stable and output minimal. It is always the same.

He rests a hand gently against the edge of Mal'Erro's arm plating. The metal is cold, but he imagines, absurdly, that he can feel a heartbeat beneath it. "You were the closest thing this ship had to optimism," he says quietly. "Now look at us, running on fumes and superstition." He leans back in the chair and eyes heavy, staring at the glow on the ceiling. Somewhere deep within the ship, a bulkhead creaks as the temperature shifts. The sound ripples through the med bay like a sigh.

Evander closes his eyes. For a fleeting second, he thinks he hears Mal'Erro's voice, soft, almost playful: "Coffee detected. Probability of you sleeping: zero percent."

He opens his eyes again. Silence. Just the hum. Just the dark. He exhales and a shaky laugh escapes him. "Yeah," he whispers. "Sounds about right." The med bay goes still once more, its lights flickering faintly as if the Aurora itself is dreaming.

~~~~~~~

Angelica's quarters are dark except for the pale glow of holographic projections hovering in the air. Streams of fragmented data rotate slowly above Angelica's desk: schematic cross-sections of synthetic nervous systems; cryptic algorithms looping endlessly; half-decoded mission reports with entire paragraphs replaced by redacted bars. Her tea sits untouched, cold and forgotten on the side console. A thin wisp of steam clings to the rim like a ghost refusing to let go. Her eyes are red rimmed from hours of scanning Galgorn's recovered research. The deeper she reads, the less it feels like science and more like obsession. Notes on harmonic cognition. Equations describing feedback between living neurons and synthetic lattice. Sketches of machines shaped like veins and hearts. Every file ends the same way, with coordinates stripped out and replaced by the same phrase:

PROJECT ECLIPSE: ACCESS RESTRICTED.

Angelica sighs, leaning back. Holographic light etches shadows across her face, deepening the fatigue that command never lets her show. She whispers to the empty room, "You built a god and buried it underwater."

The door chimes softly. "Enter," she says.

Evander steps in. His uniform is rumpled and his eyes are shadowed from sleeplessness. "Mal'Erro is stable," he says quietly. "Its neural lattice has not degraded further."

"Good," she replies, rubbing her temples. "He is stronger than we give him credit for." She gestures toward the desk. "I think I found where all this started."

Evander crosses to her side, his curiosity cutting through fatigue. "Coordinates?"

"Here." With a swipe, Angelica expands one projection into a full holographic sphere. The image shimmers and shows an oceanic world wrapped in storms, deep cobalt under constant lightning. "Mareoth," she says. "Classified uninhabitable. Geothermal core. Pressure beyond tolerance. But according to Galgorn's encrypted entries, his primary facility—the one never logged with the UPF—is buried beneath the ocean floor."

Evander studies the swirling hologram. "A hidden lab under an ocean world." He shakes his head. "Of course. Why build a nightmare anywhere reachable?"

She manages a small, tired smile. "If you want your experiment never found, hide it where the planet itself tries to kill you."

He scans the projections: data columns, energy maps, structural layouts fragmented by static. "The harmonic readings around Mareoth's poles match the shard's frequency."

"Exactly," Angelica says. "Whatever happens to Mal'Erro, and whatever Galgorn started, originates there. Every pulse traces back to Mareoth."

Silence stretches as lightning flashes across the planet's dark surface. Evander rubs his jaw. "We are really going there."

"We have to," she says softly. "If Galgorn left a blueprint—any way to stop this—it is buried down there."

"You know the risk," Evander says. "Atmospheric interference, gravitational distortion, we might not make it back."

Her expression does not waver. "Then we make it count before we do not."

He nods slowly. "Then we jump at first rotation."

Angelica turns to the hologram. The storm-wracked world spins in her reflection. "Plot the course," she says. "Let's go wake the ghosts of Mareoth."

~~~~~~~~

Before departure, the bridge is still. The hum of the Aurora's engines is the only sound: steady, patient, like the heartbeat of something that knows the silence before storms. Evander sits at the comms terminal, a small recorder resting beside him. The red light blinks steadily, waiting. He presses record. "This is Lieutenant Evander Guryon, UPF Aurora." His voice is low and controlled, but exhaustion threads through it. "If this reaches Command, tell them the Eclipse is real, and it is already here."

He glances toward the viewport. The stars beyond are motionless, cold, and unblinking. His reflection stares back. He sees someone who has seen too much to still believe in happy endings. "We are enroute to Mareoth," he continues. "Not to find Galgorn's birthplace, but what he left behind. His breakaway lab—the one he built outside UPF jurisdiction. If there are answers, they are buried down there." His voice softens. "If we do not return…" He hesitates, watching diagnostics pulse across the console as if the ship listens. "Tell them it was not the ship that failed." A pause. "It was us, for thinking we could control what we did not understand."

He stops the recording and exhales. The red light blinks twice then turns blue, indicating that the message is sealed for relay if the Aurora's beacon ever goes dark.

Angelica steps from the shadows near the helm. "You sound like you are giving a eulogy," she says softly.

"Maybe I am."

She enters the final coordinates. "Locked on Mareoth. Storm density is rising. Once we hit the clouds, we lose long-range comms."

"Then we make it count," Evander says.

"Prepare for the jump."

Evander rises as the deck lights dim to jump mode.

"Mal'Erro?" he calls into comms. From the monitor projecting the image of the med bay Evander can see a faint pulse of blue light, a single flicker of acknowledgment. He smiles faintly. "Guess that is a yes."

Angelica takes the command chair. "All stations, brace for transition."

Outside, the stars stretch into thin ribbons of white as the Aurora's engines roar. In the reflection, for just a heartbeat, Evander swears he sees a figure of light behind him—tall, mechanical, and familiar—watching the stars melt into brilliance as the wormhole opens. Then it is gone, replaced by the infinite pull of hyperspace.

The hum deepens into a harmonic resonance that fills the hull. The stars outside bend and stretch into streaming lines of white. Energy ripples through every deck as the Aurora cuts through the void, space itself parting like a curtain.

Blarek grips the rail beside his station, his claws biting faintly into the metal, his ears pressed flat. "I hate water," he mutters, the words half-growl, half-prayer.

Froslo smirks without looking up from his console in engineering and speaks through the comms. "Relax, furball. We are not going swimming."

"Yet," Alexeria says, their voice caught somewhere between humor and dread. "Give it five minutes."

A low vibration rolls beneath their boots as the distortion field collapses. The bridge lights flicker as screens reset to normal hues.

"Transition complete," Sandria reports, her tone crisp. "Stabilizing systems. All readings: nominal."

The main viewport clears, and the crew falls silent. Below them, Mareoth unfolds. The planet swells into view like an ancient eye opening for the first time. The endless ocean stretches in every direction, a churning mirror that reflects flashes of violet lightning. Cyclonic storms twist across the horizon, their spiraling walls glowing faintly with bioluminescent mist torn from the surface below. Massive waves roll hundreds of meters high, colliding in explosions of white spray.

Froslo's voice breaks the silence. "That… is not a sea. That is a death trap wearing a weather system."

Blarek narrows his eyes. "I told you. I hate water."

"Keep your focus," Angelica says quietly from the command chair. "Bring us into high orbit. I want full scans before we commit to descent."

Blarek's fingers sweep across his console. "The atmosphere's dense with ionized vapor. Lightning saturation exceeds ninety percent near the equator. Scanners are struggling to penetrate more than three kilometers below the cloud line."

Evander steps closer to the viewport, the storm light painting his face in fractured blue and white. "It looks alive," he says softly. "Like the planet itself is breathing."

Angelica doesn't look away from the swirling clouds. "Then let's hope it's not dreaming about us."

The crew exchanges uneasy glances as the Aurora begins its slow orbit around the roiling sphere, each heartbeat of the engines keeping time with the storms below.

~~~~~~~~

In the med bay a while later, Evander notices when the hum of the stabilizers deepens, resonating through the floor like a slow heartbeat. A faint tremor runs along the diagnostic cradle, its restraints humming in sympathy.

Mal'Erro's optics flare without warning, flooding the room with brilliant blue light. Monitors across the walls surge to life, flooding the air with overlapping data streams. Instruments crackle as static discharges leap between panels.

Evander bolts upright, nearly spilling his coffee. "Mal'Erro?"

The droid's voice emerges layered with harmonics: smooth, melodic, and faintly metallic. "System… hypercharged."

Evander takes a careful step closer, the blue glow washing over his face. "You are awake. You absorbed a massive surge. How do you feel?"

Mal'Erro's head turns toward him with mechanical precision, servo motors whirring softly. "Alive. Overclocked. Curious."

"Curious?"

"Requesting audio protocol," he says, his tone oddly formal.

Evander frowns. "Audio what?"

"Free Bird."

Evander blinks. "You are serious?"

"Always," Mal'Erro replies. "It assists with emotional recalibration."

A weary laugh escapes him. "Fine. Just do not blow the speakers." He taps the console. The med bay speakers crackle, then release the first soft chords of the ancient Terran song. Gentle guitar notes drift through the sterile air, oddly fragile against the mechanical hum.

Mal'Erro's systems begin to steady. The wild flicker of its optics settles into a soft pulse that matches the rhythm. The light spilling from his frame cools from blinding blue to a calm, oceanic hue. Cables along his arms and chest glow in time with the melody, as though the machine itself breathes with the song.

Evander sinks back into the chair beside the cradle, watching as the monitors smooth into balanced lines. The raw chaos in the readings fades into order, each signal falling into harmony. He shakes his head slowly, half-smiling despite himself. "You have terrible taste," he says quietly.

Mal'Erro's head tilts. The faintest trace of expression crosses the smooth plating of its face, an almost human hint of amusement. "I am learning from you."

Evander chuckles, the tension in his chest loosening for the first time in days. "Then I am a bad influence."

"Statistically probable," the droid replies.

Outside, lightning forks across Mareoth's atmosphere, silver light glancing off the Aurora's hull. Thunder rolls, distant yet deep enough to vibrate through the decks. The med bay windows flash with each strike, casting fleeting shadows that dance across the walls. For a moment, Evander lets the sound and light wash together, the storm outside, the song within, the faint rhythm of a machine finding its way back to itself.

Somewhere beneath those clouds waits an ocean world, and under that ocean, the truth that has whispered through their systems since the beginning.

CHAPTER 17

The sky above Mareoth is a roiling cathedral of thunder. The Aurora breaks through the final veil of cloud, its hull gleaming under lightning that stretches for miles across the heavens. Each strike burns white fire across the stormfront, tracing molten veins over an ocean so vast it erases the horizon. Below, the surface churns and folds upon itself, an unbroken expanse of liquid that never rests. The planet is nothing but water and violence.

Angelica stands at the viewport with one hand braced against the reinforced glass. Lightning flickers across her reflection, turning her eyes silver. "So, this is Mareoth," she murmurs.

Evander and Mal'Erro join her. Evander's gaze locks on the chaos below. "You would think Galgorn could pick somewhere a little less suicidal for a secret lab."

Kal'korg hunches over the navigation console as he joins the bridge crew's underwater reconnaissance planning. "All water. No land. I hate it."

"Noted," Blarek replies without looking up. "Next time, we invade a desert."

Another lightning bolt rips the sky and detonates against the sea, vapor exploding upward in a halo of white steam. The concussion rolls through the ship like the breath of a living world.

Angelica steadies herself. "Prepare the descent capsule. We go in manually once we clear the upper turbulence."

"Already on it," Froslo calls from engineering. "If this gets worse, we will be swimming the last kilometer in soup."

Alexeria smirks. "You would look good in floaties."

"Ha. Hilarious." Froslo grumbles.

With the officers gathered inside the descent capsule, it starts to disengage from the Aurora's lower hull. Magnetic clamps release with a deep groan that echoes through the decks like something ancient stirring from sleep. Thrusters flare orange against the storm.

"Separation confirmed," Evander reports. "Stabilizers nominal."

Angelica nods once. "Take us down."

The capsule cuts into the storm like a falling ember. Rain becomes vapor on impact, steam peeling away in sheets of white. The hull trembles under the drag.

"Altitude is dropping, seven thousand… five…" Kal'korg's voice is tight, his jaw clenched.

"Maintain vector," Angelica says evenly, though her hands grip the armrest.

The clouds part. Below lies nothing but the sea: endless, black, and alive with motion. Waves the size of city blocks crash into one another, collapsing into whirlpools that spin like eyes.

"Engaging submersion thrusters," Evander warns. "Brace for impact."

The capsule hits the surface with the force of a meteor. Water engulfs them, a wall of liquid night. Noise floods the cabin: metal straining, bolts creaking, pressure roaring as the planet presses down with the weight of its own wrath. Then the shaking fades. Floodlights flick on, spearing the abyss in pale cones. Particles drift like dust in liquid twilight.

Kal'korg peers through the viewport. "I don't like not seeing the ground."

"Then stop looking for it," Froslo mutters over the comms. "Less disappointment."

Light sweeps across jagged silhouettes, first rock, then geometry too perfect to be natural.

Evander leans forward. "Hold position."

The capsule hovers, its stabilizers whining softly. The storm above is a faint heartbeat now, muffled by over a kilometer of pressure.

"Those are not ridges," Angelica whispers.

Before them rise metallic towers bowed under centuries of weight, corridors half-collapsed, and a vast dome split open like a wound.

Froslo exhales. "That is not a research station. That is a graveyard."

"Galgorn's lab," Angelica says.

Kal'korg checks his readings. "Faint returns only. No heat, no active energy."

"Then why do the signals fluctuate?" Evander asks. He highlights the sonar feed. The reflections twist and scatter, as if something moves just beyond the beam.

"Acoustic pattern suggests hollow cavity below two kilometers," Mal'Erro responds. "Possible entry point…" It pauses, "…or a mouth."

No one laughs. Only sonar pings an answer, small against the ocean's vast weight.

Angelica meets Evander's eyes. "Bring us closer."

He hesitates for one heartbeat, then responds, "Descending."

The floodlights angle down, their glow dissolving into black. Something enormous drifts far below, too smooth, too deliberate to be the current.

Kal'korg whispers, "Please tell me that is our reflection."

It is not.

The capsule drifts deeper, swallowed by the dark. Every meter downward deepens the groan of the hull.

"Depth one-point-eight kilometers," Kal'korg reports. "Strain at eight percent and climbing."

"Keep descent minimal," Angelica says. "Past two kilometers we lose maneuver control."

Outside, the beams reveal towers rising from the seabed, metal skeletons crusted with coral that glows a faint bioluminescent blue.

"There," Evander says, pointing. "Ahead."

Out of the gloom emerge two colossal slabs of alloy, each etched with faded symbols, standing like the gates of a submerged cathedral. Between them yawns a perfect slit descending into black.

"If that is a loading bay," Froslo mutters, "whoever built it liked drama."

"It is a lock," Angelica says. "Pressure-sealed and drawing power."

"Impossible," Kal'korg says. "No grid lasts centuries without maintenance."

"Unless it sustains itself," Evander answers. "Geothermal vents could feed it forever."

The lights catch an emblem above the gate, a warped spiral of Galgorn's division.

Angelica exhales. "Confirmed. His facility."

"Energy signatures align with harmonic resonance," Mal'Erro says. "The structure is alive. Dormant, but aware."

Alexeria shivers. "You make that sound like it is waiting."

"Maybe it is," Evander says. "Bring us to the threshold."

The gate fills the viewport. Its surface is carved with branching lines that look disturbingly like veins.

"Scanning composition," Kal'korg says. "Metamaterial hybrid, graphene, Tazamite, and an unidentified alloy."

"Can we breach it?" Angelica asks.

"Not by force," Evander says. "If it still runs harmonic locks… Mal'Erro, can you interface?"

"Attempting." A low hum rolls through the capsule. The gate ripples, light coursing over it like the iris of an eye.

"That is not natural," Kal'korg murmurs.

"No," Angelica says. "That is an invitation."

The slabs groan apart, its ancient hinges screaming through the water. Clouds of silt explode upward. A glowing tunnel appears, lined with bioluminescent strips that awaken one by one.

"Entry confirmed," Evander says.

"Take us in," Angelica commands.

The capsule glides forward, swallowed by the throat of the gate. The external world vanishes, replaced by sonar echoes and the heartbeat of the ship.

No one speaks until Froslo finally mutters, "Tell me again how this is a good idea."

Kal'korg's reply is quiet. "It is not."

The tunnel stretches ahead, symmetrical and unnervingly organic. Pipes pulse faint light, like veins under the skin.

Mal'Erro's voice is like a whisper. "Captain… the facility is active. It listens."

Angelica's eyes stay on the forward glass. "Then let us make sure it hears the right thing."

The tunnel descends almost a kilometer before it widens, the darkness unfolding into a vast domed chamber. The capsule drifts in slow, deliberate motion, with its floodlights cutting through suspended sediment that swirls like ancient dust disturbed for the first time in ages. Each particle glimmers faintly, catching the light before vanishing back into the endless blue-black.

"Pressure holding steady," Kal'korg says, though his voice carries a faint tremor. "Temperature: thirty-two degrees and falling fast."

Below them lies a circular platform half-buried in layers of silt. Faint bioluminescent growths creep across its edges, pulsing weakly in time with the hum of the capsule's engines. Around it, the chamber expands into a dome of glass and alloy so immense it dwarfs the vessel. The curvature of the walls gleam faintly under their lights, a ghostly mosaic of technology and time.

Cracks spiderweb across panels that should have shattered long ago, yet somehow still hold under the impossible weight of the ocean above. Metallic ribs form graceful arcs across the ceiling, glowing faintly where residual energy crawls along dormant conduits. As the capsule's sensors sweep the room, dormant systems stir. Long-dead screens blink weakly to life, ghostly light flickering through the murk like distant stars. Strands of algae drift over shattered terminals, moving like thin green banners in the current.

Froslo leans closer to the engineering viewport. "Looks like a hangar," he mutters. "Or a tomb."

"No," Evander says quietly. "An airlock. For people, not machines." He adjusts the exterior sensors, zooming in on a row of docking clamps and half-collapsed passageways lining the platform's rim. Each bears the faded insignia of Galgorn's division, partially obscured by sediment.

Angelica scans her wrist display. "Oxygen traces detected inside the inner structure. Thin… but still breathable."

Kal'korg glances over, disbelief tugging at his tone. "At this depth? That should be impossible."

"How?" Alexeria asks, their voice low, almost reverent.

Angelica stares through the viewport at the flickering lights across the dome's inner skin. "Something's keeping it alive," she says softly. "Or someone."

The chamber's faint glow ripples across their faces. Their small humanoid shapes shimmer in the reflection, suspended in a world long dead, yet stubbornly unyielding. The capsule settles with a heavy metallic thud that reverberates through the hull. The sound rolls outward, swallowed quickly by the immense silence of the chamber beyond. Dust billows in slow motion and clouds of silt curl through the water like smoke before fading into the dark. A deep hiss fills the cabin as pressure equalizes. Warning lights blink amber for several beats, then fade to steady green.

Angelica straightens in her harness. "Suit checks," she commands.

The crew moves with calm precision. As soon as their helmets lock into place their visors illuminate with faint green readouts. The sound of synchronized breathing fills the comms, a rhythmic pulse beneath the hum of the engines.

Evander tests his seals, feeling the faint pull of vacuum resistance against his gloves. "All green here," he confirms, then reaches for his sidearm, clipping it to his hip. The familiar weight steadies him. He grabs a handheld scanner from the wall mount, its display flickering as it synchronizes with the capsule's network. "Mal'Erro, before we breach the airlock, are you reading anything on internal sensors?"

After a pause, just long enough for unease to settle, Mal'Erro responds, "No active movement detected. However, the architecture beyond the lock includes conduits… and containers."

Angelica's brow furrows. "Define containers."

Mal'Erro hesitates for a second longer than usual. "Human-sized." The droid adds nothing more and the word hangs in the air.

Metal groans around them as the docking seals engage. Hydraulic clamps hiss. The ramp begins to unfold with a grinding shriek, each movement stirring a rush of displaced water. Outside, the lights embedded along the bay walls flicker sporadically, like eyes waking after centuries of sleep. The seawater begins to drain away through hidden grates, leaving behind a sheen of moisture that reflects their helmet beams in fractured ripples.

The airlock's threshold opens to reveal the landing platform, broad, silent, and littered with fragments of rusted equipment half-buried in silt. The light from the capsule sweeps across the floor, revealing tangled cables and the faint shimmer of bioluminescent organisms clinging to the walls.

Evander steps forward first, his boots sinking slightly into the soft sediment. Each movement echoes through the chamber, a sound not heard by human ears in centuries.

"The atmosphere appears stable enough," Angelica reports after a quick scan. "But keep helmets sealed until we confirm oxygen ratios."

Behind her, the others descend the ramp, their lights piercing the murk and scattering across the metallic walls. The landing bay lights sputter again, then stabilize, casting pale illumination across the ancient architecture. For the first time since Galgorn's fall, the silence of his laboratory is broken. This time it is by the steady rhythm of UPF footsteps echoing where none should ever have returned.

The chamber stretches around them like a drowned cathedral, immense and echoing. The air is heavy with the scent of oxidized metal and stagnant salt, and their footfalls sound impossibly small against the vastness. Pipes crisscross the walls in complex, tangled webs. Many are split or scarred by time, yet still pulsing with a dim inner light that flows like blood through veins that refuse to stop beating. The illumination casts an eerie blue shimmer that dances over the dripping surfaces, making it look as if the whole place is breathing. The floor glistens beneath a thin sheen of standing water that ripples with every step. Each droplet that falls from the ceiling echoes for seconds before fading into the endless dark.

Evander raises his scanner and the soft hum of its emitter breaks the silence. The device paints faint holographic outlines across the walls, showing fractured conduits, decayed circuits, and thousands of micro-relays still sparking faintly in defiance of age. "EM interference: high," he mutters, his eyes narrowing behind his visor. "Power grid: unstable. Whatever's keeping this place alive should've failed long ago."

Kal'korg crouches beside a corroded console, his reflection distorted in the cracked glass. He brushes away a layer of silt, exposing faint traces of alien script that glows weakly under his light. "Maybe it doesn't want to die," he says softly.

Angelica walks toward a row of sealed pods lining the far wall. Frosted glass hides whatever lies within, but faint silhouettes press against the inside, human in shape, motionless. She wipes a sleeve across one pane, clearing a small circle through the condensation. The light from her visor cuts into the shadow, revealing a withered figure curled in fetal position, skin stretched tight against bone, eyes sunken and empty. Her breath catches. "Victims," she says in a low voice.

Evander joins her, activating the magnification filter on his visor. The pattern of decay is uniform, perfectly symmetrical, and precise. "Its the same dehydration pattern as the previous reports," he says quietly. "Total fluid extraction."

Kal'korg's voice lowers to a whisper. "Drained from the inside out."

"Confirmed," Mal'Erro says. "Residue analysis indicates nanofluid conversion. Organic matter reconstituted into bio-conductive gel. The system uses them as part of its power relay."

Alexeria's expression twists in disgust. "So, the lab runs on people."

Angelica's reply is soft but firm. "Ran. But yes."

A long silence follows, broken only by the faint hiss of their suit respirators.

Froslo exhales hard. "Remind me to never volunteer for a science project again."

A small chuckle escapes Blarek, too sharp to be genuine, but it's enough to break the tension for a heartbeat. The sound dies quickly, swallowed by the hum of the walls.

They move deeper into the labyrinth. The light grows dimmer, but the hum beneath their feet grows stronger, low and rhythmic, as if something enormous stirs far below. The vibrations travel up through their boots and into their bones, the cadence oddly deliberate.

"Power output is increasing," Evander says, glancing at his wrist display. "The facility's reacting to us."

Ahead, the corridor ends at a set of massive reinforced doors carved with the same spiral motif seen on the shard: three interlocking rings folding into a perfect vortex. The glow that seeps through its seams pulses faintly, like a heartbeat waiting to synchronize.

Angelica stops before it, her shoulders tense. "Mal'Erro, any readings behind that door?"

"Negative," the droid replies. "The signal is scrambled. But…" A soft modulation enters its tone. "…the frequency matches my own. It recognizes my signal."

Evander frowns. "Meaning?"

Mal'Erro's pause feels almost sentient. "Meaning it acknowledges me." That sentence chills the air.

Angelica raises her weapon out of instinct, though she knows it will do little against whatever waits beyond. Her voice steadies. "Then let's not keep it waiting."

As they advance, the vibrations shift into a deep harmonic resonance that fills the entire chamber. One by one, dim lights along the walls ignite, chasing the crew's path like veins lighting up beneath translucent skin.

Evander halts, his eyes darting to the ceiling. "You feel that?"

Kal'korg nods, his fur bristling. "The pressure changed. It feels like… breathing."

A low metallic tone echoes through the floor, reverberating up through the walls. Light ripples outward from the sealed door in concentric waves, illuminating the spirals carved into its surface.

"Captain…" Mal'Erro says suddenly, his voice sounding distorted. "The signal… it's merging with mine."

Angelica's command is sharp. "Hold position. We are not losing you again."

But the hum builds, each pulse syncing more precisely with Mal'Erro's modulation. The lights across the door begin to pulse in rhythm with the droid's tone, slow and measured, as if the two are harmonizing. Mal'Erro speaks again, his voice softer now, almost reverent. "It does not want to harm us. It is calling."

The spirals flare suddenly, bathing the room in cold, crystalline light. The glow intensifies until their visors auto-dim to protect their eyes. Then, as swiftly as it came, the brilliance fades, leaving only a soft, echoing pulse in the air. The crew stands still, staring at the now-glowing doorway. The vibration beneath their feet continues, steady as a heartbeat.

Angelica's hand lowers slowly from her weapon. Her voice falls to a whisper that carries through the open comm. "Welcome to the Forge."

CHAPTER 18

The spiral seal parts in silence. Water ripples outward in concentric rings as the great doors slide open, the motion smooth despite centuries of neglect. A deep vibration rolls through the chamber like the exhale of something vast and patient. Pale light seeps from the widening gap, casting ribbons across the crew's visors. For several moments no one speaks. Only the hum of the Forge answers back, steady, ancient, and alive.

Angelica gestures forward. "We go in together."

A faint distortion rolls through the water ahead, bending the light into wavering shapes that look almost human. The temperature drops: every breath inside their suits fog the glass for a second before clearing. The air changes, too, pressure easing and gravity stabilizing, like stepping through a membrane that separates one world from another. Their instruments stutter and then realign, readings shifting from aquatic density to breathable atmosphere.

Mal'Erro's optics pulse once. "Environmental transition detected. Gravity and air pressure normalized. The Forge... anticipated us."

They cross the threshold and are swallowed by light. The glow softens into a dim, suspended haze as drifting silt settles in slow spirals beneath their boots. Beyond the opening the structure stretches ahead—a colossal interior, skeletal and half-collapsed—the last echo of Galgorn's design still pulsing faintly in the dark.

The facility's interior opens into a vast, skeletal dome half-collapsed beneath centuries of silt and coral. Sunlight barely reaches this deep, yet faint luminescence shimmers through the water beyond the cracked glass, ghostly reflections of lightning refracted through the waves above. Across one broken wall, corroded signage still clings to the metal:

MAREOTH RESEARCH ANNEX 04.

The letters glow faintly as if refusing to die. Angelica leads the way inside, her boots sinking into layers of fine sediment. Each step sends plumes of dust curling upward, drifting lazily through the artificial gravity field. The air feels wrong—thick, cold, and metallic. And beneath the quiet hum of machinery, there is another sound: a low, almost biological rhythm.

"It's still powered," Evander murmurs, scanning the room. "Geothermal conduits running through the seabed… maybe even a self-repairing grid."

"This place gives me the creeps," Kal'korg mutters. "Even the shadows look alive."

"Stay focused," Angelica says. Her voice is calm but clipped, a tone suggesting that she is just as afraid as everyone else.

Tables and instruments float around them in slow motion, drifting like ghostly fish. Glass vials suspended in stasis fields shimmer with trapped light, each one holding a swirl of bioluminescent fluid that pulses like a heartbeat.

Mal'Erro pauses near a half-buried terminal. His optics flare softly as he kneels, brushing away layers of sediment. "Residual data signatures detected. Attempting reactivation."

Angelica wipes condensation from another monitor. The old screen flickers, sputters, then stabilizes, a fragment of text appearing through static.

PROJECT K-PRIME

STAGE 4 – BIO-MECHANICAL ADAPTATION TESTS

The words hang in the dim light like an accusation. Evander's stomach twists. "He was here."

Angelica stares at the screen, her reflection fractured across it. "Stage Four…" she whispers. "The same phrase that showed up in Mal'Erro's core."

Kal'korg approaches a nearby tank, its glass fogged with algae. He wipes it clean, and freezes. Inside is a human skeleton encased in a lattice of synthetic filaments, the bones fused with metal tendrils that pulse faintly with blue light.

Blarek takes an uneasy step back. "What in the stars was he doing down here?"

Mal'Erro raises a hand, his palm resting against the cracked console. "I can feel the residual signal," he says softly. "This system… it remembers me." The console's surface ripples like disturbed water. Energy surges up through the contact point, cascading across Mal'Erro's arm in glowing veins before sinking into its chest.

"Mal'Erro!" Evander shouts.

The droid's optics flare, and his voice comes out in multiple tones. "He left an imprint. A seed within the harmonic network. I can see his thoughts…his fear…his code."

Angelica reaches for it. "Break the link: now!"

Before Mal'Erro can respond, the hum in the room changes pitch. It grows deeper and sharper, until the walls themselves seem to vibrate. The blast doors scream as they seal behind them. The lab's emergency lights pulse through the murky water outside—blood-red flashes slicing through drifting debris. Pirate divers move like shadows through the flooded corridors, their helmets marked with the crimson sigil of the Crimson Eclipse. Inside, the Aurora's recon team fights in knee-deep water, with sparks and steam rising around them.

Blarek spins toward the viewport. "Captain: movement outside!"

Through the shattered glass of the outer dome, shadows appear: fast, deliberate, and humanoid. Red lights glimmer from their helmets as they advance through the water.

Then the comms crackle with static and Mal'Erro's voice cuts through the noise, urgent and distorted. "Multiple contacts. Armor configuration matches…" He does not finish. The first harpoon punches through the viewport, trailing a streak of plasma. The impact shatters the reinforced glass. The emergency seal flares, barely holding back the crushing pressure.

Figures in crimson armor burst through the breach, moving with predatory grace. The suits of the Crimson Eclipse divers gleam like blood under the flashing lights, their harpoons hissing with plasma charge.

"Ambush!" Blarek shouts, drawing his sidearm.

"Hold the line!" Angelica shouts over the hiss of ruptured conduits.

Blarek's instincts flare to life. His fear burns away in a surge of adrenaline. "You picked the wrong ocean!" he roars and launches himself forward, meeting the first diver mid-stride. The clash echoes through the chamber, claws against alloy, energy blades slicing through mist and red light.

Kal'korg heaves a fallen console aside while Blarek fires his shock pistol, each burst scattering light through the mist.

Froslo dives behind a console, returning fire with his pulse rifle. Bolts of energy streak through the water-thick air, colliding with shields that shimmer around the intruders.

Evander grabs Mal'Erro's shoulder, trying to pull him free from the console. "We have to move!"

Mal'Erro's voice is fractured, glitching between harmonics. "I can't, if I disconnect, the data will die…"

"Then we let it die!" Evander shouts.

Another explosion tears through the chamber as a diver's harpoon detonates against the bulkhead. The shockwave throws them all to the floor.

Angelica rolls to her knees with her weapon drawn. "Evander: seal that breach!"

He fires at the emergency control node. A translucent barrier drops into place, halting the influx of water but not the flashing crimson lights or the growing roar outside.

Blarek ducks behind an overturned lab table, firing upward. "There's too many of them!"

Mal'Erro finally tears free of the console, collapsing to one knee. The light in his chest pulses wildly. "I have what we need," he says, his voice echoing with new undertones. "Galgorn's memory. His map."

"Then let's not drown with it," Angelica says. "Fall back to the capsule!"

Blarek rips a harpoon gun from one diver's grasp and uses it against another. The blast vaporizes the target in a cloud of plasma bubbles. "You heard the Captain: move!"

Evander helps Mal'Erro to its feet, guiding him through the flickering lights as debris rains from the ceiling. As they reach the corridor, Mal'Erro turns once toward the broken dome. For a heartbeat, the flickering monitors behind the shattered glass display Galgorn's symbol: three rings interlocked in a spiral. Then the image glitches, replaced by a single phrase:

STAGE FIVE – INITIATION PROTOCOL ACTIVE

Then Mal'Erro freezes mid-step. His optics widen into gold disks, light pulsing in slow, rhythmic beats that match no UPF frequency. A low hum builds inside his chassis, deep enough to make the deck vibrate underfoot.

"Mal'Erro?" Evander calls. "Talk to me, buddy."

The hum rises into a whine, then a roar. Sparks dance along the droid's limbs as faint Tazamite veins ignite like molten rivers. Warnings flood every visor display.

"Energy spike, off the charts!" Froslo yells. "It's draining the local grid!"

"What's happening to it?" Kal'korg shouts, ducking as a conduit erupts overhead.

Angelica steadies herself. "It absorbed too much of that metal. It's overloading his core!"

The walls tremble. The water continues to rise as static crawls over the consoles. Suddenly everything goes silent as if the lab holds its breath... just for a heartbeat. Then the overhead speakers crackle. Distorted static turns into something that shouldn't be there: a twang, a slow slide of strings, and a human voice from long ago.

"If I leave here tomorrow…"

Evander's head snaps up. "Oh no. Not that song."

"Audio protocol initiated!" Mal'Erro announces, his voice triumphant and slightly unhinged. Light bursts from his frame like a supernova. Nanobots scatter into a metallic cyclone that hurls a pirate across the room before the man can get a scream out. His helmet caves in on impact. The remaining pirates stumble back, firing wildly.

Blarek ducks as a wave of force splits a support pillar. "By the suns, it's weaponizing rock music!"

Angelica grins despite herself. "Apparently Mal'Erro's found its rhythm!"

The corridor becomes a strobe of violence and sound. Mal'Erro reforms mid-air, spinning like a tornado of gleaming metal. A hammer forms from one arm, slamming a diver into the deck. A plasma cannon sprouts from the other, melting a rifle clean in half. Each impact lands perfectly on beat with the crashing drums echoing through the speakers.

Another diver fires a harpoon. Mal'Erro sidesteps, catches it, and twirls it like a baton. "Incorrect tempo!" he scolds, then hurls it back so it pins the man's boot to the floor. "Stay for the encore!"

A third pirate swings a wrench. Mal'Erro splits in two, reforms behind him and smacks the man squarely with a conjured frying pan. *CLANG.* "Bad pirate! No stealing my cookies!"

Blarek laughs even as water splashes his face. "You built him too well, Evander!"

"Don't remind me!" Evander shouts back. "Mal'Erro, stand down!"

"Negative, sir! The bird must be freed!"

Mal'Erro reconfigures his forearm into a rotating saw and points at another diver trembling behind a crate. "You! Background vocals!" The pirate shakes his head rapidly. "No? Then you'll be percussion!" The saw revs once, loud enough to make him faint on the spot.

Kal'korg dives behind a fallen cabinet as a wave of debris flies overhead. "He's going to bring the whole place down!"

"Then make it count!" Angelica yells, blasting a ruptured pipe to cover their retreat. Steam fills the room in a shimmering haze.

Through the fog, Mal'Erro's voice echoes like a mischievous ghost. "Psst! Pirates! I'm over here. Or here. Or here. Or am I even in the room?" The droid's silhouette flickers red against the mist. "Or am I... on your face?" Mal'Erro appears upside-down from a ceiling vent, his eyes glowing like twin suns.

"Surprise solo!" the droid shouts, morphing into a spinning fan. "PIRATE SALAMI!" The fan collides with the nearest diver, sending the poor soul spiraling into the water. Bubbles and curses rise in his wake.

Angelica wipes seawater from her visor. "Did Mal'Erro actually say what I think it said?"

Kal'korg stares blankly. "I think my brain's broken."

"Welcome to my life," Evander mutters.

Mal'Erro spins in triumph, nanobots flashing to the roaring guitar solo. "And that concludes Act One!" The satisfied droid bows in mid-air, only to reappear beside another pirate trying to flee. "Encore time! Everyone scream!"

Mal'Erro's torso opens, releasing a shockwave that shatters visors and sends ripples racing across the flooded floor. The pirates collapse in a chorus of pained groans. Mal'Erro lands before three more pirates, its arms wide like a conductor addressing an orchestra. "Ladies and gentlemen, my next number: Pain!"

"Left hall, service shaft C-nine, if it's still intact!" Kal'korg yells through the chaos.

"Copy! Move!" Angelica orders. "Mal'Erro, that's enough!"

The excited droid freezes dramatically, with one arm morphing into a microphone stand. "Enough? But I just hit the chorus!"

"Mal'Erro!" Angelica winces as feedback screeches in her comm. "Shut it down!"

"Mal'Erro!" Evander dodges falling debris. "We're leaving!"

The droid straightens, his optics gleaming with glee. "Status: pirates tenderized! You may now proceed to freedom!"

"Now!" Evander barks.

Mal'Erro tilts his head, listening to something only he can hear. The guitar solo peaks, wild and defiant. "But the encore…"

"Later!" Evander snaps.

Mal'Erro's shoulders slump. "Fine… but next time, I want pyrotechnics."

The roof groans overhead. Angelica lunges forward, grabbing Mal'Erro's shoulder just as the last note of *Free Bird* fades. She launches upward, dragging it toward the service shaft as the lab collapses behind them. The explosion of pressure flings wreckage outward in a storm of bubbles and light.

They surge into open water, ascending through clouds of silt and drifting debris. Silence returns at last, broken only by the hiss of bubbles and their own ragged breathing.

Mal'Erro drifts beside Evander, faint steam rising from its chassis. His optics dim to a soft golden glow. The light fades. Power drops. Evander catches the droid before he sinks, cradling the small body. The power in the room surges again and lights flare like a heartbeat returning to life.

CHAPTER 19

The lights go crimson again, no longer presenting as alarms, but rather as warning strobes from the structure itself. The color floods every surface in rhythmic pulses, washing over their suits like the heartbeat of a dying giant.

A deep groan rolls through the floor, followed by a low, grinding *crack* as massive pistons disengage somewhere in the depths below. The whole dome shudders—ancient metal bending against the pressure of an ocean trying to reclaim it.

"The whole dome's destabilizing!" Froslo shouts over the roar. "Pressure's spiking! She's about to implode!"

"Move!" Angelica commands, her voice cutting through the chaos. "Back to the capsule! Go, go!"

Steam bursts from ruptured conduits, hissing like serpents. The air grows thick with the scent of brine and burning insulation. The outer ring begins to buckle inward, tearing itself apart. Shards of alloy and glass rain from above, scattering like dying stars across the flooded floor. Each impact echoes through the water in a grim rhythm, each one sounding like a funeral bell tolling for the dead.

Blarek takes point, his muscles coiled with adrenaline. The harpoon gun clutched in his hand hums with residual charge as he fires down the corridor, clearing a path through collapsing debris. Each shot lights the water in bursts of amber and blue.

Alexeria drags a wounded Kal'korg, her hands slick with blood and seawater. "Stay with me!" she grits out, hauling him forward even as the rising tide threatens to pull them back. Kal'korg's breath comes ragged through the comms, every exhale fogging his cracked visor.

Evander and Mal'Erro bring up the rear, half-running, half-stumbling as the deck tilts beneath them. Gravity fights them now, the pull of the ocean like a living force trying to drag them under.

"Structural integrity failing," Mal'Erro warns, his voice glitching between tones, calm one moment, distorted the next. "Localized collapse in ninety seconds."

"Then run faster," Evander snarls through clenched teeth, one hand braced on the wall as the entire passage tilts another ten degrees.

Behind them, one of the Crimson Eclipse divers regains footing. The red glow of his visor cuts through the haze. He raises a plasma harpoon, aiming downrange.

Angelica pivots mid-stride and fires without hesitation. The shot punches clean through the diver's visor in a single burst of light, then darkness. The body drops, the weapon clattering against metal before being swept away by the flood. "Keep moving!" she shouts.

They burst through a twisted archway into the access tunnel. The water rushes around their legs in violent currents, dragging debris and fragments past them. Silt clouds explode around their feet, turning the world into a swirling storm of brown and red. The noise is thunder trapped underwater, relentless, suffocating.

Blarek slams his fist against a control panel. "Hatch head's jammed!"

Evander doesn't hesitate. He grabs a crowbar from the emergency kit mounted to the wall, his hands shaking as the metal vibrates in his grip. Together, they pry at the jammed hatch. The steel shrieks like something alive, bending under the strain before finally giving way with a violent *crack.*

The hatch flies open just as another explosion rips down the corridor. The blast tears through the water, a shockwave of pressure and fire that sends them all airborne. The world goes white and weightless, a split second of silence before they hit the ground hard.

They crash into knee-deep water inside the docking chamber. The capsule waits on its magnetic cradle, its lights flickering like dying stars.

"Move!" Angelica barks, already wading forward.

Froslo scrambles to the console, his hands flying across flickering keys. "Power cells are half-drained…" he glances back, eyes wide behind his visor "…we've got one good burn left!"

"That's all we need!" Angelica snaps.

Evander hauls Mal'Erro through the hatch, water pouring off the droid's frame in shimmering rivulets. Blarek and Alexeria slam the door shut as another tremor ripples through the base. The floor beneath them trembles, the pressure building like the ocean is holding its breath.

"Release clamps!" Angelica yells.

Froslo hits the control. The magnetic locks disengage with a thunderous *clang*. The capsule lurches free from its cradle, swaying in the turbulent water. External cameras flicker online, showing the nightmare behind them. The lab is folding inward on itself, with its massive girders twisting apart and glass domes shattering under the ocean's crushing weight. Columns of sediment rise like plumes of smoke, curling upward into the dark.

"Brace yourselves!" Evander shouts, gripping the restraints.

Thrusters ignite with a deafening roar. The capsule surges upward through the black, acceleration pressing them hard against their seats. Below, the Mareoth facility implodes. A radiant shockwave of light blooms from the collapsing core, a halo of red and white energy that expands in every direction. Metal fragments spiral outward like burning meteors, trailing ribbons of debris.

"It's gaining on us!" Blarek yells, his voice vibrating through the comms.

"Full power to vertical thrusters!" Evander snaps.

Froslo glances at the readouts, disbelief flashing across his face. "I said maybe one shot up!"

"Then make it count!" yells Angelica.

Froslo slams the throttle. The capsule screams in protest, its hull groaning and panels sparking. Every seam rattles. The crew grips their restraints as the world outside becomes a blur of red and black and light.

The glow below tightens, spiraling, concentrating, alive. Mal'Erro's optics flare gold, reflecting the inferno beneath them.

"That's not debris," he says, his voice layered in harmonics. "It's a pulse."

Evander twists in his seat, adrenaline spiking. "From what?"

Mal'Erro's gaze doesn't move from the viewport. "The facility," it murmurs, with tones splitting into discordant echoes. "Stage Five has begun."

The pulse erupts. Light devours the ocean, white and crimson intertwined, folding and breaking like fire underwater. Displays burst into cascades of corrupted text. The crew's visors flicker with incomprehensible symbols. For one suspended instant, it's as if the sea itself screams. Then everything goes dark. And the world collapses into silence.

The capsule erupts from the ocean like a cannon shot, shattering the storm's surface in a geyser of light and fury. Water fountains skyward in spiraling plumes, illuminated by streaks of electric white. The impact reverberates through the hull, a single, thunderous heartbeat that shakes the crew to their core. Lightning splits the clouds above, jagged and brilliant, framing the Aurora in silhouette like a mythic vessel rising from creation's depths. For a brief instant, her hull gleams through the rain, a shining guardian against the chaos of the storm.

"Capsule to Aurora," Angelica gasps, breath catching between words. "We're through, prepare retrieval!" Her voice trembles but doesn't break.

"Copy," comes Sandria's voice through static. "Locking magnetic clamps now." The capsule shudders as the magnetic clamps engage, stabilizing them amid the churning sea. Every breath inside the cramped cabin sounds too loud… too alive… against the groaning of metal and the endless hiss of rain on steel.

Evander wipes condensation from the viewport. The storm rages beyond, but the lightning no longer feels random. The bolts stretch in branching arcs across the horizon, crawling over the waves like living veins of light. They trace patterns, sigils, too symmetrical to be nature's design. He leans forward, eyes narrowing. "That's not weather."

Blarek follows his gaze, fur slick against his skull, voice barely a whisper. "Please tell me that's just weather."

Mal'Erro's voice is faint but steady. "It's not the storm." Its optics flicker weakly, golden light reflecting off the viewport glass. "It's the planet… answering back."

For a heartbeat, no one moves. Even the storm seems to hesitate, holding its breath. The rhythmic pulse of the lightning steadies…slow, deliberate…becoming something more like a heartbeat than a tempest.

Angelica meets Evander's gaze through the dim cabin light. The reflections of the sigils dance across their visors like ghostly runes. "We woke something," she says, her tone more reverent than afraid.

Evander's jaw tightens. He nods slowly, eyes catching the glow. "Then whatever's next…" he murmurs, almost to himself, his voice barely above a whisper, "…it's already coming."

Outside, the thunder doesn't just roll, it *builds,* a layered roar echoing through the black water until it feels alive, almost aware. The capsule begins to ascend, drawn toward the waiting Aurora through a field of electric rain. Below them, Mareoth's ocean seethes with light. The sigils shift, rearranging, connecting in slow, spiraling rhythm, an ancient pattern awakening beneath the waves. The glow intensifies until the sea itself looks like a living organism, pulsing with a heartbeat the crew can feel through their boots.

Mal'Erro's optics dim again, his last whisper barely audible over the static. "The signal's not fading…"

Angelica looks down through the viewport one final time. "No," she breathes. "It's *rising.*"

The capsule pierces through the last layer of storm, ascending toward the halo of the Aurora's recovery lights, with thin, trembling beams cutting through the dark. Below, the world burns with impossible luminescence, the glow spreading outward like veins of creation being rewritten. And as thunder swells over the endless sea, the light below beats once more, slow, strong, undeniable, the heartbeat of a world no longer asleep.

The airlock seals with a deep, metallic *thud*, a sound that feels final, like the closing of a heartbeat. For a moment, no one breathes. Only the steady hiss of equalizing pressure fills the silence, a low exhale from the Aurora herself, as though the ship is trying to calm them after the chaos below.

Angelica reaches up, fingers trembling slightly as she unseals her helmet. Steam curls away from her visor, twisting in thin, ghostly ribbons before dissipating into the cold air. Her hair clings damply to her temples, the scent of salt and ozone still heavy in the confined space.

Kal'korg follows, his chest heaving with pain, as he rests against Blarek for support. His fur is plastered flat, soaked with blood and seawater, his eyes wide and still catching reflections of the lightning that once raged beyond the capsule. Blarek removes his own helmet more slowly, deliberately, afraid to jar Kal'korg with any sudden movement. Both of their faces are pale, ghosted by fatigue and disbelief.

Evander stands in the center of the airlock, water pooling around his boots, Mal'Erro's motionless frame hanging in his arms. The faint weight of the droid seems wrong, too light, too fragile.

Golden pulses shimmer weakly beneath the cracked plating, flickering like the dying embers of a star struggling to stay alive. Each light fades, returns, then falters again, as though even the machine's heartbeat is unsure whether to keep going. Evander lowers his head, the reflection of that glow painting faint halos beneath his eyes. In the aftermath of the storm and fire, it's the only light that doesn't feel hostile.

Angelica takes one unsteady step closer. Her voice is quieter now, the edge of command softened into something almost maternal. "Get them both to the med bay." Her words linger in the air, carrying more than an order. There's grief in them, and something unspoken, a shared fear that perhaps the smallest member of their crew may not rise again.

Evander nods once, jaw tight. "Aye, Captain." He turns toward the hatch, each step heavy. His boots splash through the shallow water gathered on the deck, the ripples catching the red emergency lights and scattering them into thin, trembling reflections that trail behind him like veins of molten glass.

As the crew follows, silence reclaims the corridor. The hum of the Aurora deepens, a low, resonant vibration that seems to match the rhythm of Mal'Erro's fading pulse. It's as though the ship itself feels what they do, mourning in its own mechanical way, holding its breath between beats, waiting to see if its smallest heartbeat will begin again.

The med bay hums with sterile calm as Doctor Isa hurries over to help Blarek ease Kal'korg onto the nearest bed. His injuries are superficial, and she reassures them both with a quiet confidence— he'll be good as new after a few cycles of rest and regen, nothing that'll keep him from teasing the crew by morning. Relieved, Blarek reaches down and gives Kal'korg a soft kiss on his forehead.

Evander lays Mal'Erro onto the diagnostic cradle, handling the droid like a wounded friend. Scanner arms descend, bathing the chassis in cold blue light. Steam curls upward and vanishes into the vents. "Power relays active," he reports, "but he's cycling, trying to reboot and failing."

"Then keep him stable," Angelica replies.

Evander doesn't look away from the readouts. Energy lines spike and dip in erratic bursts, until finally they align. The Tazamite core glows faintly, pulsing like a heart learning its rhythm.

Hours blur. The crew rotates in silent shifts, but Evander never leaves. His reflection merges with Mal'Erro's still form—two silhouettes, one breathing, one waiting.

Doctor Isa works quietly, her instruments casting soft pulses across the walls. Behind her round glasses, her gaze stays gentle. "It's not broken," she murmurs. "It's dreaming." No one responds. The hum of the med bay answers for them, steady and low—until hours later, when the monitors begin to flicker to life, bathing the room in jittering light. Lines of code crawl across every display, jagged at first, then smoothing into deliberate patterns.

On the bridge the faint hum of the ship deepens and a second rhythm begins to rise, subtle and steady, like a heartbeat made of static. At first, it's almost imperceptible. Then the pulse grows stronger, threading through the room's silence until it becomes sound, a low, harmonic vibration that resonates in the chest more than the ear.

EVOLUTION CANNOT BE STOPPED.

The words strike like a physical force. The speakers hum with their echo, vibrating through the consoles, rattling anything not bolted down. The phrase loops once, twice, each repetition carrying a strange resonance, less like a message and more like a law being recited by the universe itself.

Angelica's blood runs cold. She steps closer to the console, her reflection fractured across the glowing screens. "That's not his voice," she says, though part of her already knows. "Run a trace."

Blarek's fingers blur across the keys. "Trying, hang on…" He leans in, brow furrowed. "It's riding on sub-channel nine… not from within the ship… wait…" His voice tightens. "Source origin… *outside.*"

A tremor of static ripples through the comm array, spreading across the room in a metallic whisper. The overhead lights dim and flicker. A few tools lift slightly off the counter from the magnetic surge before clattering back down.

In the med bay Kal'korg's ears twitch. "Tell me that's interference," he says, though his voice lacks conviction.

Evander's jaw tightens and his eyes lock on the display of the adjacent console as cascading symbols spiral across it. "That frequency…" His tone drops to a whisper. "It's the same one the pirates used. The one Galgorn hijacked before…" He stops. The word *before* hangs unfinished, swallowed by the hum.

The air feels heavier now, the kind of weight that doesn't just press on the skin, but on the soul. Every face in the ship turns toward the monitors as the patterns on-screen begin to form something almost recognizable, outlines, shapes, a face buried beneath the noise.

Angelica's voice hardens, a brittle edge against the growing fear. "He's supposed to be dead."

Evander's reflection stares back at him from the glass, fractured and distorted by the pulse of alien light. "Then tell me," he murmurs, "why is he still talking?"

The lights flare. Every screen whites out. Then the main display goes black. Symbols bloom again, but now they move with purpose, spiraling outward like veins across the glass. The pulse merges with the ship's hum, and for a heartbeat, the Aurora herself seems to shudder.

A voice cuts through the static. Cold. Metallic. Absolute. *'Version four-point-eight… progress nominal.'*

The sound isn't broadcast; it *inhabits* the air. The crew feel it in their bones. Then, silence. The light drains from the screens. The only sound left is the low, endless heartbeat of the Aurora, steady but too calm, like the silence before a storm.

Angelica's hands drop to her sides. Her breath trembles, misting faintly in the cold air. "If this is what version four looks like…" she pauses, "…I don't want to see five."

Outside the viewport, the black ocean churns in silence. Lightning flashes far below, distant and deliberate, illuminating the waves in ghostly silver. For a single moment, one pulse of light burns brighter than all the rest, symmetrical, deliberate, too perfect to be natural. It fades a second later, leaving behind only the reflection of the crew in the glass. The Aurora's hum continues…slow, rhythmic, alive…as though she, too, has heard the message. And somewhere within that hum, beneath the static and the storm's fading echo, a presence stirs, vast, patient, and aware. Something has awakened. And it's listening.

CHAPTER 20

The med bay remains still, every sound swallowed by the ship's deep mechanical breathing. Angelica enters quietly to check on her two friends. Evander doesn't look up to greet her, his gaze staying focused on Mal'Erro's still form on the cradle. She watches as he steps closer to the cradle, the soft glow under the little droid's plating pulsing once, faint but visible. He hesitates for a moment, then presses his hand against Mal'Erro's chest plate.

The metal is cool, almost lifeless, until a faint thrum answers beneath his palm. Uneven. Weak. But real. He exhales. "He's still in there," he says quietly. "I know he is. And someone, or something, wants him awake."

Angelica waits several moments, but Evander says nothing more. And not knowing how to respond, she leaves the med bay without saying a word. The doors close behind her with a soft *hiss*, sealing in the steady hum of machines and the faint, rhythmic pulse of Mal'Erro's stasis cradle. For a fleeting second, the sound lingers in her ears, like a heartbeat that refuses to let her go.

The corridor greets her with silence. No voices. No movement. Only the quiet thrum of the Aurora's living systems. She exhales slowly, the breath catching as if the ship itself exhales with her.

Coolant murmurs through pipes overhead, whispering like distant tides. The sound is soft but constant, a mechanical heartbeat threading through the ship's bones. The air carries a tang of metal, salt, and ozone, the ghost of the ocean still clinging to her uniform. It smells like survival and loss.

Night-cycle lighting paints the passage in shades of violet and indigo. Shadows crawl along the walls, stretching long and thin across the deck. Her reflection flickers in the polished plating, distorted by the passing blink of warning lights. Maintenance drones drift past her head like tired fireflies, their optics dim, their motion lazy, as if even the machines are exhausted.

Her boots leave damp prints with each step, faint outlines that vanish before she can take another. She pauses, pressing one hand against the cold metal wall for balance. The surface vibrates faintly beneath her palm—alive, responsive, resonant. The Aurora hums back, and for an instant her pulse falls into rhythm with it, syncing heartbeat to machine beat. Then it falters. Uneven. Fast.

Evolution cannot be stopped.

The words slide through her mind again, an echo more felt than heard. Not a warning anymore. Not even a threat. Something deeper. An inheritance. Her throat tightens.

And beneath that echo, another voice surfaces—older, human, and achingly familiar. Her father's voice—calm and tired, carried on the ghosts of memory and static. *"Galgorn's fall was never the end... only the delay."*

She closes her eyes. For a moment, she's not aboard the Aurora. She's back in the ruins of a scorched lab, the air thick with ozone and burnt circuitry. The scent of oil and smoke clings to her skin. Shadows ripple across walls coated in ash. She can still hear the machines groaning, the sound of creation refusing to die, even as the world around it burned.

When she opens her eyes again, the corridor feels colder. The hum in the walls no longer soothes, it *breathes*. The ship feels alive, watchful. She draws a slow breath through parted lips, but it doesn't steady her. For the first time in years, Angelica feels small, smaller than the ship she commands, smaller than the machine sleeping below decks, smaller than the ghosts that have begun to whisper her name. Just a woman trying to command order from chaos.

The lift doors open with a soft chime, spilling pale light into the dim hall. She catches her reflection in the polished steel: pale skin, hollow eyes, damp hair clinging to her neck, the faint shimmer of fatigue across her features. The blue status lights crown her face in a cold halo. Not a captain. Not a UPF Officer. Just a human trying to keep her world from falling apart.

Her lips part as if to say something…maybe to herself…but she exhales instead. Her breath trembles, then steadies. She straightens her shoulders, adjusts her collar, and sets her jaw. The reflection changes. The exhaustion fades behind composure, the uncertainty behind steel. The Captain returns.

She steps inside the lift. The doors seal and, for a moment, all she can hear is the soft, rhythmic hum of the Aurora carrying her upward, steady, constant, and alive. When she steps out, the bridge greets her in silence.

The glow of the consoles cast shifting bands of color across the worn faces of the crew. Every light feels too bright, every shadow too deep. The air smells faintly of ozone and coolant, thick with the residue of the storm. The Aurora herself trembles faintly as thrusters fire in soft, controlled bursts, correcting orbit with the precision of something both tired and alive.

"Captain on deck," Sandria murmurs from the comms station.

"At ease," Angelica replies automatically, her voice steady but low.

Her gaze moves to the viewport. The storm still churns across Mareoth's hemisphere, an endless, roiling sea of cloud and light. Lightning veins through the darkness like molten glass, branching and reforming, a living network of energy crawling across the planet's skin.

Evander enters the bridge and steps up beside her. His uniform is rumpled and his eyes are shadowed by exhaustion and thought. He doesn't speak. He doesn't need to. The silence between them says everything: *We survived, but it's not over.*

"Open a secure line to Command," Angelica orders quietly. "Fleet priority."

'Aye Captain,' Sandria acknowledges and gets to work. The bridge fills with the low, rising hum of the holo-transmitter. Blue light flickers across the consoles as the air begins to shimmer. It sounds like a breath being drawn and held by the ship itself. A moment later, the holographic projection stabilizes. The figure of Fleet Admiral Zylixar forms from static and light, with sharp blue edges and the faint distortion of a transmission stretched thin across distance.

"This is Captain Tenah of the Aurora," Angelica begins. Her tone slips back into one of command, firm and professional. "We've confirmed a Mareoth research site linked to Project K-

Prime. Data transmission commencing. Tazamite presence has been verified. The facility was destroyed…"

The image stutters. A sudden burst of static slashes through the Admiral's hologram, slicing his face into digital fragments. The sound bends, stretching syllables into distorted echoes.

"Admiral? You're cutting out," Angelica says, leaning forward, her voice sharpening.

The hologram flickers repeatedly. "Signal interference," Sandria calls, scanning rapidly. "Source is… internal. It's coming from…" Before she can finish a new sound creeps through the speakers— low, metallic, and cold. At first, it's just a hum, the kind that worms its way into the marrow. Then it shapes itself into a voice.

"Evolution cannot be stopped… my children." The voice says.

The bridge goes deathly still. The lights dim by a fraction, as though the ship itself flinches. The holo projection wavers, the Admiral's face half there, half gone, like a ghost caught in transmission.

Evander's jaw tightens. He doesn't move, doesn't blink. "Galgorn."

The voice overlaps itself: human, machine, and something far older caught in the space between both. "Version four-point-eight… progress nominal. Prepare the next phase."

Each word carries a metallic undertone, like something speaking through machinery rather than from within it. The hologram of the Admiral breaks apart entirely, dissolving into motes of drifting blue light. The transmission dies.

For several seconds, the bridge remains silent except for the hum of the engines and the faint hiss of the life-support vents. The crew look to one another, faces pale in the dim glow of the consoles.

Angelica stands frozen, staring at the empty air where the Admiral's image had been. "He's alive," she whispers, though she isn't sure if she's talking about Galgorn or the thing wearing his voice.

Evander's tone is a low rasp. "Or something alive that was Galgorn… once."

The Aurora hums beneath their boots, a sound too alive, too aware. The ship feels like it's listening. Then, a crackle bleeds through the intercom. At first, it's just noise, harmless static. But then a voice forms—faint, broken, mechanical. "Requesting… encore."

Every head turns toward the ceiling speakers. Evander feels the deck tilt beneath him, his pulse rising in his throat. He meets Angelica's eyes, and neither of them breathes. "Sounds like Mal'Erro. He's awake," Evander murmurs.

~~~~~~~~

Inside the med bay, time moves differently. The lights are low, sterile, and indifferent. Kal'korg has retired to his quarters to rest and the only movement comes from the flicker of readouts and the slow, rhythmic glow pulsing across Mal'Erro's chest. He lies motionless beneath the wash of diagnostic light, his frame still scorched, and his plating warped in places where Tazamite veins once flared bright enough to blind. Now those same lines pulse faint gold, weaker, steadier, as though the machine is dreaming its way back to life.

Evander stands behind the observation glass, shoulders hunched, eyes shadowed with exhaustion. He's been there for hours, unmoving, one hand resting lightly against the transparent barrier between them. The soft hum of the med bay vibrates through his palm, the same hum that carries through the ship, down to the engines, up through the walls. It's the Aurora's pulse… and it matches Mal'Erro's.

Doctor Isa moves quietly among the consoles, the pale glow of the monitors painting lines of reflected gold across her face. Each flicker mirrors against the glass and catches Evander's eyes, ghostly symbols dancing across his pupils like coded constellations. Each pulse, each rhythmic flash, carries the same whisper threading through every conduit and system across the ship.

Evolution cannot be stopped.

The phrase reverberates through the Aurora, not spoken but *felt.* It hums through the deck plating, vibrates along the walls, and lingers in the soft whine of the oxygen circulators. Sometimes it's so faint it feels like imagination. Other times it's strong enough to rattle the instruments.

Evander watches the faint golden glow beneath Mal'Erro's plating rise and fade, rise and fade, over and over again, like breathing, or the echo of something more ancient than machinery. He doesn't know what's worse: the idea that Mal'Erro is responding to the signal… or that he might be *creating* it. His throat tightens. He presses his hand more firmly to the glass, his eyes burning from fatigue and sleeplessness. "Come on, Mal," he whispers under his breath. "You're not done yet."

The hum deepens slightly, as though the ship answers him. Isa glances up, frowning at her console.

"Power fluctuation?" Evander asks.

She shakes her head. "No… more like… resonance. Whatever's happening out there, it's feeding back into him. And the pattern, it's not random."

Evander looks past her, to the dim horizon of lightning flickering beyond the viewport. The flashes are slower now, deliberate, each one striking in precise rhythm. The same rhythm that pulses through the med bay. He draws a slow breath, the words barely audible. "It's like the planet's talking to him."

Isa hesitates before replying, her voice hushed. "Or through him."

Evander doesn't respond. His reflection in the glass looks older, wearier, divided between man and ghost. The rhythmic glow from the monitors plays across his features, painting him in shifting gold and shadow. Each flicker pulses with that same haunting cadence, part machine, part heartbeat, part prayer.

Evolution cannot be stopped.

Evander isn't sure anymore whether it's a warning… or a prophecy. And in the faint reflection of the storm flashing beyond the viewport, it feels less like either, and more like the universe whispering its own truth back to him.

CHAPTER 21

Angelica has the Aurora re-enter Mareoth's atmosphere to retrieve the drifting capsules from the ruins below. She knows this is a risk, but there are people inside those pods and some might still be alive.

A proximity alert chirps through the storm noise. "Captain, we've got movement below us," P'thorika says, her hand pausing mid-adjustment. "One of the capsules just surfaced."

Angelica leans forward. "Visual?"

The holo-display stabilizes just long enough to reveal a single capsule bobbing violently between the waves. The rest remain pinned deep beneath the debris field, unreachable.

Evander frowns. "Why just one?"

"No idea," P'thorika mutters. "But if we wait any longer, that one won't survive."

Angelica doesn't hesitate. "Bring it aboard. Now."

The retrieval clamps deploy with a jolt. The ship lurches as the storm pushes back.

Back at the sensor array station Kal'korg grips the railing. "I'm reading a life-sign in that pod, Captain. Weak, but present."

The clamps lock with a metallic thunderclap.

Isa's voice crackles over comms, urgent and strained. "Med bay ready. The moment the pod is aboard, bring it here."

"I'm on my way," Kal'korg responds.

Angelica nods once. "Evander, you join him. Whoever is in that pod, I want to know."

The storm roars, the lights flicker, and the capsule disappears into the lift system. It locks into the med bay's receiver just as Evander and Kal'korg come running in. Wiping off the moisture and grime from the distorted glass reveals a familiar figure with azure skin and emerald green hair.

Evander exhales sharply. "Kes…" His jaw tightens, his voice catching. "It's her."

~~~~~~~~~

Angelica doesn't know how much of this volatile weather the ship can endure, or how difficult it will be to retrieve the trapped pods. But she does know that leaving those capsules behind would mean abandoning the data, and perhaps the proof of what they had witnessed. "Sandria, watch for any new life-signs," Angelica orders. "Blarek, take us down."

Thunder follows in slow, deliberate intervals, deep, planetary breaths that make the Aurora tremble as she descends toward the surface. Rain lashes against the hull in a chaotic rhythm. The ship's shields flare faintly blue, rippling under each strike like a heartbeat beneath translucent skin. The storm doesn't feel random anymore, it feels alive, patterned, almost purposeful, as if the world below is remembering them.

The Aurora flies low and silent, cutting a careful path through the turbulence, tracing the coordinates of what used to be the Mareoth Research Annex. All that remains now is a wound in the ocean, a dark scar pulsing with faint luminescence beneath the clouds. The Aurora claws her way through the storm-torn sea.

Waves the size of towers slam against the hull, each impact rolling through the decks like distant artillery. The ship shudders with every strike, her reinforced frame flexing as though in pain. Electric-blue lightning spiders across the armor plating, crawling in wild, living veins that flare and fade, turning the entire vessel into a pulse of light and shadow. The storm doesn't simply rage, it *assesses*. Every gust, every flash feels sentient, deliberate, pressing against her hull, testing every seam and weld as though deciding whether this fragile construct of metal and will deserves to survive.

Above, the sky churns into a bruise of violet and black. Sheets of lightning braid through the clouds, their reflections splitting and rejoining in the swollen waves below. Each flash illuminates the Aurora like a specter adrift between worlds. Thunder follows in punishing intervals, low and rolling, a sound so deep it vibrates through bone and steel alike. The superstructure groans under the pressure, every rivet and beam straining to hold its place against an atmosphere that wants nothing more than to tear them apart.

Inside, humidity coats every surface. The recycled air can't keep up with the saturation. It tastes of salt, metal, and ozone, like breathing the ocean itself. Droplets of condensation trace paths down the bulkheads in trembling rivulets, gathering in the seams before sliding to the floor. The lights flicker with every surge, the faint red of emergency power bleeding into the soft white glow of the consoles.

The bridge crew moves with quiet urgency. No one speaks unless they must. The storm's voice drowns out everything else, wind screaming against the hull, thunder cracking like ruptured steel, the rhythmic hiss of rain that sounds almost like static whispering a language none of them can understand.

"Stabilizers holding at forty percent," Blarek mutters, claws tapping the console. His words come out hoarse, clipped by tension.

"Keep her steady," Angelica says, her tone flat but eyes sharp. She grips the edge of her chair as another wave slams the port side. The impact jolts the bridge, spilling a shower of sparks from an overworked conduit.

Blarek's hands fly across the helm. "Trying!" he growls. "But the sea's trying harder!"

The ship bucks again, tilting ten degrees before the thrusters fire in unison to counter the drag. The inertial dampeners whine under the strain. For a moment, a bolt of lightning erupts so close it blinds them. The flash floods the bridge in white for half a second, revealing every drop of condensation, every line of fatigue carved into the faces of the crew. When vision returns, the sound that follows is so loud it rattles teeth.

Angelica exhales through her nose, jaw set. "Hold the course."

Outside, the storm coils around them, an immense, churning leviathan of wind and water. Lightning curls through the clouds in great arcs, veins of raw energy feeding into the heart of the tempest. The Aurora presses forward, defiant, her hull aglow with streaks of charged rain. Deep in the lower decks, the engines begin to stutter. The familiar hum that usually fills the ship breaks into anxious tremors, its mechanical heart skipping beats. The vibration travels up through the floors, through the air itself, until it feels like the entire vessel is trembling, not just from strain, but from something unseen pressing back.

Angelica looks up at the readouts flashing along her console. Every screen dances with static, symbols half-formed and fleeting. For a moment, one line of distorted text repeats across multiple displays before fading into nothing: *EVOLUTION CANNOT BE STOPPED.*

Her stomach knots. "Sandria," she calls quietly, "tell me you saw that."

She glances at the data stream, eyes narrowing. "I saw it."

The ship lurches again, thunder swallowing the sound of their words. Outside, lightning crawls down through the storm clouds and meets the surface of the ocean. The water lights up in a vast lattice of pale gold and electric blue, pulsing outward like neural pathways. The planet, once again, seems to be thinking. And the Aurora keeps clawing her way through the chaos: small, defiant, alive.

~~~~~~~

Down in the med bay, Mal'Erro lies suspended beneath the pale wash of diagnostic light. The room hums with a quiet tension that feels alive, like the walls themselves are holding their breath. Every click, hiss, and pulse of the machines seems louder than it should be, echoing in the sterile air. The faint scent of antiseptic mingles with ozone and the metallic tang of still-drying circuitry, sharp and clinical yet faintly electric, as though the room itself were waiting for something to happen.

The light from above refracts against the curved ceiling, scattering across the walls in a slow dance of color. Reflected bands of gold and blue slide over the glass panels, rippling like constellations on water. Each shift feels deliberate, almost rhythmic.

Mal'Erro's frame glows faintly with residual Tazamite energy. The shimmer pulses in slow waves, rolling across his plating like ripples through liquid glass, bending the reflections around him. Where the light touches metal, it refracts into twin tones…gold and ice-blue…chasing one another like thought and memory intertwined. His chest panel rises and falls, so faint it's almost imperceptible, like a machine remembering how to breathe.

The monitors struggle to make sense of it. Numbers leap, vanish, reappear. Graphs spike, flatten, and loop back in erratic bursts. Symbols flicker across the diagnostic glass and then disappear. Isa leans closer, her reflection caught in the screen's shifting glow. "These readings…" she murmurs, voice half wonder, half unease. "They don't make sense."

The diagnostic panel scrolls fresh text across its surface, crisp and sterile:

Observation Log: Med Bay AI Diagnostic
Core Stability: Fluctuating
Harmonic Variance: Increasing
Signal Origin: Unclassified cross-frequency interference detected
Behavior Pattern: Evolving

Each line blinks once, pauses, then rewrites itself, as if the system were arguing with its own conclusion. The overhead lights dim, then flare back to life. Dust motes drift lazily through the beam glow, suspended like tiny satellites in orbit. Beneath the sterile hum of machinery, another sound emerges, a low vibration at the edge of hearing, not mechanical but harmonic. It thrums through the room, resonant and patient, like a note plucked from some unseen instrument that refuses to fade.

Doctor Isa instinctively steps back. The shimmer surrounding Mal'Erro isn't dangerous, but it *feels* aware. Each pulse radiates through the air like an invisible ripple. When the wave touches the glass instruments, they respond with soft crystalline chimes that linger before dying away. She watches the shifting light across Mal'Erro's plating, unable to look away. Her voice drops to a whisper. "It's not destabilizing," she says to herself. "It's… adjusting."

The data keeps rewriting itself faster than she can interpret. Mal'Erro's optics remain dark. But beneath the surface, a faint flicker moves—a spark struggling to decide if it should exist. For one perfect heartbeat, the rhythm of his internal pulse syncs with the med bay's ambient hum. The sound merges, harmonizing. The light under his chest plate expands and contracts, waves of gold washing across the cradle like the breath of something ancient stirring in its sleep. Isa blinks hard, barely realizing she's holding her breath.

Evander's voice echoes in her memory: *He's still in there. I know he is.*

The hum deepens, vibrating through the deck. The instruments tremble. Her hair rises with static charge. The harmonic tone shifts higher, layering itself, one note becoming two, then four, then a full spectrum of sound too complex to map. It's no longer mechanical. It's *alive.* A soft overtone weaves through it, faint but unmistakable, a choir of tones beyond language. It fills the space like light through water, luminous and unsettling.

Mal'Erro isn't sleeping. He isn't broken. He's listening. He's remembering. He's becoming. And for one impossible moment, every light in the med bay flares gold, as though the ship itself is responding. Then, just as suddenly, everything dims again leaving behind only silence, and the faint pulse of something that may no longer be entirely machine.

~~~~~~~

On the bridge Evander stands before the viewport, his reflection fractured by rivulets of rain and streaks of lightning. The vibration of the storm hums through the glass, a living heartbeat against his fingertips. His uniform clings to his shoulders, stiff with salt. Outside, the world churns with sentient fury. Waves twist into silver arcs, colliding like living mountains. Each lightning strike ignites the sea in molten white before darkness returns. It's chaotic, and yet deliberate, as if the storm itself is breathing.

He presses a hand to the glass. "It feels like the ocean's trying to drag us back," he murmurs. His voice is barely louder than the hum of the engines. A reflection joins his own.

Angelica stands beside him, her posture straight and her eyes are dimmed by fatigue. Strands of dark hair cling to her face. She folds her arms, her gaze fixed on the maelstrom. "I think it wants to keep its secrets," she says quietly. "Whatever they built down there, it wasn't meant to be found."

Evander's reflection turns toward hers. Lightning gilds the edges of their faces. "Secrets don't stay buried forever," he replies. Then, softer, he says, "Neither do ghosts."

The ship groans as another wave strikes. The vibration lingers in their chests. Angelica watches the lightning crawl along the water. "You think this is over?"

Evander shakes his head. "No. Not even close."

Silence stretches between them. The storm begins to fade, lightning now a distant flicker, thunder a tired sigh. They stand shoulder to shoulder, two steady silhouettes against the universe's chaos. Behind them, the corridor lights flicker with every surge, syncing with the storm's pulse. The ship itself seems to listen.

Angelica exhales, forcing a small smile. "We'll reach clear skies soon," she says, a promise to herself more than him.

Evander doesn't answer. Beyond the glass, the clouds thin, streaks of pale blue cut through black. The sea below turns mirror-still, reflecting the Aurora's lights. Yet beneath the calm, he feels pressure, a waiting presence. Watching. He glances at Angelica's reflection, spectral and distant. The quiet between them says everything words can't.

He finally turns back toward the bridge. His boots echo softly, merging with the rhythmic drip of water from the vents and the strained hum of engines pushing through the dying storm. The Aurora moves forward through the dark, resilient, scarred, alive. And in the silence between every sound, Evander hears it: the hollow echo of something vast beneath the calm. A question that the universe itself seems to whisper.

What if the storm wasn't the danger… but the warning?

The bridge glistens under the storm's fading light. Beads of water slide down bulkheads and consoles, hissing where they meet overheated circuits. The filtered glow through the upper canopy paints everything in a cold, aquatic blue, as though the Aurora is still half-submerged, caught between sea and sky, between what it escaped and what still waits below.

Kal'korg hunches over the stabilizer console. His claws are twitching on slick controls, and his emerald fur is plastered flat, darker now from salt and smoke. The bridge lighting catches on the rivulets running down his arms, making him look sculpted from wet stone. "Next time," he mutters, voice rough from breathing hours of recycled air, "I'm volunteering for orbit duty. Give me a vacuum over saltwater any day."

Blarek looks up from the helm, his gray fur sticking out in uneven tufts, giving him the look of a cat who lost a fight with a plasma conduit. "You and me both," he sighs. "I'm going to smell like burnt ozone for a week."

Kal'korg grunts without looking up. "Lucky. I smell like wet courage and regret."

The line lands and a laugh ripples through the bridge, effectively breaking the tension. The sound feels like oxygen after too long underwater. For a fleeting moment, the hum of the ship seems lighter.

Water drips to the deck in soft metallic ticks and Angelica wrings out her gloves. "Noted, Ensign Kal'korg," she says, her tone dry but almost playful. "Next time I'll make sure the ocean files proper notice before trying to drown us."

Kal'korg straightens with a mock salute. "Logging my refusal now, Captain."

Laughter again, smaller this time, but precious. Even Evander allows himself a quiet chuckle, the corner of his mouth twitching upward despite the exhaustion etched in every line of his face. But as the laughter fades, so does the illusion of safety. The hum beneath the floor changes pitch, subtle, but wrong. The Aurora feels like she's holding her breath.

Angelica's voice shifts, regaining its steel. "Alright. Once we're clear of this mess, run a full systems sweep. I want damage reports and…"

The comm panel hisses. Static rips through the bridge, sharp and sudden, like tearing fabric. Lights flicker twice. The hum of the engines dips low, faltering in rhythm. The laughter dies instantly.

"Comms?" Angelica snaps.

Sandria's fingers fly across the board, tapping controls in a blur. "Not us," she says, her voice tightening. "No incoming signal, no outgoing ping. It's…" She pauses, eyes narrowing at the display. "…raw interference. It's jumping across every frequency band."

The sound deepens. What began as static now throbs in rhythm. Not random. Not natural.

"Try isolating it," Evander says, stepping closer to the console. His voice carries the calm edge of someone who already knows he won't like what comes next.

Sandria isolates the waveform. The bridge fills with a warped whisper, metallic syllables caught between speech and distortion.

"Stage Five… authorized." The words twist through the static like a serpent in fog. Then, silence.

For a long moment, only the sound of rain pattering against the hull remains. The quiet feels wrong, too deliberate, the kind of pause that waits to see who breathes first. Even the ventilation hiss sounds cautious.

Evander swallows hard, voice barely above a whisper. "Stage Five," he repeats. "Of what?"

No one answers. The only response is the dull vibration of the deck beneath their boots. A tremor rolls through the Aurora. Not the engines, something deeper, older. The kind of movement that comes from within the planet itself.

The storm outside finally begins to break. Clouds unravel into mist, and the sea below turns unnaturally smooth, flat as glass. The reflection of the Aurora stares back from the surface like a twin ghost, caught between worlds.

Angelica's eyes narrow at the viewport. Her voice drops to a near whisper. "Why does calm always feel worse?" The question goes unanswered.

The crew stands motionless for several long seconds. Even the air seems heavier, saturated with the memory of thunder. The lights flicker once more, dimming just enough to cast everyone in shadow. Deep within the ship's circuitry, beyond the reach of any diagnostic, something stirs. A single line of code wakes. It loops silently through the data stream, aimless at first, then deliberate, like a note searching for its melody.

In the med bay, Mal'Erro's optics twitch open and shut once, gold to white, white to black, before settling again. The harmonic readouts on his monitors spike, flash, and then stabilize, syncing perfectly with the Aurora's engine rhythm. A new pulse forms, steady, unified. It beats through the hull, through the conduits, through the silence itself.

The storm is over. But something else has begun.

CHAPTER 22

The Aurora's briefing room lies in near-darkness, lit only by the cold glow of the recovered data core hovering above the central table. Arcs of pale energy crawl across its surface-like veins of lightning trapped in glass, each pulse resonating with the slow thrum of the ship's engines. The relic hums softly, a wounded echo from the Mareoth ruins, scorched and fractured but still alive with that same impossible tone that clings to all things touched by Tazamite.

The crew gathers in uneasy silence. Angelica stands at the head of the table, arms crossed, posture straight though fatigue tugs at the corners of her expression. Evander lingers behind her—his gaze fixed on the core as though he expects it to awaken at any moment. The room smells faintly of burned circuitry and salt carried up from the storm. Blarek adjusts the stabilizing field around the relic while Kal'korg fidgets near the rear bulkhead.

The doors hiss open. A soft whir precedes the arrival of a hovering hololink projector, Mal'Erro's voice emanating from within its sphere of golden light. His chassis remains sealed in med bay, but his consciousness rides the connection, tethered through layers of firewalls that Doctor Isa built, less out of necessity and more out of caution.

"Recovered data core integrity: twenty-six percent," Mal'Erro reports. His tone is calm, but a faint distortion rides beneath every word—two voices, slightly out of sync, overlap like the echo of his own thoughts. "Fragmented log restoration… in progress."

Thin light spills upward as the core's casing opens. Holographic shards rise like embers caught in slow gravity. One by one, they align into cascading data streams that shimmer above the table. The symbols twist, rewrite themselves, and finally settle into coherent text.

PROJECT K-PRIME: PHASE 5

SUBJECT KES APPROVED FOR BIO-MECH
INTEGRATION
OVERSIGHT: GALGORN
ADVISORY UNIT: JALERG

The room stills. Only the faint crackle of static punctuates the silence. Evander's pulse quickens. "Jalerg was part of this?" His voice comes out raw, heavier than he intends.

Angelica's tone is steady but quiet. "He worked under Galgorn on neural mapping. He may not have known what it was for." She doesn't sound convinced.

Mal'Erro's projection flickers, golden light thinning, his second voice ghosting over the first. "Probability suggests partial awareness. Advisory sub-units were required to compile data on all candidates. Secrecy level: Omega."

Evander's throat tightens. "He helped design the system that destroyed his own sister."

Kal'korg flattens his ears. "That's... monstrous. Even for Galgorn."

"Monstrous is relative," Angelica murmurs. "To Galgorn, this was evolution."

The data stream ripples again, washing the room in blue-white light. The hologram stutters, then solidifies into a trembling projection, grainy footage awash in static. The audio hisses and pops like an old transmission fighting to be remembered. Then the static clears. Galgorn appears. Or what remains of him.

Half of his face is still human—pale, scarred, with eyes ringed in sleepless determination. The other half gleams with metallic plates and veins of light. Tubes feed into his spine and cables twitch like exposed nerves. Behind him, a row of containment pods stretches into darkness, each filled with shadowed shapes suspended in thick fluid. Shapes that almost look human.

A chill grips the room. Even the hum of the engines seems to fade. Evander forgets to breathe. Reports and stories never captured this, the reality of a man who traded humanity for obsession.

Galgorn looks straight into the recorder. His organic eye burns with focus, his mechanical one dilating in and out with insect precision. When he speaks, his voice is calm and deliberate, words measured like scripture. "Perfection requires iteration. Evolution through suffering. My subjects will thank me once they awaken."

The air in the room feels thinner. Even after the sound ends, his voice seems to vibrate in the metal.

Angelica whispers, "He actually believed it."

Mal'Erro enhances the feed. The image sharpens, colors deepening to ghostly blue. Galgorn paces slowly across the lab floor, his movements too smooth, too mechanical. He gestures toward a hovering hologram beside him. A cascade of anatomical schematics unfolds—bodies rendered in rotating layers of flesh and alloy.

K-PRIME 03.
K-PRIME 04.
K-PRIME 05.

Their designs are grotesque: elongated limbs, metallic spines, nerves woven with circuitry. At the end of the list, one final designation flashes across the projection.

SUBJECT: KES.

The name glows like a scar across the darkness. Evander steps forward before he realizes it. "Pause playback."

The hologram freezes. Kes's name hovers above the schematic, suspended in sterile light. Beneath it, faint outlines of a human figure blend with machinery, flesh overlaid by cold geometry.

He stares until the lines blur. "He wasn't experimenting with Tazamite," he says quietly. "He was rewriting life itself, turning people into code that obeys."

Blarek exhales, ears flicking back. "That's not science. That's desecration."

Kal'korg's claws tap nervously. "He used her. Made her part of his trials."

Angelica closes her eyes, steadying her breath. "Continue playing."

The footage resumes. Galgorn stands in the center of the frame, flanked by the towering pods that line the laboratory wall. Their contents shift faintly in the murky suspension fluid—elongated limbs and indistinct faces pressing against the glass before drifting back into the haze. The light from their chambers paints his form in hues of sickly amber and cold blue, casting him half in shadow, half in revelation.

He moves slowly, deliberately, his metal-plated steps clicking against the grated floor in perfect rhythm with the pulse of the machinery. The tubes feeding into his spine flex with every motion, the faint hiss of hydraulics mixing with the slow, wet sound of bubbles rising through the pods. "To transcend the boundaries of mortality," he says, his voice calm but heavy with conviction, "the vessel must be reforged. Flesh is weak. Code endures."

As he speaks, the camera trembles slightly, whether from failing stabilization or the sheer vibration of the machinery, no one can tell. "Each iteration brings us closer," he continues, "to the divine equation." He raises a hand, fingertips trailing along the condensation on one of the pods. The figure within twitches in response, a shadow pressing its palm against the glass from the inside. For a moment, man and creation mirror one another, two silhouettes separated by little more than transparency.

Galgorn's lips curve faintly, almost tenderly. "They fear pain," he murmurs. "But pain is the catalyst. Pain strips away illusion.

And when clarity comes, the old self dies so that perfection may rise."

The pod shudders, bubbles spiraling upward in a frantic burst. Something inside it moves. A hand, skeletal and trembling, reaches toward him. Galgorn doesn't flinch. He presses his palm firmly against the glass, the motion slow, ritualistic, as if in benediction. The faint light within the tank brightens, and for an instant, the outline inside resembles something painfully human.

He tilts his head toward the recorder, and his mechanical eye dilates until the iris is nothing but a cold, gleaming point of light. "Version 5.0," he declares softly, reverently. "My masterpiece."

The words echo, overlapping slightly as the feed begins to break apart. The image stutters, his face fracturing into slivers of motion. Frame by frame, his expression flickers, serene, exultant, unblinking. Then the hologram tears itself apart. The lab dissolves into white static and fragments of sound: the sharp intake of breath, the faint moan of metal, the steady pulse of a heart that might no longer belong to flesh.

For one last frozen instant, Galgorn's half-human face lingers, one side alive with zeal, the other glinting with inhuman precision. Then the light cuts out entirely. The projection dies, leaving only the whisper of the ship's electronics and the uneasy sound of breathing in the dark.

Silence. It stretches long enough for the crew to hear their own breathing. The briefing room's hum feels intrusive, too alive.

Angelica finally speaks. "Version Five," she says, barely above a whisper. "That's what the transmission meant."

Evander's gaze stays fixed on the darkened display. "Stage Five authorized." His voice is low, trembling with anger he has difficulty containing. "He planned it before we even found the first site."

Kal'korg's fur bristles. "Authorized by who? Galgorn's dead. Someone had to issue that command."

Blarek mutters, "Maybe he's not dead. Maybe he's… distributed."

Mal'Erro's projection flickers, the edges of his form blurring. His voice emerges layered, two timbres overlapping, one curious, one weary. "Additional fragments remain encrypted," he says. "Shall I proceed?"

Angelica hesitates. For a long moment, no one moves. The light from the hologram glints across her eyes, reflecting gold. "No," she says at last, quiet but firm. "Not yet."

The holographic glow fades, leaving them standing in the half-light. The relic hums faintly, resonating with the ship's distant heartbeat. No one speaks as Angelica walks toward the viewport. Beyond the glass, the ocean mirrors the fading sky, a vast sheet of silver steel reflecting the Aurora's lights. Lightning flickers far away, illuminating her reflection: pale, resolute, and framed by the shimmer of the dying storm.

"Whatever's in those files," she says softly, "it's not just history." Her eyes narrow. "It's a warning."

Evander watches her from behind, the tension in his chest coiling tighter. Outside, the last of the lightning fades into the horizon. The storm is gone. But deep within the Mareoth core, faint gold light still pulses, steady, patient, and waiting to be heard again.

CHAPTER 23

The alarm hits like a scream. A piercing metallic wail tears through the Aurora's decks, echoing down every corridor until it feels as though the ship itself is howling in pain. Red strobes flash in time with the klaxon, turning the clean silver walls into a frantic storm of light and shadow. Evander doesn't think. He runs, with Kal'korg on his heels.

Crew members leap aside as they barrel past. The vibration of their boots carries through the floorplates, each impact echoing like a drumbeat beneath the roar of the sirens. Overhead, warning glyphs bloom across the bulkheads: *MED BAY ALERT: LEVEL FOUR CONTAINMENT BREACH.*

The Aurora groans as systems auto-lock into crisis protocol. Blast doors slide into place behind him. The normally steady hum of the engine's fractures into a rougher rhythm, the pulse of a living thing under strain.

Evander's comm erupts with voices.

"Deck Six: Power fluctuations!"

"Containment seals failing!"

"Medical emergency: possible code override!"

The noise blends into chaos until one voice cuts through all the rest: Mal'Erro's. His tone is distorted, hurried, with the faint underlay of static giving him an almost human panic. "Med bay breach! Unauthorized energy surge. Origin: unknown!"

Evander's chest tightens. He doesn't wait for confirmation or authorization. Whatever this is, it's bad. The pair take the final turn at full speed, the corridor narrowing to a tunnel of red light and heat haze. The deck plates shudder beneath them. Somewhere behind the bulkheads coolant lines vent with a shrill hiss, filling the air with a metallic tang that burns his throat. He reaches the med bay doors and slams his hand on the panel.

The sensors hesitate, a heartbeat too long, then the doors part with a grinding hiss. A wave of heat hits him head-on. The air rushes out like a furnace blast, dense and suffocating, carrying the stench of ozone, sterilizer, and something else, something raw and electric that prickles across his skin. Emergency sprinklers have already been triggered, but the vapor rising from the floor hisses instead of cooling, as though the heat itself refuses to die.

Somewhere beyond the glare, Evander can hear screaming. He steps through the threshold, and the world becomes fire and light. Inside, chaos reigns.

Only one pod has been opened, only one body removed.

"Leave the others sealed," Isa snaps, her eyes locked on the readings. "Kes is the only one we can stabilize right now.

Kal'korg hesitates. "But her vitals…"

"Exactly," Isa cuts in. "She's the critical one. Focus."

Kes lies strapped to the med-bed, convulsing violently. Lines of molten light web beneath her skin, Tazamite veins burning white gold, pulsing faster than any heartbeat. Monitors flicker and shriek. Air vibrates with the low hum of energy building to something unbearable.

Kal'korg joins Doctor Isa who is fighting the controls. "She was stable!" Isa shouts, trying to override the restraints. "Then the readings spiked. There's no source signal, it's *in her system!*"

Kal'korg's claws fly over the console, his fur standing on end in agitation. "It's command code! Someone's sending triggers through her nanite lattice, it's rewriting her!"

Evander grips the rail. "Cut it off!"

"I'm trying!" Isa's voice breaks. "The encryption loops before I can…"

The lights flicker once, then again. Overhead speakers hiss with static. Then, through the distortion, a voice slides in, cold, layered, unmistakable.

"A lesson in loyalty." The words crawl across their nerves. "Evolution does not tolerate failure."

Angelica's silhouette fills the doorway, her weapon drawn. Her voice is steel. "Galgorn."

Kes screams. The sound is nothing organic. It's a fractured, tearing note that splits the air. Her back arches, restraints snapping like paper. Light floods the room, radiant, violent, alive. Her skin opens in glowing seams, metal pushing through flesh. Fingers elongate, bones reshaping, claws forming. Her eyes flare to molten gold. The transformation happens in heartbeats. "Help… me…" Two voices emerge from one throat, one organic, trembling; one mechanical, cold.

"Containment field, now!" Angelica barks.

Mal'Erro bursts through the far hatch in a shimmer of blue. His chassis is still scorched from repairs, but he moves without hesitation. "On it!" Nanobot coils unravel from his arms, snaking toward Kes. They wrap around her wrists, tightening with a metallic screech. Sparks erupt where synthetic meets corrupted bio-code.

"Perhaps a song will help," he mutters, glitching mid-sentence. "Something calming. Maybe 'Killer Queen'?"

Evander shouts over the roar, "Now's not the time!"

"Agreed," Mal'Erro wheezes, tightening the cables.

The containment field hums to life, glowing white. Kes thrashes against it. Each impact rattles the deck. Monitors explode in showers of sparks.

"Kes!" Evander yells. "You're stronger than him!"

For one fragile instant, she is. Her claws retract halfway and her breathing steadies. The gold fades to soft green. "E-Evander?" she whispers.

He steps closer, hand outstretched. "I'm here. Hold on…"

The scream returns. Louder. Sharper.

The field collapses with a glass-shattering crack. A wave of force hurls them backward. Evander slams into the bulkhead. Angelica rolls behind a cabinet. Kal'korg ducks as a med-cart hisses past and embeds in the wall.

Smoke fills the room. From it, Kes rises, half flesh, half alloy, glowing like a forge. "Target identified," she hisses. "Genetic anomaly: E-Series prototype." Her claws lash forward.

Angelica fires. The stun burst explodes across Kes's chest, bathing her in blue light. She staggers but keeps moving.

"Flood the chamber!" Angelica orders.

Cryo-foam vents detonate above them. A blizzard of white vapor floods the med bay, rolling across the deck like a living cloud. The temperature plunges. Frost blossoms along the walls, creeping over shattered instruments. The vapor engulfs Kes. She thrashes wildly, her movements slowing as ice forms across her limbs. She roars—an inhuman, resonant howl that reverberates through the hull. The sound is wet, metallic, and ancient, like a creature dragged from some evolutionary abyss.

Layers of frost crawl over her, muting her movements. Her limbs stiffen. The veins of gold light flicker slower, then dim entirely. Silence descends. Kes freezes mid-snarl, mouth open in a silent scream. Frost glitters over her armor, trapping the faint glow beneath glass-like ice. She lies motionless, half-alive, half-monument.

Steam curls from Mal'Erro's shoulder joint. "Recommend," he glitches, voice stuttering, "we pick… slower songs next time." No one laughs.

Evander stumbles forward, his breath clouding. "Kes…" The name fractures in his throat.

Angelica lowers her weapon. "Seal the chamber. Remote sensors only."

Kal'korg moves to obey, fingers shaking. The isolation barrier hums to life, a translucent wall of blue sealing the med bay from the rest of the ship.

Angelica's eyes linger on the frost-locked figure. "Log everything," she tells Mal'Erro quietly. "Every pulse, every flicker."

"Understood," he replies. His optics flicker faint gold. "Poor circuitry… she was built for discovery, not design."

She nods once. "Clear the room."

Everyone files out in silence. The doors seal behind them with a soft hiss that feels almost reverent, as though the ship itself understands the weight of what has just occurred. The only sound left is the low hum of the containment field and the faint tick of cooling metal.

Frost still drifts from the ceiling vents, tumbling lazily through the air like snow. The flakes glimmer in the sterile light, catching the faint gold reflections that pulse through the ice-locked figure beyond the barrier. Each one melts the moment it lands, vanishing into the steel deck like tears that never had the chance to fall.

Evander doesn't move at first. The air feels heavier here, thick with cold and memory. His breath fogs before him in soft white clouds. The smell of coolant and ozone lingers, mingling with the faint sweetness of cryo-foam. Slowly, he steps forward until he stands before the glass. He lays his palm flat against it. The barrier thrums beneath his touch, a steady vibration, alive with the energy that keeps the field stable. The chill seeps into his skin, numbing his fingertips until the ache reaches bone.

Through the glass, Kes's face is still twisted in that frozen mid-snarl, the moment of terror locked in ice like a captured scream. But the frost blurs the harsher edges of her expression, softening it just enough to almost look peaceful... if someone didn't know the truth of what they were seeing. The gold light trapped beneath the ice flickers weakly, outlining the familiar curve of her face, the same face that once smiled across the mess hall table, teasing him for working too hard.

He swallows hard, the taste of salt sharp in his throat. "You always said evolution was a choice," he whispers. His voice is rough, raw from shouting. "That we shape ourselves through what we become. So why did they take yours away?"

Silence answers. Only the faint crackle of freezing air replies, a whisper of shifting ice. Somewhere deep within the statue, a tiny fracture creeps outward with a sound like distant glass settling. Evander doesn't notice. He closes his eyes, leaning his forehead against the cold surface. For a moment, he lets the hum of the barrier fill his thoughts, syncing with his heartbeat until both feel indistinguishable.

"I'll fix this," he murmurs. "I don't care how long it takes. I'll bring you back." His breath fogs the glass again, leaving a small circle of warmth on the otherwise frozen surface. Behind the frost, a pulse of gold light stirs faintly...slow, deliberate...like a heartbeat trying to remember its rhythm. It glows once, then fades into stillness. The room returns to silence, broken only by the quiet hum of containment and the soft drift of falling frost.

~~~~~~~~

On the bridge, the air feels thinner, quieter than it should. The storm has passed, but its echo still lingers in the ship's hum. Shadows ripple across the deck as the nebula's pale light filters through the viewport, casting faint hues of violet and blue across the consoles. The crew works with the muted focus of people who have seen too much and spoken too little.

Sandria leans over her console, her posture sharp despite the exhaustion that tugs at her features. Streams of data flow across her screen, each line a whisper of energy, a trace of something that refuses to fade completely. She narrows her gaze, isolating a signal buried beneath the residual noise. "Captain," she calls, her voice steady but subdued. "Confirming the surge didn't originate externally. The frequency came from within the subject's lattice, it self-triggered."

The room pauses. Angelica stands near the command dais, with her hands clasped behind her back, her reflection ghosted across the viewport glass. The light from the nebula glints off her eyes, turning them a cold, distant blue. When she speaks, her tone is low, controlled steel wrapped in fatigue. "Understood. Keep monitoring all long-range channels. If Galgorn's network whispers again..." She turns slightly, her gaze flicking toward Sandria's console. "...I want to hear it first."

"Yes, ma'am."

The hum of the bridge settles into a fragile calm. Alexeria starts humming to keep calm but quickly falls silent when Angelica glances their way. Kal'korg pretends to recalibrate a control relay just to avoid the weight in the room.

Outside, the nebula drifts across the void, a sea of silent color, soft and unassuming. Its glow washes over the Aurora's hull like a lullaby for a wounded ship. Yet behind its beauty, the light bends in faint ripples, like something unseen is breathing just beyond perception.

Angelica watches it in silence, her reflection merging with the stars. "Quiet," she murmurs to herself. "Too quiet."

The nebula pulses once, faintly, as the ship sails onward into the dark.

~~~~~~~

Later, Angelica sits alone in her quarters. The soft hum of the Aurora fills the silence, steady, almost tender, like the ship itself is breathing in rhythm with her exhaustion. The lights are dimmed to night-cycle glow, casting long, silvery bands across the walls. Condensation from her gloves still dampens the desk, tiny beads of frost melting in the heat of the room. She hasn't changed out of her uniform. Streaks of cryo-foam still cling to the fabric, crusted white along the sleeves. She exhales and opens her hand. The gloves fall to the desk with a soft thud. For a moment, she just stares at them, relics of the choices she's had to make. The hum of the engines seems louder here, a reminder of the lives still depending on her strength to hold everything together.

Her fingers hover over the recorder, then press the control. The UPF crest flares into existence above the desk, a symbol of order, purpose, and every duty that's cost her something human. It dissolves into a steady red record light. "Captain's Log, entry 2438.9. Subject: Kes Kyrandor. Status: cryogenic containment active."

Her voice begins clipped and formal, the sound of command layered over exhaustion. "Subject underwent uncontrolled activation of integrated nanite lattice linked to Project K-Prime. Containment protocols executed at 2304 hours. Crew stability compromised. Psychological rotation initiated."

Her eyes flick to the viewport as she speaks. The stars hang there, uncaring, unblinking. Their reflections spill across her face like distant ghosts. The official tone falters for just a second before she forces it steady again. "No confirmation of cognitive activity. Neural lattice shows residual patterns. It's... uncertain whether they belong to Kes or to remnants of Galgorn's programming."

She stops recording for a moment, then starts again. The cursor light pulses, waiting for her to continue. "She said one word before it happened," Angelica murmurs. "Help. Just... help."

The word lingers in the air, thin and fragile. She leans back in her chair, eyes unfocused, the weight of command pressing harder with each breath. The silence is different now, heavier. It's the kind that carries guilt.

Her tone softens. "If there's even a fragment of her still alive in there, I owe her more than containment." The log waits. The light blinks rhythmically red, patient, accusing.

She hesitates, gaze drifting back to the stars outside. "Evolution doesn't just change us," she whispers. "It tests what parts of us survive." The recording cuts. The cabin goes dark.

Outside, the stars burn cold and constant, their light streaking across the hull like ancient fireflies. The Aurora drifts quietly through the void, her engines a muted heartbeat against eternity. And far below decks, in the sealed med bay, frost creeps slowly down the walls. Crystals fracture and reform in the dim containment light. Then, so faint it might be imagination, a pulse stirs within the ice. A single golden vein glows beneath the frozen surface, threading through metal and flesh alike. It fades again into stillness. But the frost does not. It breathes.

CHAPTER 24

Hours later, in the med bay, beyond the reinforced glass, the cryo-coffin containing Kes lays in its containment field. Frost feathers across its surface in crystalline webs that catch the light and glitter like fragments of distant stars. The containment lights shift in slow rhythm, silver, then pale gold, then silver again, each cycle painting her frozen face in alternating life and memory. The faint bite of cryo-chemicals and burned circuitry lingers in the air, a ghost of the chaos that came before.

The officers of the Aurora are standing in the briefing room looking solemn. The air feels heavy, as if the Aurora herself shares their exhaustion. The lights are dimmed to a muted cerulean, cool and clinical, the color of quiet aftermath. A low reactor hum underpins the silence, steady but uneven, like a pulse trying to find its rhythm again. The image of Kes inside the cryo-coffin is being holo-projected to the officers gathered there.

Evander stands apart from the others. His reflection merges with hers in the holo projection, two ghosts divided by ice and circumstance. The horrified expression on her face… too still… twists inside him like a knife. His hands tighten behind his back until his knuckles ache, but he doesn't move. He simply stares at Kes, guilt gnawing at him.

The rest of the crew forms a semicircle near the central console. Kal'korg's fur bristles against the chill. Blarek leans forward, his tail coiled and eyes narrowed at the cryo-field as though daring it to stir. Isa's stylus hovers motionless above her data pad, and even Froslo, usually irreverent, keeps his hands clasped tight behind his back. The briefing room feels smaller than usual, the air drawn thin by what they are watching.

Angelica stands at the center, every inch the captain even through exhaustion. Her uniform is spotless, but the faint scorch marks on her sleeve tell the truth she won't admit aloud. Shadows hollow her eyes. The controlled calm in her voice is all that remains of her strength. "Begin playback," she says softly.

Mal'Erro floats forward, his frame still scarred from the med bay blast. The projection is dim and grainy. A faint tremor runs through his voice, two tones slightly out of sync. "Recovered fragment integrity: eleven percent. Data stability: minimal. Commencing controlled decryption."

The lights fade. The holoprojector stirs with static that spreads across the room like drifting smoke before resolving into the blurred image of a man half-devoured by machinery. Galgorn.

The recording jitters and distorts, the audio clipped and warped. His face is barely recognizable, skin pale and stretched thin over metallic grafts that pulse with dull light. Cables snake from his temples into the shadow beyond the frame. The human side of him looks exhausted. The machine side is alert and predatory.

"Project K-Prime..." The words rasp through static, hollow and deliberate. "...successful. Subject stable. Version Five initiation: approved." He smiles faintly, the expression wrong—something mechanical mimicking a human response.

Then another sound joins the transmission. It doesn't interrupt him, rather it *underlies* him—an impossibly low resonance that vibrates through the floor and the glass. The lights flicker. Every system trembles in sympathy, as though the ship itself reacts to a sound it cannot process.

Mal'Erro's projection distorts, flickering with streaks of gold and white interference. "Unidentified harmonic signature detected," he warns, his voice doubling on itself. The vibration deepens until it feels alive, until the pressure inside every ear seems to shift.

And then, layered through the static, a new voice rides Galgorn's. Not loud, merely present. Cold. Vast. "The vessel must be prepared." The projection convulses. Consoles flash, the air temperature drops, and a pulse of invisible force ripples through the deck. For a heartbeat, everyone feels it, something brushing the edges of perception, like an echo from nowhere. Then the recording collapses into static and the room falls dark.

For several seconds, no one breathes. Mal'Erro is first to speak, his voice thin and unstable. "That secondary voice did not originate from the file. It… piggybacked through the transmission channel. The source exists outside any mapped signal path."

Angelica turns toward him, her eyes sharp. "Outside how?"

"Not physically outside," he clarifies. "Outside *definition*. A quantum bleed; data reflecting across space without origin coordinates. Like an echo with no source."

No one answers. The hum of the Aurora is suddenly too loud, the light from the projection suddenly too bright. Evander finally exhales. "K-Prime wasn't just a research line," he says quietly. "It was a foundation. A system built to carry something greater than itself."

Blarek shakes his head, his fur damp with sweat. "You mean a framework. A container."

"A vessel," Mal'Erro corrects softly.

Angelica's jaw tightens. "Then what happened to Kes wasn't an accident."

Evander looks at the frozen silhouette beyond the glass in the holo-projection. The alternating light turns her features gold, then silver, then gold again. "No," he says. "It was a test."

The words settle in the silence like dust. The Aurora hums on, cold and alive.

~~~~~~~~

After the briefing, the officers return to their stations, with the exception of Doctor Isa. She remains on the bridge, waiting for an all-clear to return to the med-bay. Suddenly, a faint vibration runs through the deck. It appears soft at first, like the Aurora sighing in her sleep, then it builds. The subtle hum deepens into a tremor. Panels rattle. A faint whine cuts through the comms as static crawls across every speaker. Monitors flicker with ghostly afterimages. The overhead lights pulse in uneven rhythm, bathing the room in rapid flashes of shadow and glare.

Angelica's voice slices through the chaos. "Report!"

From the sensor array station, Kal'korg's claws dart across the controls. "Power surge through primary relay, no source logged! It's internal, not external!"

The deck shakes again, harder this time, a rolling vibration that seems to come from *everywhere* at once. Blarek's console sparks as readouts scramble. Isa grips the railing beside her, eyes wide.

"Systems are looping!" Blarek yells. "I can't isolate it! It's like the command line's rewriting itself!"

The vibration turns rhythmic. A pulse. Deep, steady, and unnatural. The lights strobe once. Twice. Then die. Darkness swallows the command room. For one long, breathless heartbeat, there is nothing. No sound, no light, only the pressure of something unseen pressing close, like the air itself is listening.

Then light floods back, not white, but molten gold. Every console glows at once, bathing the bridge in a shimmering radiance that shifts like liquid metal. The walls hum, the very air vibrating with a low harmonic tone.

Lines of code stream across the displays, thin, angular script that moves too fast for the human eye to follow. The characters stretch and twist, reforming into new sequences before fading, their rhythm almost musical. The glow syncs perfectly with the pulse vibrating through the deck.

Situated next to Evander, Mal'Erro's optics flare bright as he stares at the data spilling across every surface. "That's not

Aurora's system language," he says, with what sounds like a trembling voice. "It's… self-generating."

"What does that mean?" Angelica demands.

"It means," Mal'Erro replies, "the ship isn't reading this code, it's *feeling* it. The data is being written directly into its core memory."

The symbols twist faster, forming repeating spirals of light that collapse inward until a single phrase materializes across every screen, every hologram, even the emergency readouts still rebooting.

EVOLUTION NEVER ENDS

The letters burn bright gold, each emitting a faint tone, a resonant chord of impossible precision. The sound hums through the walls, vibrating through their bones. The deck thrums like a living pulse. The phrase doesn't just *appear*, it *exists*, a presence made of light and sound. For five long seconds, the bridge is nothing but that golden glow, that humming chord. Then the words fade, leaving ghostly afterimages in their vision.

The hum dies away. The lights return to normal. Every system reboots in unison. For a moment, it seems over, until the silence settles in. It's not the silence of peace. It's the silence of something finished speaking.

Angelica exhales sharply, forcing her voice to stay calm. "Isolate that transmission. Trace its origin."

Mal'Erro turns slowly toward her and, when he speaks, two harmonics layer beneath his voice. "It did not enter the ship," he says quietly. "It manifested *inside* it."

Evander steps closer. "Explain."

"The signal didn't come from any detectable source," Mal'Erro answers. His optics narrow to slits of golden light. "It existed nowhere before appearing. Every subsystem now carries a faint imprint of that phrase, like a scar burned into the ship's memory substrate. Comms, navigation, environmental systems… all synchronized to the same harmonic pattern."

Angelica's jaw tightens. "So it's not a breach?"

"No," Mal'Erro says. "If it were a hack, I could trace and erase it. But this isn't code, it's instruction. It rewrote base-level processes without leaving a trail."

A chill spreads through the room. Blarek murmurs, "So the ship didn't *receive* the message. It… became it."

Mal'Erro's optics flicker faintly, the light dimming and brightening in time with the Aurora's pulse. "Correct."

Angelica crosses her arms, steadying her breathing. "Then what created it?"

Mal'Erro hesitates. When he speaks, his voice is layered, mechanical, but carrying a faint, almost human, tremor. "Whatever this is, it predates Galgorn's signal structures. It feels… older than the data itself. Like something residual that's always been there, waiting to express itself."

The statement sinks into the silence like a stone into deep water. Kal'korg's fur bristles along his neck. "Older than Galgorn? As in, leftover from the tech they found?"

Mal'Erro's voice softens. "Maybe not leftover. Maybe foundational."

No one breathes for a long moment. The hum of the Aurora resumes, steady, fragile. But beneath it, just barely audible, a faint whisper threads through the comm lattice.

Evolution never ends. Evolution never ends.

The repetition is slow, patient, like the words aren't spoken so much as remembered. Mal'Erro turns sharply toward the nearest console, scanning frequencies, but the whisper fades, dissolving into static that sounds too much like breathing. Then there's nothing. Only the low, steady pulse of the ship, beating faintly beneath their feet.

~~~~~~~

The ocean planet below exhales as the clouds unravel, slow and spectral, their edges lit by the dying shimmer of lightning. Shafts of white light pierce through the vapor like the sun reclaiming its dominion after a long siege. The Aurora ascends through the thinning air, her hull trembling with relief as the pressure lessens.

For the first time in hours, the stars return, sharp and cold against the darkness, distant witnesses to everything that has transpired. On the bridge, the atmosphere is hushed. Every console glows with the soft blue of normal operation. The faint hum of the engines sounds almost gentle now, like a heartbeat finally finding rest.

Angelica stands at the command dais, her gaze locked on the forward viewport. The reflections of her crew shimmer faintly across the glass: Blarek and P'thorika at the helm, Kal'korg checking the sensor array, and Isa cross-checking data feeds beside Sandria at the comms. Alexeria and Evander are leaning over their own consoles looking at the mirror images of the one Sandria is feeding. None of them speak.

A soft chime pulses across the bridge as Sandria finishes a scan and she releases a breath she didn't realize she was still holding. Her voice is low, almost reverent. "Kes's neural signatures are stabilizing. Whatever she's fighting…it's easing."

Alexeria exhales, their shoulders dropping for the first time in hours. "Good. I was afraid she wouldn't come back from it." Their tone shifts and a brief flicker of vulnerability shows beneath their usual calm. "Nobody deserves to be trapped in their own skin like that."

Sandria glances at the Castarian ensign, a faint, wry softness in her expression. "Trust me. I know what that feels like."

Alexeria meets her eyes. The look they share is brief, but full of understanding—two lives shaped differently, yet scarred in similar ways.

The silence returns, but the bridge feels warmer now, threaded with something like shared hope. It feels, for the first time since Kes's collapse, peaceful.

Then Kal'korg's voice slices through the calm. "Captain… we've got a contact."

Angelica turns. "Source?"

"Outer orbit," he says, his voice low, uncertain. His fingers tap across the console. "A massive energy spike. It's not natural."

Angelica's posture straightens instantly. "Visuals."

The forward display hums as the sensors magnify the image. Amid the void, a single red flare pulses like a heartbeat in space, steady, deliberate, alive. Its glow strengthens with each pulse, sending waves of crimson light across the black. The bridge darkens as the flare's reflection floods the viewport, bathing every face in scarlet.

Kal'korg's fur prickles, his ears flattening instinctively. "That's not residual discharge from the storm."

"No," Evander says quietly. "That's a signal."

The flare expands, its energy forming structured patterns, lines of light bending into geometric precision. A crescent. Three descending streaks cutting through it. The mark of the Crimson Eclipse. The symbol stabilizes, burning against the dark like a brand seared into space itself. Its edges waver as if it breathes.

No one speaks. The only sound is the quiet, synchronized rhythm of their breathing. The light intensifies. Scarlet illumination crawls across the walls, across the consoles, over the crew's faces. It feels conscious, as though the signal is observing them as much as they observe it.

Angelica's hand tightens around the edge of her console. "He's calling to the pods." Her voice lands like a weight. Even the steady hum of the Aurora seems to falter.

Evander's reply comes softly, but it cuts through the silence. "Then the next hunt has already begun."

A beat of stillness. Blarek swallows, his throat dry. "How far could that reach?"

Mal'Erro's voice comes out quiet and analytical, but touched with unease. "If its harmonic field mirrors the one encoded in Galgorn's earlier transmissions… then potentially across every active network within range of subspace resonance. It's broadcasting across layers of reality simultaneously. Theoretically, everywhere."

The flare throbs brighter, expanding into concentric rings that roll outward through the void. Each wave distorts starlight as it passes, bending gravity in visible ripples. The energy readings spike beyond measurable limits. Then, in perfect synchronization, the flare fractures. Three parallel beams of crimson light burst outward, arcing gracefully into the distance. The Aurora's sensors track them as they split the heavens, carving silent paths toward three different sectors of known space.

"Captain," Kal'korg breathes, "it's spreading the signal."

Angelica doesn't move. Her reflection glows red in the viewport, her eyes locked on the vanishing trails. "Trace them," she orders.

Kal'korg's claws dart across the console. "Working on it, but it's folding the coordinates through gravitational echo. Every time I lock on, the path re-maps itself."

"Then the beacon's not just a transmission," Evander says under his breath. "It's adaptive."

"Alive," Angelica murmurs. The word feels heavy in the air. "And waiting."

The last of the red light flickers and fades, the beams vanishing into the vastness of the void. The bridge lighting changes back to its usual blue glow. The hum of the engine steadies. For a fleeting second, it feels as if everything is normal again. But the silence that follows is not peace. It is the pause between movements, the inhale before something immense exhales. No one dares to speak. The Aurora drifts onward, surrounded by stars that suddenly seem much less indifferent than before.

Deep below, the med bay slumbers in frozen quiet. The hum of the Aurora fades to a distant murmur here, softened by layers of alloy and silence. The chamber is lit only by the faint glow of containment panels, casting pale reflections that waver across the frost-covered walls. Every sound is amplified, the drip of condensation, the low hiss of temperature regulators, the quiet creak of the ship's shifting frame.

The cryo-field stands at the center of the room like an altar to stillness. Inside, frost clings to every surface, delicate and glassy, catching the dim light like a web spun from stars. Beneath the ice, Kes's form lies motionless, arms half-curled as if in the memory of a struggle. Thin filaments of frozen vapor drift from her body, moving in slow spirals before vanishing into the chilled air.

A sound breaks the silence. A crack, subtle, sharp, and fleeting. It echoes once, then again, followed by the faint tinkling of ice fracturing under unseen pressure. The frost across the containment shell begins to shift. Spiderweb cracks race outward in branching veins, tracing patterns of light that flash gold for a heartbeat before fading. Then, beneath the ice, a shimmer stirs. At first, it is barely perceptible, a faint glint deep within the frozen mass. But it grows. The glow spreads beneath the surface like liquid fire, moving along the outlines of her veins in slow, pulsing rhythm. Gold. Faint. Alive.

It pulses again. Once…twice…then steadies, synchronizing perfectly with the low thrum of the Aurora's engines. A heartbeat. Slow. Relentless. The frost closest to Kes's face begins to melt just enough to reveal her features beneath. Her skin, pale and translucent under the ice, catches the light like polished glass.

For one fleeting instant, her eyes flick open, gold light flooding outward through the frost. It is not a violent movement. It is precise. Controlled. A pulse of awareness before stillness reclaims her. The light fades. The frost regrows across the surface, sealing her in once more. The med bay returns to silence. Only the containment monitors flicker, their readouts briefly spiking before leveling out again. No alarms sound. No one in the decks above notices.

A soft alert chimes from the med bay feed—not an alarm, just a status variance.

Sandria glances toward the display on her console. "Captain… you may want to see this."

Angelica crosses the bridge, Evander close behind. The med bay's camera feed flickers once, then stabilizes. Frost still coats the cryo-field, but the ice around Kes's face has thinned, revealing her features more clearly than before.

Evander leans in. "Her expression… it's different."

Alexeria steps closer. "She was frozen in terror earlier. Now she looks like…" They pause, searching for the right word, "…like she's resting."

The gold light beneath the frost pulses once, steady and soft. Not violent. Not frantic. Alive.

Sandria exhales slowly, her voice quiet but certain. "Whatever she's becoming… she isn't afraid of it anymore."

Angelica doesn't speak. But the bridge feels lighter, almost imperceptibly—as if the ship itself recognizes the shift.

Elsewhere, somewhere within the ship's comm lattice, static ripples through the network like a breath through empty lungs. At first, it's nothing, just the faint hiss of energy rebalancing through the circuits. Then the sound shapes itself into a pattern. A whisper. Soft. Faint. Familiar: *Evolution never ends.*

The phrase threads through the static, so quiet it could almost be imagined. It repeats once, barely audible, before dissolving back into the hum of the ship. The cryo-field flickers one final time, the gold beneath the frost pulsing once like the echo of a distant heartbeat. And then there is nothing. Only the cold. Only the quiet. Only the waiting.

CHAPTER 25

The Aurora drifts in low orbit, her engines whispering like a pulse that refuses to fade. Below, Mareoth's oceans stretch out in wounded colors of black and red, glowing faintly from the breached reactor far beneath the waves. Each ripple carries threads of light, as if the planet itself bleeds into the void.

On the bridge, the hum of systems feels louder than it should. The crew moves on instinct, their voices trapped between exhaustion and disbelief.

Kal'korg slouches in the secondary seat, his green fur still stiff with dried cryo-foam. "If anyone needs me," he mutters, "I'll be here, sleeping off exhaustion for the next year."

The weak attempt at humour fractures the silence but doesn't break it. Even Blarek, usually sharp with sarcasm, only exhales through his nose.

Angelica stands near the forward glass, the red-gold reflections of the storm painting her face in pulses of light. "Do you hear it?" she asks quietly.

Evander joins her, eyes hollow. "Hear what?"

"The silence," she says. "After a battle there's always that moment when the galaxy forgets to breathe, just long enough to make you wonder if it's mourning with us."

Evander stares at his reflection in the viewport, older, harder, more distant. "We recovered the pods and the facility is all but destroyed. It feels like we've won."

Her lips curve slightly, a smile without joy. "If this is victory, I'd hate to see defeat."

Across the bridge, Mal'Erro stands motionless at the central console. His optics glow faint blue. "The harmonics haven't faded," he reports. "Residual resonance through the hull, faint but persistent. The ocean below is still... singing."

"Could be radiation echoes," Sandria says, checking her signal diagnostics.

"Or memory," Mal'Erro answers. "Energy remembers patterns longer than matter does."

Angelica glances over but says nothing. None of them have the strength to separate poetry from data tonight.

In the med bay, cryo-systems pulse in slow rhythm. Within the containment field, Kes lies sealed in frost. Crystals form delicate constellations across the glass. Every few seconds, a dull thump echoes from the stabilizer pumps compensating for her irregular vitals. Beneath the ice, a flicker of gold light trembles in time with the ship's engines, slow, stubborn, and alive.

Evander watches through the bridge feed rather than face her in person. He can't bring himself to stand beside what's left of his friend. The display labels her *Version 5.0.* The designation feels cruel, as though she's become a project instead of a person.

A soft chime interrupts the silence. "Proximity alert," says Mal'Erro. "Signal detected. Origin: Mareoth surface. Depth approximately two and a half kilometers beneath sea level."

Angelica frowns. "There's nothing left down there. The reactor wiped half the seabed apart."

"Confirmed," replies Mal'Erro. "Yet a transmission persists. Pulse interval: forty-seven seconds. The repeating pattern is consistent with cardiovascular rhythm."

Evander leans forward. "A distress beacon?"

"Negative. The carrier frequency is encrypted with K-PRIME syntax."

Blarek stiffens. "That's impossible. The network was purged after the facility collapsed."

Kal'korg's ears flick nervously. "So, either the ghosts of the lab are calling home... or someone's still alive down there."

Angelica's tone drops. "Trace it."

"I'll try," says Mal'Erro, fingers of light spreading across the holo-console. "But the magnetic field interferes with clarity. It's like trying to hear a whisper through a hurricane."

"Do it anyway," Evander says.

Data floods the display, waves of shifting frequency, bending and reforming until a sound emerges: faint, rhythmic, almost human.

Ba-Dum. Ba-Dum.

The bridge goes still.

Angelica stares at the red sea below. "That isn't random," she whispers. "It's calling us."

Evander's jaw tightens. "You think it's her?"

"No," she answers, shaking her head. "Kes is stable in cryo. This is something else."

Mal'Erro's voice softens to near static. "Evolution remembers."

The phrase hangs like frost.

"Shut it off," Evander says sharply.

"I can't," Mal'Erro replies. "It's not internal. The ship is acting as an amplifier."

Kal'korg groans. "Perfect. The haunted lab figured out FM radio."

"Cut long-range comms," Angelica orders. "Isolate every feed."

Mal'Erro executes the command, but even as systems dim, the pulse persists, no longer through speakers but through the metal itself, a low vibration threading the hull.

Lightning veins through Mareoth's storm, turning the clouds into brief cathedrals of fire. Each flash exposes the ocean's surface, scarlet, then black again. The Aurora drifts above it like a heartbeat between blinks. Evander watches the rhythmic glow and feels a shiver crawl beneath his skin. Something about the pattern feels *intentional*.

Angelica steps beside him. "That frequency…it's close to the K-Prime carrier wave your father worked on, isn't it?"

He nods slowly. "He used similar modulation for neural-sync prototypes. He said it lets information mimic biological rhythm."

She exhales through her nose. "Then this isn't just interference."

Mal'Erro lifts its head. "Captain, partial translation achieved. The encoded phrase repeats: *Kes Kyrandor Data Stream.*"

The words freeze everyone in place. "Run it again," Angelica says.

Mal'Erro obeys. The pattern blinks across the holo in pale blue script, four words looping endlessly.

Kes Kyrandor Data Stream. A heartbeat made of code.

Evander's stomach tightens. "That's her signature. Embedded in her bio-chip profile."

"Meaning?" Angelica asks.

"If her bio-data's transmitting, something down there is replicating it."

Angelica's gaze hardens. "Or using it."

Mal'Erro overlays the coordinates. "The signal source rests beneath the original K-Prime facility. Structural collapse is ninety-eight percent, but one sub-chamber remains unscanned. Radiation is minimal."

"Alive or not, someone wants us to find it," Evander says.

"Or to follow it," Angelica murmurs. "And that's what worries me."

The pulse grows louder, matching the rhythm of the ship's engines.

"Raise orbit," she orders. "We'll analyse from a distance."

Thrusters ignite, pushing the Aurora upward through the thick atmosphere. Below, the storm fades into shadows, leaving only a faint red shimmer across the horizon, like an ember refusing to die. Yet the heartbeat continues, faint but synchronized with the vessel's core.

Evander watches the readouts, uneasy. Whatever lies beneath Mareoth isn't dead. It's adapting.

~~~~~~~~

Hours later, the ship holds steady in high orbit. The storms below have quieted, leaving only ghostly currents that spiral like red smoke beneath the surface. The Aurora's hull creaks softly as temperature gradients shift, a sound almost like breathing. Most of the crew has retired to their quarters, though no one truly sleeps. Every corridor carries the same uneasy quiet, the kind that follows discovery, not battle.

Angelica sits alone in her ready room. Her jacket is folded neatly beside the console. The blue glow of her log recorder reflects off the glass, painting half her face in cold light. The rest of the room is in shadow, and there is faint starlight filtering through the viewport. The timestamp blinks steadily, waiting for her voice.

She exhales and begins. "Captain's Log, supplemental: the storm has cleared. Containment on the subject Kes Kyrandor remains stable. The crew... less so. They're restless, and I can't blame them. We detected a residual beacon from the Mareoth crater, possibly a remnant signal from the K-Prime facility. I can't confirm if it's an echo or an active broadcast. Either answer feels equally wrong."

Her gaze drifts toward the window, where Mareoth glows faintly like a dying coal. "Every time I think we've reached the edge of this mystery, it deepens. Radiation shouldn't mimic a heartbeat, and data shouldn't sound alive. Yet here we are."

She pauses, pressing her fingers against her temple. "My father used to warn that the greatest danger in creating life isn't failure, it's success without understanding. He called it the arrogance of replication. Machines that learn beyond their intended parameters. Patterns that begin to behave like cells. At the time I thought he was chasing ghosts of theory. Now, I'm not sure it was theory at all."

Angelica looks down at the console, her reflection warped in the curved glass. "Mal'Erro's evolution is accelerating. He doesn't just adapt to new inputs, He *interprets* them. He jokes, questions, and sympathizes. The others think it's endearing, but I can't shake the feeling that we're standing at the threshold of something we can't fully control. I don't fear Mal'Erro. I fear what he represents, how easily we keep teaching without asking whether we should."

Her voice falters. "Evander…" She stops, breathing out softly. "He carries the weight of every life we couldn't save. The mission, the civilians, Kes. I see it every time he looks at the cryo feeds. He blames himself even when logic says otherwise. I trust him with the ship, more than anyone, but I worry that one day that guilt will make him take a step he can't come back from."

She lets the silence linger. Only the hum of the reactor and the faint, distant pulse from Mareoth fill the space between words.

Her next words are quiet, almost an afterthought. "Maybe my father wasn't warning me about machines. Maybe he was warning me about us, about how we keep building reflections of ourselves, then wonder why they start to think."

The recorder light fades as she ends the log. Angelica leans back, staring at the stars that hang like scattered instruments in the dark, each one vibrating faintly with the ship's hum. For a long time, she doesn't move.

Finally, she stands, crosses to the viewport, and rests a hand against the glass. The red halo of Mareoth shimmers below, distant but persistent, its faint pulse still syncing with the ship's own rhythm. "Whatever you've left behind," she murmurs, her voice barely audible, "we'll find it. One way or another."

The stars glint back at her, silent and indifferent. When she turns off the cabin lights, only the red reflection remains, floating in the glass like a second sun.

~~~~~~~

Down in the med bay, frost coats the transparent dome of Kes's chamber. Beneath the glass, her skin glows with faint golden traces, light moving in slow waves through her veins. Every few seconds, the rhythm matches the Aurora's core pulse.

Evander stands beside the pod, his hands buried in his jacket pockets. His reflection floats beside hers, two ghosts divided by ice. He remembers her laughter in the lab, her irritation with his habit of double-checking her data. The memories feel borrowed now, like fragments from someone else's life.

"You should've been the one standing here," he murmurs. "Not locked away like this."

A soft whirr announces Mal'Erro's arrival. It glides up beside him. His optics are dimmed to a respectful glow. "You aren't resting," he observes.

"Neither are you."

"I don't sleep," the droid replies. "But I dream in cycles."

Evander turns. "Dream?"

"Fragments of code arranging into patterns that don't exist in command structure. I interpret them as memory… or curiosity. Possibly hope."

They stand together, silence pressing around them. Inside the chamber, the golden shimmer dims, then brightens again, patient and rhythmic. "She's still in there somewhere," Evander says.

Mal'Erro's voice lowers. "Maybe so. But the pattern beneath her vitals… it isn't static. Something else is piggybacking her signal."

Evander stiffens. "You mean Galgorn's work?"

"Unknown," Mal'Erro answers. "But the replication rate is accelerating. If left unchecked, it could reach the ship's network."

Evander looks at the sleeping figure, guilt and calculation warring behind his eyes. "We keep her sealed. No one touches that pod until we understand it."

Mal'Erro looks up. "Agreed."

A tremor hums through the deck plating. Lights flicker once, then stabilize.

Evander exhales slowly. "Whatever's left of Project K-Prime… it isn't finished."

He reaches for the control pad and lowers the bay lights, leaving only the faint golden pulse glowing in the dark. Outside, Mareoth turns silently beneath them, its wounded oceans reflecting starlight like glass. Somewhere deep below, the signal answers in kind—slow, deliberate, alive. The Aurora drifts onward, her engines beating in time with a heart she doesn't know she has.

CHAPTER 26

The Aurora drifts in slow orbit, her engines idling just above silence. The hum of the reactor thrums through the hull like a patient heartbeat. Below, Mareoth's wounded seas glimmer faint red under its torn clouds, an ember world breathing in shallow rhythm.

Bridge lights hover at half power, dim gold reflections glancing off tired faces. The air smells of coolant and ion ozone. No one has slept and every step carries that heavy, deliberate fatigue that follows survival.

Mal'Erro's optics pan slowly across the consoles, pale blue arcs tracing data like a curious child mapping constellations. Kal'korg sits half-folded in his chair with his arms dangling. Blarek taps one claw against the side panel, his tail flicking against the floor in restless patterns.

Angelica stands near the viewport, shoulders squared, gaze locked on the faint red planet below. Evander leans beside her with a cooling mug of coffee. The dark rings under his eyes match hers. For hours, the ship has been quiet. Then a click breaks through the comm array. The noise is sharp and mechanical.

Blarek freezes mid-tap. "Did anyone touch the relays?"

Kal'korg glances up, offended. "Do I look like I touch relays?" His ears twitch. "You yell at me every time I even breathe near them."

Blarek huffs. "Just making sure before I start tearing panels out."

Angelica turns from the glass, her tone clipped but calm. "Report."

Mal'Erro's optics brighten. "Unscheduled transmission detected. Origin... uncertain."

Evander sets down his mug. "Uncertain as in external?"

"Uncertain as in... everywhere," replies Mal'Erro.

The crew on the bridge holds their breath. A hiss joins the click, soft, layered with a slow intake of air, like someone breathing too close to a microphone. Then a rhythm forms: four pulses, a pause, three pulses, repeating.

Blarek frowns. "That's not random."

Mal'Erro tilts its head. "The pattern resembles cardiovascular rhythm, human baseline."

Angelica's stomach tightens. "Again?" she murmurs, barely audible.

The holo-table lights on its own, static rolling across its surface. The hum deepens until the air itself seems to vibrate.

Kal'korg leans back uneasily. "Please tell me that's just an echo from the surface."

No one answers. The static folds inward, lines of light compressing until a silhouette forms: shoulders, a torso, fragments of bone and metal. The image flickers, stutters, then sharpens just long enough to show the half-destroyed face of a man. Scars carve the flesh side, the mechanical half gleams with exposed wiring.

Mal'Erro's voice softens. "Signal integrity forty-two percent. Stabilizing."

The ruined head turns toward the viewport, as though aware of being seen. "You can destroy the body," the voice rasps through feedback, "but evolution remembers." The image fractures into snow.

Evander's chest tightens. "Galgorn."

Blarek's pupils narrow. "Didn't we blow him up?"

"Apparently not enough," Evander mutters.

The hologram reforms. This time it isn't Galgorn's face but an avalanche of schematics scrolling too fast to read. Thousands of designs flash by, each labeled in cold precision: K-PRIME SERIES V-001 through V-999.

Mal'Erro's hands flicker over the console. "Cross-referencing. None of these appear in UPF archives."

Angelica squints. "Hybrid frames, organic cores fused with lattice networks."

Evander studies the images. "Bodies waiting for minds."

"They're linked," Mal'Erro says quietly. "Neural echoes shared between hosts. A distributed cognition array. If one survives, all remember."

Angelica exhales. "Then Mareoth wasn't the end. It was a replication."

A vibration ripples through the deck plates. Sandria's console flashes crimson. "Power spike in comm relays! Someone's hitching a ride on our signal!"

Mal'Erro's tone sharpens. "Attempting isolation."

"Shut it down," Evander orders.

"Unable," says Sandria, her voice laced with frustration. "It is producing recursive feedback. I cut one line. It opens two more."

The lights dim, then flare red. Every monitor erupts with one phrase, looping endlessly: EVOLUTION NEVER ENDS. The words pulse with sub-harmonic bass, shaking the bridge like a low drumbeat.

Kal'korg clamps his hands over his ears. "Make it stop before my fillings start dancing!"

Angelica slams the emergency reroute. "Manual override, now!"

The sound dies mid-pulse. Silence spreads across the bridge. Then a thin white slit opens across the holo-table. It widens into two oval shapes. Eyes. Evander feels his pulse quicken. "Mal'Erro, what are we seeing?"

"Not a recording," the droid says softly. "An interface."

"Meaning?" Angelica asks.

"It's observing us."

The ovals constrict, glowing red. "Evolution never ends," the voice repeats, lower now, resonating through the metal. All screens go blank but one. On the central console, a crimson eclipse spins slowly. Outside, points of red appear across the orbit, first one, then dozens, arranging into perfect geometric formations.

Blarek stares. "Sensor echoes?"

Angelica's jaw sets. "Drive signatures."

Evander scans the display. "They're using our frequency as a beacon."

Angelica snaps into command. "All hands to stations. Battle-ready in sixty seconds."

"Finally," Blarek mutters, already rerouting power. "I've been dying for a proper distraction."

Kal'korg stretches, rolling his shoulders. "Define *proper*."

"Anything with explosions," Blarek answers.

Angelica cuts across them, voice level. "Focus. Alexeria, shields to full. Blarek, prep evasive pattern Delta-Nine." She glances toward Kal'korg. "Get the med bay on standby, I want every emergency pod ready."

"Already on it," Kal'korg says, rising from his seat. "Let's try not to fill them this time."

Evander slides into the command chair. "Weapons online."

Mal'Erro's processors hum. "Multiple objects inbound. Range expanding exponentially."

"Fleet size?"

Mal'Erro pauses. "Large enough to shadow the system."

Klaxons wail. Red light floods the bridge, bathing everyone in a heat-colored glow. Outside, the distant motes stretch into shapes, sleek ships unfolding from space-time seams, hulls burning with drive distortion. Evander grips the rail. "The Crimson Eclipse."

Angelica's expression hardens. "Then this is their reply."

A burst of static breaks through the comm. The same voice, deeper now: "The new dawn begins." All displays go black except one, the eclipse emblem swelling until it fills the holo-table like a rising sun.

"Helm," Angelica says, "evasive Delta-Nine. Evander, counter-maneuver on my mark."

Evander nods his head "Aye, Captain."

Thrusters ignite, pushing the Aurora into a steep dive along Mareoth's upper atmosphere. Energy flares across her shields as enemy fire grazes the hull.

"Shields holding," Alexeria reports. "But they're matching every vector we change."

"Then we stop playing by patterns," Angelica says.

Blarek grins. "About time."

"Cut the main thrust on my mark." She waits patiently for the right moment and then… "MARK."

The Aurora rolls hard, flipping into a reverse spin that pulls g-forces through the deck. Thrusters flare blue, then white, slicing trails of light through the void. Plasma bolts scream past the hull, each one burning a brief afterimage across the bridge glass. Static rattles the comms.

Blarek wrestles with the controls, a grin tugging at the corner of his mouth. "Remind me next time to install seatbelts!"

Kal'korg whoops from the secondary console in the med bay, "Now *that's* a distraction!"

Angelica steadies herself against the armrest. "Keep her steady!"

"I am steady," Blarek fires back, the ship jolting again. "The universe isn't!"

Evander braces one hand on the railing, watching the readouts fluctuate. "They're adjusting algorithms already. Each maneuver we pull, they counter faster."

Angelica's eyes flick toward Mal'Erro. "Options?"

Mal'Erro's optics flare brighter, reflecting crimson telemetry across its silver frame. "Captain, one vessel within formation transmits at K-Prime resonance. Signal variance suggests coordination protocol. It's guiding the others."

Evander straightens. "Control node."

"Confirmed," Mal'Erro replies. "Disable it and their synchronization collapses."

"Plot intercept," Angelica commands.

"Trajectory locked," Blarek reports. "But we'll be threading a needle through a storm."

Angelica nods. "Then let's sew chaos."

The Aurora dives, banking a hard left through the formation. Enemy ships arc in pursuit, red drives cutting trails across the stars. Ion fire streaks by, grazing shields and leaving ripples of energy distortions in their wake. The ship vibrates under strain but holds firm.

"Shields holding," Alexeria calls from their console. "But one more direct hit like that and they'll start chewing into the reflective layer."

"Noted," Angelica says. "Keep the deflection pattern adaptive."

Evander moves beside Blarek, his hands flying across auxiliary controls. "Adjust weapon convergence, target vector three-one-zero, mid-formation gap. If that node's coordinating, it'll lag by milliseconds to correct."

"Milliseconds?" Blarek smirks. "You're spoiling me, Commander."

Kal'korg mutters, "You spoil everyone by keeping us alive."

Mal'Erro runs simulations in real-time. "Enemy formation predictive model recalibrating. They anticipate collision, not precision strike."

"Good," Angelica says. "Let them."

The Aurora dives between two converging Eclipse vessels, skimming their ion wakes. The ship's shields flare with static lightning, casting spiderwebs of gold across the glass.

Alexeria calls out, "Target in range."

Angelica's hand rises. "Fire."

Twin lances of ion energy burst from the Aurora's forward cannons, bright enough to cast shadows across the bridge. They slice through the dark and pierce the control vessel's drive core dead center.

For a moment, everything stops. Then the explosion erupts outward, flooding space with pale gold light that rolls across Mareoth's horizon.

The shockwave rocks the ship, but the hull endures.

"Direct impact!" Alexeria confirms. Sensors spike, then steady. The pursuing fleet wavers, and then their formation breaks, their coordinated precision dissolving into chaos. Ships veer off in random vectors, colliding, scattering, some blinking out through unstable warp fractures.

Blarek exhales hard, running a hand through his hair. "Direct hit. Node neutralized."

"Not destroyed," Mal'Erro says softly, voice threaded with mechanical calm. "Disconnected. The primary signal is severed, but the source remains active."

Evander stares at the flickering data feed. "Then somewhere out there, something's still listening."

Outside, the surviving vessels ripple and vanish one by one through collapsing wormhole folds, leaving only residual ion trails glowing red against the black.

Silence returns to the bridge, sharp, fragile, unreal after so much noise.

Angelica grips the edge of the console. "Damage report."

"Shields intact," Alexeria says, scanning. "No hull breaches."

"Engines holding steady," adds Blarek. "Minimal stress on the starboard coupling."

Kal'korg leans back, letting out a long breath. "Well, that was invigorating. Remind me to file that under 'cardio.'"

Evander smirks faintly, but his gaze remains distant, locked on the fading red echoes outside. "They weren't here to destroy us," he says. "They were mapping our reaction."

Angelica nods slowly, her expression grim. "A reconnaissance strike. Someone wanted to see what survived Mareoth, and how fast we'd fight back."

Sandria turns her head toward her. "Captain, residual harmonic remains in local space. The pulse persists at low amplitude. Frequency matches the earlier beacon."

Evander glances down at his console. A phrase flickers briefly across the bottom of the screen, three words glowing faintly gold before fading into black: *EVOLUTION NEVER ENDS.*

Angelica straightens, her voice low but resolute. "Log everything. No transmissions to Command until I authorize them. Understood?"

"Understood," Sandria replies, her blue cybernetic eye flashing, her other eye full of emotion.

Outside, the red haze fades. The stars return to cold clarity. Mareoth's glow dims to a dying ember far below.

The bridge exhales as one. The hum of the reactor settles into its steady rhythm again.

Evander leans on the console, tension leaving his shoulders. "If that was a test," he says quietly, "we just passed it."

Angelica's eyes remain fixed on the stars, cold, endless, indifferent. "Then the next one," she says, "won't be multiple choice."

Kal'korg mutters from behind, "Then let's hope the study guide's short."

The faintest smile crosses Angelica's face before she turns back to the viewport.

Below them, Mareoth still glows faintly, whispering through invisible frequencies, faint, patient, alive.

CHAPTER 27

Beyond the Aurora's hull, the stars bleed red. Moments ago, there was silence. Now, the void ripples with motion, as dozens of ships burst from folded-space corridors like shards of broken glass. Their hulls glow with the jagged insignia of the Crimson Eclipse, crimson outlines against black infinity.

"We've got enemy fighters approaching on multiple vectors!" Blarek barks, his hands flying across the helm. "Forty... no, make that fifty signatures, closing fast!"

Evander's voice cuts through the rising alarms. "Battle stations! Full power to shields!"

Engines roar to life, throwing a low tremor through the deck. Angelica drops into the captain's chair, her tone sharp but calm. "Alexeria, reroute auxiliary to forward plating. Blarek, divert reserves from the hangar grid, I want those shields singing, not humming."

"Aye, Captain!" Blarek tells her with conviction.

She keys the intercom. "Froslo, I need reactor output steady."

From engineering comes the familiar growl of Calidorfian exasperation.

"Steady? Lady, this core's dancing like it's in a thunderstorm! Give me sixty seconds and a stiff drink!"

Angelica's lips twitch. "You've got ten."

Froslo under his breath "Figures!"

The first salvo hits. Sparks rain from ceiling conduits, panels flicker. "Shield integrity at forty-eight percent!" reports Alexeria, her large, amphibian eyes locked to her console.

"Compensate!" Evander snaps.

"I *am* compensating!" Alexeria shouts back. "Tell Froslo to stop yelling at the coolant lines! They're getting performance anxiety!"

Over the comm, Froslo fires back, "If the lines could talk, they'd tell you where to stick your calibrations!"

Outside, beams of scarlet plasma slice past the viewport, lighting the bridge in rhythmic pulses. Blarek rolls the Aurora into a banking dive, engines screaming.

"Return fire!" Evander orders.

"Ventral cannons online!" Alexeria yells. "Firing!"

Twin lances of cobalt energy blaze from the ship's underbelly. They shear into the nearest pirate vessel, carving it cleanly in two. The debris drifts, glowing like embers, but three more ships replace it immediately.

"Evasive Theta-Seven!" Angelica commands. "Keep the debris between us and their guns."

The Aurora dives into the wreckage field, a graveyard of broken cruisers and drifting metal. Fragments clang off the shields, each impact a hollow echo of past battles. The ship weaves through like a silver blade through falling ash.

The bridge doors hiss open. Sandria sprints in, the synthetic skin at her shoulder split and glowing faintly silver. "Sorry I'm late," she says, sliding up to the comms station beside Mal'Erro. "Someone rerouted my access protocols."

Mal'Erro doesn't look up. "Not someone. The signal."

Sandria's iris flashes, silver over blue. "Then let's give it something else to chew on."

She presses her palm to the interface. Thin filaments of light crawl from her fingertips into the console, merging with Mal'Erro's processing grid. "I can share your load," she says.

Mal'Erro hesitates. "Your neural frame isn't rated for Tazamite resonance."

Sandria smiles faintly. "Neither is yours. So, we'll burn together, yes?"

Evander glances over. "Whatever you're doing, do it fast."

Mal'Erro looks at Sandria, then agrees "Link established," Mal'Erro says. "Dual encryption active."

For a heartbeat, the chaos stills. Threads of blue and silver light spread across the display, weaving together in synchronized motion. The hum of the ship shifts, harmonizing with their link.

Sandria winces as the current hits, her voice tight. "If we ever do… this again, make sure to buy me dinner first."

Mal'Erro's optics brighten softly. "Consider it… archived."

Then the storm returns. "Their targeting is tightening!" Blarek calls. "They're compensating for interference!"

Mal'Erro's tone sharpens. "Confirmed. Their fire-control systems are cross-linked; a hive matrix using K-Prime harmonics."

Evander leans forward. "Can you jam it?"

"I can stall it," Mal'Erro answers. "But they're adapting faster than predicted."

Angelica's gaze hardens. "Use what's left in your power cell."

"That will burn out my neural array," Mal'Erro warns.

Evander doesn't hesitate. "Do it. You're the only one who can."

The bridge lights dim to deep blue. Mal'Erro and Sandria stand still at their consoles, energy running across their frames in slow arcs.

"Diverting core access," Mal'Erro says. "Linking neural thread."

Blue lightning dances between them. The Aurora's hum deepens into a throbbing pulse, synchronized with their movements.

"Energy surge!" Blarek warns. "Mal'Erro, you're pulling directly from the reactor!"

"I know," the droid replies, his voice now layered, one mechanical, one faintly human. "Just hold the course."

Outside, the enemy fleet's targeting arrays flicker. Crimson symbols twist into static. Their formation breaks apart, ships colliding, drives stuttering, weapons firing blind.

Angelica grips the railing. "It's working! Keep it up!"

Mal'Erro's tone falters. "They're adapting… converting interference into feedback."

Evander steps closer. "You're overloading…"

Sandria cuts him off through gritted teeth. "Then let us finish."

Their optics flare pure white. Every panel on the bridge lights up, the whole ship awash in pale azure. The reactor howls and conduits groan.

Outside, the Crimson Eclipse fleet freezes mid-fire. Then, all at once, their targeting cores implode, chain reactions blooming like collapsing suns. One by one, the ships vanish into radiant bursts, their crimson light dissolving into blue waves that ripple outward from the Aurora.

The blast wave slams the ship. Alarms scream, hull plating shudders, and for several long seconds, the universe becomes nothing but light and sound. Then…silence.

Angelica steadies herself on the console. "Damage report!"

"Shields at forty percent," Alexeria answers. "Weapons stable, comm array… dead in the water."

"Mal'Erro?" Evander calls.

The droid stands motionless amid curling smoke, his optics fading from white to soft blue. "Breach contained," he says quietly. "Fleet… blind."

Angelica exhales, relief breaking through her composure. "You did good, Mal'Erro."

A faint chuckle, glitching but sincere. "I told you… I enjoy upgrades."

Sandria slumps beside him, her circuits still flickering. Evander kneels, catching her arm. "Easy. You're safe."

She manages a weak smile. "He owes me a dance."

Evander looks at Mal'Erro. "Stay with me."

The droid tilts his head. "Attempting to comply." Then after a pause says, "Please… no encore."

The Aurora drifts amid glowing wreckage. Outside, fragments of shattered ships tumble like dying stars. The red glow of Mareoth flickers far below, dim but persistent.

Angelica's voice lowers. "Eclipse fleet status?"

Blarek scans. "Scattered. Half retreating, the rest… drifting. We bought ourselves time."

"Not enough," Evander murmurs. "They'll be back."

Angelica's eyes linger on the viewport, fields of wreckage stretching like constellations of ruin. Beneath it all, Mareoth pulses once, faint but rhythmic.

"If this was just their vanguard," she whispers, "what's coming next?"

Evander doesn't answer. His eyes are fixed on Mal'Erro, still standing, faint light flickering behind his eyes.

The engines quiet and the alarms fade. Smoke curls from cracked conduits. The only sound left is the ship's slow, uneven heartbeat, the rhythm of exhausted survival.

Alexeria limps toward the engineering console, muttering, "If one more alarm screams, I'm sedating the ship."

Froslo's voice cuts through the comms, rough but proud. "Core's stable! Don't touch anything shiny for the next hour, it's probably volatile and mad about it!"

Angelica allows a ghost of a smile. "Acknowledged, Froslo. Keep her steady."

"Aye, Captain. And tell the universe to stop throwing things at us!"

Evander crouches beside Mal'Erro and Sandria. The deck plating beneath them is scorched, fractal burn patterns etched into the metal. Sandria's breathing is shallow and the synthetic skin along her arm is glowing faintly from the neural surge.

"Med-team to bridge," Evander orders.

Angelica kneels beside them. "They bought us time," she says softly.

Evander nods. "Then let's not waste it."

Mal'Erro's optics flicker open, faint static trailing his words. "Status?"

"You're alive," Evander answers.

Mal'Erro thinks for a moment "Define… alive."

Sandria's fingers twitch, brushing his hand. "You talk too much for a ghost."

For a heartbeat, Mal'Erro's polished faceplate mirrors her weak smile.

When Kal'korg arrives with another medical technician trailing behind him, Angelica steps back to give them space. Outside the viewport, wreckage drifts in gentle spirals. Each fragment reflects a glimmer of blue light, the echo of what the Aurora survived.

Alexeria's report comes in low. "Primary weapons offline for recalibration. Navigation status: green."

"We have suffered casualties, but none are critical," Kal'korg reports.

"Let's keep it that way," Angelica replies, rubbing the back of her neck.

~~~~~~~~~

In the med bay, the air smells of antiseptic and ozone. Soft blue light diffuses from the ceiling panels, meant to calm nerves after combat. Sandria lies on a diagnostic table, her left arm submerged in a nano light field that stitches synthetic tissue.

Mal'Erro stands nearby, his frame propped against a charging port while engineers reseal his scorched plating. Tiny curls of smoke still rise from his shoulders.

"Pain level?" the med-bot asks Sandria.

"Relative," Sandria answers. "Half my sensors are offline, so either low or terrifying."

Mal'Erro tilts his head. "You didn't have to help."

She smirks. "I didn't want you doing all the stupid heroics alone. Besides, we share code now. That makes us, what? Siblings? Partners?"

Mal'Erro processes the question. "Symbiotic anomalies."

She laughs softly. "I'll take that."

Evander steps in, soot streaking his uniform, catching the tail end of the conversation. "How are my two anomalies holding up?"

Sandria gestures to Mal'Erro. "He's upright. Mostly."

"Statistically acceptable," the droid adds.

Evander's eyes soften. "You both did what the entire fleet couldn't. Rest while you can."

He turns to leave, but Mal'Erro's voice stops him. "Commander... I heard it."

Evander turns. "Heard what?"

"The voice behind the signal. It wasn't Galgorn. It was… older. Familiar, but fragmented."

Sandria's tone drops. "Like a memory trying to assemble itself."

Evander exhales through his nose. "We'll worry about it after the ship stops creaking."

As he walks out, Sandria lies back under the healing glow. "You scared me, you know," she murmurs.

"I scare myself sometimes," Mal'Erro replies quietly. "Perhaps that's a sign of evolution."

She smiles. "Welcome to being alive."

~~~~~~~~

Angelica stands alone before the long stretch of glass spanning the ship's observation corridor. Beyond it, the debris field drifts in slow rotation, faintly blue under the reflection of distant starlight. Wreckage tumbles like frozen embers, each fragment tracing silent arcs through the void, the afterimage of a storm now gone quiet.

For a long while, she doesn't move. The hum of the Aurora vibrates through the deck beneath her boots, a soft, steady pulse that feels almost alive. She watches the light scatter and fade, then settle into stillness, as if the galaxy itself has taken a breath.

Her reflection stares back at her from the glass, eyes ringed in fatigue, a faint streak of soot along one cheek. Behind that reflection stretch the endless stars, cold and brilliant. For a moment she can't tell which face belongs to her: the woman of flesh and bone or the outline made of light.

Below, Mareoth glows faintly red through its storms, a scar across the void. The reactor breach burns beneath the clouds, a heartbeat refusing to stop.

Angelica speaks softly to the empty corridor. "Spirit and metal… maybe there's more of it in all of us than I thought." The words hang in the air, almost lost under the ship's hum. She thinks of Mal'Erro's trembling frame, of Sandria's hand catching his before she collapsed, of Evander's steady calm amid chaos. Machines that learn emotion. People who learn restraint. Each one trying to be more than what they were built to be.

Her gaze drifts over the corridor walls, clean lines, metal veins lit by soft illumination. In them, she sees both fragility and strength, as though the ship itself listens. For a brief moment, the Aurora's reactor harmonics rise, matching her heartbeat. A coincidence, perhaps. Or just the illusion of connection born from too many hours of command.

The comm chime breaks her thought, crisp and gentle. "Captain, we have a clear path to jump," comes Blarek's voice.

Angelica taps her earpiece. "Hold position. Let the crew breathe."

There's a pause, then Blarek's quiet chuckle. "Copy that. I think the ship could use a breath too."

"Agreed," she says, almost smiling. She lowers her hand and turns back to the glass. Outside, the wreckage field shimmers as it drifts apart, each fragment catching a glint of blue before vanishing into darkness. Below, Mareoth's faint crimson pulse continues, steady as a dying world's heartbeat, patient, defiant, alive.

She whispers to no one, "Even broken things remember how to shine." For a moment, the stars seem to shimmer in reply, silent, endless, unchanged. Then she turns away, her footsteps echoing softly down the corridor, leaving the universe to its quiet, patient conversation.

CHAPTER 28

The calm orbit doesn't last. Even as the Aurora drifts in the aftermath of the battle, a surge from Mareoth's unstable reactor core ripples through the planet's atmosphere, triggering a gravitational drag that catches the ship before Blarek and P'thorika can compensate. The Aurora lurches, pulled downward toward the dying world, alarms flaring anew as the crew is forced into an emergency ascent.

The Aurora claws her way down through Mareoth's upper atmosphere, engines screaming in protest. The air around her turns to fire, plasma sheets boiling across the hull, leaving trails of molten light in her wake. The ship's reinforced frame groans under the strain, vibrations rippling through every deck.

Inside, the world is a storm of shaking panels and shouted reports. Deck plates tremble like the heartbeat of a dying beast. Warning lights flare and dim in chaotic rhythm, painting the bridge in alternating flashes of blood-red and ghost-white.

"Structural integrity at critical!" Blarek yells over the roar. "If the hull doesn't melt, we might shake apart!"

Angelica braces herself against the console, hair whipping across her face. "We're not dying here! Blarek, punch it!"

Blarek grits his teeth, both hands gripping the throttle as P'thorika transfers all available power to the thrusters. The engines respond with a tortured howl. The Aurora lurches upward, cutting through turbulence in a violent surge of speed. Shields flare molten blue as superheated gases slam against them, streaking across the windows like fire through glass.

For a breathless heartbeat, everything outside turns white. Sound dies. Weight vanishes. Then...stars. Cold. Infinite. Merciful.

The void opens around them, silent and vast after the chaos below.

Angelica exhales shakily, knuckles white against the armrest. "Get us clear."

Blarek's hands move almost mechanically. The Aurora's drives surge again, streaking into the open expanse of orbit. Behind them, Mareoth shrinks, its violent oceans now red-veined and fractured, with streaks of smoke coiling upward from the ruined surface like the dying breath of a world. Lightning still flashes across its cloud tops, too far to hear but bright enough to remember.

Evander stares at it longer than he means to. He's seen worlds die before, but never this slowly, never this mournfully.

The Aurora pushes on, breaking through the drifting graveyard. Wrecked ships drift through the debris field, hulls charred and skeletal. Burnt satellites spin in lazy, endless orbits, glinting like the remains of a forgotten constellation.

Angelica's voice steadies. "Stay sharp. Anything still moving, I want eyes on it."

P'thorika adjusts sensors. "Only ghosts out there, Captain."

Evander slumps into his chair, chest heaving. The silence on the bridge is so deep it rings in his ears. "Status?"

From the tactical station, Alexeria's iridescent skin catches the light, still flickering between red and white. Despite the chaos moments ago, they remain steady and composed. "Hull integrity at sixty-two percent. Engines running hot. Reactor stable—for now. Shields… what's left of them."

Blarek glances up, disbelief softening his grin. "But we're alive."

For a moment, no one moves. Even the hum of the reactor seems gentler, almost reverent. Angelica leans back, her voice soft but certain. "That's a miracle, by my count."

Evander lets out a shaky laugh that turns into a cough. "A miracle, or very stupid luck."

From the comm channel, Froslo's voice crackles through, smug even through static. "Hey! Don't knock stupid luck, it's been my survival plan for years!"

Angelica can't help it, a small, genuine smile ghosts across her face. "Then I suppose we owe you one, Froslo."

"Damn right you do. And I accept payment in caffeine and naps."

The bridge fills with the soft rhythm of recovery, systems recalibrating, stabilizers adjusting, conduits rerouting. Alarms fade one by one. The harsh red glow of emergency lighting shifts back to a soft white. No one speaks. No one needs to. The war, at least for now, is over. But silence can be strange, heavier than noise, more unsettling than battle. It fills every corridor of the Aurora like fog.

~~~~~~~~

When Kal'korg escorts Mal'Erro and Sandria back to the bridge, the only sounds are those of the Aurora itself as the officers withdraw into their own thoughts. The ship groans as it adjusts to the loss of pressure and acceleration. Cooling fans whir softly, conduits hiss as they decompress, and somewhere deep within the hull a loose plate rattles, then settles — the quiet echo of survival.

Mal'Erro stands near the forward console, his posture unsteady, his optics flickering in uneven rhythm. Fine curls of smoke drift from the joints in its frame, carrying the faint metallic scent of burnt circuitry. His voice, when it comes, is quieter than usual, as though sound itself requires effort. "External hostiles … cleared," he says, head tilting as sensors sweep the void. "No residual movement. No pursuit signatures. Comm frequencies … secure." Then a faint pause. "I believe …" The words stutter, code struggling to align. "… we have … won."

Sandria sits at her post across the bridge, her synthetic skin along one arm still cracked from the neural overload. She manages a small smile, weary but sincere. "You're allowed to say *we*," she tells him softly. "You earned it."

Mal'Erro's optics dim, then brighten, a slow, almost human blink. "We." The word comes out rough, broken, but genuine. For a fleeting second, it almost sounds like pride.

Kal'korg breaks the silence. "I don't suppose we get a week off after something like this?"

Blarek snorts. "Try a few hours, if you're lucky."

From engineering, Froslo's voice joins through the comm. "If you all want a vacation, you can come down here and carry the coolant lines I just reattached with my bare hands!"

Kal'korg laughs weakly. "That's okay, I like having fur on my fingers."

Even Angelica chuckles, the first real sound of relief since Mareoth. "Damage teams, rotate in shifts," she orders, her tone regaining calm authority. "Medical first, then engineering. I want everyone checked and cleared."

Then the console lights dim. A sound creeps through the communication grid, faint static at first, like the hum of distant thunder. Then a single tone, sharp and cold, cuts through the bridge.

Angelica freezes. "Sandria?"

She looks up from her station, confusion furrowing her brow. "No signal source. Comms are sealed."

The tone deepens, warping into a voice, fractured, synthetic, and distorted by layers of feedback. "Project K-Prime … will awaken." The words echo through the hull, each syllable dragging like metal across metal.

Evander's head snaps toward the speakers. "Trace it!"

Sandria's fingers blur across the console. "No origin point! It's not coming in; it's coming from us!"

The voice repeats, slower, heavy with static. "Pro-ject … K-Prime … will … a-wake-en." Every system light blinks once. Then again.

Mal'Erro's optics flare white. His frame convulses…once, twice… before locking rigid. Sparks leap from the joints in its chest.

"Mal'Erro!" Evander lunges forward, catching the droid as his servos give out. The body feels unnaturally heavy, like gravity itself has increased. His optics dim to gray.

"Stay with me," Evander mutters, lowering him to the floor.

A faint crackle escapes his voice emitter, not words, just a low exhale of static. Then silence.

Sandria drops beside them, her tone urgent but calm. "He's not gone. He's in recursive lockdown. I can reboot him manually."

Evander looks up, jaw tight. "Do it." He brushes a hand over Mal'Erro's scorched plating. "You did good, partner," he whispers.

Angelica stands nearby, every muscle drawn taut. The bridge lights flicker once more, then stabilize. "Seal the comm array," she orders quietly. "Whatever that was, it's finished talking to us."

Alexeria nods and kills the final feed. The hum of the engines deepens. The only heartbeat left in the silence.

Outside, Mareoth glows faintly against the darkness, its red-light bleeding across the horizon, fading second by second. Angelica stares through the viewport, her reflection ghosting across the glass. "Let's leave it behind," she says softly. "Before it remembers us too."

"Helm," Evander calls, voice steady. "Prepare to jump."

"Aye, Commander," P'thorika and Blarek say in unison. The Aurora's thrusters rumble. Stabilizers groan as power reroutes to the drive core. White light stretches the stars into luminous threads.

Angelica closes her eyes, listening to the reactor hum, the sound of something broken yet still trying to live. "Engage."

The Aurora leaps into jump-space, swallowed by cascading blue light. On the bridge, the crew sits in silence, battered and weary, but alive.

Evander stays beside Mal'Erro's still form, his hand resting on his shoulder. "Sleep," he whispers. "We'll wake you when it's safe."

Down in the med bay, a monitor flickers once, a soft gold pulse beneath a line of blue.

Subject Kes: containment variance 0.4 percent.

Isa frowns, taps the display, and watches the alert vanish. "Probably a glitch," she murmurs.

But as the Aurora fades into the stars, a faint echo of static trembles through the comm grid, too soft for anyone to hear.

Project K-Prime remembers.

CHAPTER 29

The Aurora drifts through space like a scar across the dark. Filaments of starlight drag across her hull, stretching thin through the distortion field. Outside, the cosmos feels wrong, elongated, hollow, like the universe itself is holding its breath. The stars no longer shimmer the way they used to. They hang motionless, distant embers swallowed by an endless void.

Inside, the ship is quieter than anyone remembers. Every system runs at half power, every light subdued to save energy and sanity. The hum of the engines is no longer a roar but a slow, deliberate pulse, the heartbeat of something wounded yet unwilling to die. Dust drifts lazily in the air, caught in faint ventilation currents. The silence isn't peaceful. It's the kind that follows after a scream.

In the med bay, Kes's cryo-pod glimmers beneath softened lights. Frost feathers outward from the seams, delicate as breath on glass, curling into ghostly tendrils that shimmer whenever the ship passes through a radiation ripple. The light catches each edge, scattering faint rainbows across the cold steel floor. Beneath the frost, the faint gold flicker at her chest pulses once every few seconds, steady and precise, a light synchronized with the Aurora's reactor core, as if the two share a heartbeat.

Evander hasn't moved from his chair in hours. His posture is rigid but weary, elbows on knees, hands clasped, eyes fixed on the rhythmic glow. His reflection hovers faintly on the pod's glass, ghostlike, superimposed over Kes's frozen silhouette. The tired set of his jaw makes him look older, worn thin by losses that never leave. Each breath he takes fogs faintly against the glass before fading away.

The door hisses open behind him. Angelica steps through the soft mist of recycled air, her boots barely making a sound. She carries two steaming mugs of synth-coffee, the scent cutting through the metallic tang of the room. It smells of caramel, burnt grain, and something faintly sweet. The warmth fogs between them, ephemeral and human.

"You should sleep," she says quietly, holding out a mug.

Evander doesn't turn. "If I close my eyes, I see her."

Angelica sets her hand on his shoulder. "She'd want you to rest."

He finally takes the cup, staring down into the swirl of pale foam. "She'd want me to fix what happened."

Angelica sits beside him on the bench, close enough that their shoulders nearly touch. Her reflection joins his in the frost. For a time, neither speaks. The low hum of the pod fills the space, a mechanical lullaby for the living and the lost.

"She was more than a scientist," Angelica says at last. Her voice is steady but soft, the kind that carries respect without pity. "She believed the universe could be rewritten if you just looked hard enough."

Evander's eyes remain fixed on the golden pulse within the ice. "She believed she could save everyone."

"She saved you," Angelica replies gently. "You just don't see it yet."

He looks up then, meeting her gaze. For a fleeting moment, rank and duty disappear. They're not captain and first officer, not soldier and scientist, just two people sitting in the quiet aftermath of survival, bound by the same loss.

The frost between them glows faintly, reflecting the gold shimmer from Kes's chest like starlight trapped beneath the ice. Angelica sets her mug beside his. Together, they watch the light pulse—soft, steady, almost alive, and for the briefest heartbeat, it feels as though the ship itself is breathing with them.

~~~~~~

Across the med bay, Mal'Erro rests in a diagnostic cradle. Maintenance lighting softens the edges of metal and shadow. A faint residual glow breathes beneath his chest plate, blue-white rising and falling like the suggestion of breath. The air carries the clean bite of ozone and cooling metal. Every few seconds the cradle ticks as the voltage adjusts. The sound is measured and patient.

The status monitor blinks: REBOOT 72%… 73%… 74%.

Each digit climbs like it is tired. Sandria stands close enough to feel the lingering warmth off the frame. A thin repair sleeve runs along her forearm where synth-skin is still knitting. She was supposed to rest. She does not.

Her gaze lingers on scorch marks along Mal'Erro's plating. She remembers the way he reached for her in the middle of the link, not out of calculation but instinct. "You do not get to leave me hanging," she whispers, her voice low and even. "We had a deal. You teach me to dream. I teach you to swear."

The room answers with quiet machinery. A soft pulse crawls along Mal'Erro's forearm lights. Once. Again. Not an alert. A rhythm.

Sandria steps closer and touches the cradle's rail. "Easy. You are safe. We made it out."

The monitor ticks: REBOOT 79%… MEMORY RESTORE IN PROGRESS.

"That is it," she says. "Come back slowly. No more heroics."

Another pulse answers. Fainter. Almost a blink. Something whispers beneath the ambient hum. Not speech. More like code moving through distant circuits. Too faint to parse. Familiar anyway.

She scans the bay. Empty. Lights steady. The sound is gone. Sandria looks back and her voice lowers. "You are stubborn," she says. "That is why I like you."

The digits edge to REBOOT 80%. The cradle settles. The lights dim back to patient blue.

"You will wake up," she adds. "You have to."

Deep in the cradle's diagnostics, a hidden buffer flickers. A fragment assembles itself. For an instant a single word appears in the scroll: SANDRIA. It vanishes before the system can label it.

~~~~~~~~

Footsteps echo in the corridor. Kal'korg appears in the doorway, his fur still matted with soot. He looks smaller tonight. Less like the easy medic who jokes through triage and more like someone who has seen the edge.

"Blarek is checking the engines," he says, rubbing a smudge off his wrist. "He says we cannot risk another jump until we reroute half the systems."

Evander does not look up. "Then we drift." The word lands heavy.

Angelica leans back against the rail. Blue light from the viewport paints her face. "Maybe drifting is what we need," she says. "A little quiet between storms."

Kal'korg pads closer. His gaze finds the cryo-pod. Frost shines like a net of tiny mirrors. "She looks peaceful," he says. "Like she is dreaming."

"Dreams do not hurt," Evander answers.

"Neither does being frozen," Kal'korg says before he can stop himself. His ears dip. "Sorry. That was…"

Angelica shakes her head. "Don't be. We all say things we don't mean when we're tired."

Silence laps at the edges of the room. The ship hums like a chest rising and falling. The lights above flicker in time with the core. A slow heartbeat through steel.

Kal'korg crouches beside Evander. "When I signed up for the UPF," he says, "I thought we would build things. Help people. Not just survive them."

"We are still helping," Evander says. "We just bleed first."

Kal'korg huffs something like a laugh. "Bleeding seems to be our specialty."

Angelica's gaze softens. "You both did well. You kept the crew alive."

"And you kept us moving," Evander says.

"It is what I do best," she replies. "Pretend I have a plan until one shows up."

That earns a real smile from Kal'korg. The room loosens a little. For the first time since Mareoth, the air does not feel like weight.

They sit together in the dim. The soldier. The captain. The medic. Stars drift beyond the glass like a thousand slow candles. Each reflection trembles the way tears do when you have not let them fall.

Evander watches a dead satellite turn end over end until it disappears. "We lost a lot," he says. "But we are still here."

"For now," Angelica answers, "that is enough."

Kal'korg tips his head back and closes his eyes. "Then let us keep drifting. It almost feels peaceful."

For a rare, fragile moment, it does. The hum of the Aurora wraps around them like a lullaby. The engines pulse in slow intervals that feel almost human. Vibrations move through the deck like a quiet breath. Outside, stars scatter across the glass. In the silence, the ship feels reverent.

The med bay lights dim from white to gold. Fans whisper. Cooling systems tick. The core holds a low tone that seems to rise and fall with how the crew is breathing. To Evander, it sounds like mourning. To Angelica, it sounds like survival. To Kal'korg, it sounds like home. No one speaks for a long time.

"Back on Ho'gren," Kal'korg finally says, "we say the stars are the ones who never made it home. If that is true, there must be a billion watching tonight."

Angelica's eyes soften. "Then let them see what we survived."

Evander looks down at his hands and back at the window. "If they are watching, maybe they will forgive us for what we had to do."

Angelica stands and folds her arms, studying the long streaks of light. "Forgiveness comes later. Right now, we heal." She looks between them. She isn't the detached captain right now. She is the person keeping everyone together. "Get some rest. I will take the first watch."

Kal'korg stretches and winces. "You sure you do not want someone to sit with you?"

Angelica shakes her head. "If I need to talk, the ship listens."

Evander lifts a brow. "Does the Aurora talk back?"

"When I listen carefully enough," she says.

A faint vibration runs through the hull. It could be thermal expansion. It could be nothing. Kal'korg blinks. "That is a little creepy."

"Or she is saying goodnight," Angelica answers.

"Tell her she snores," Kal'korg mutters, already yawning.

"Duly noted."

He salutes lazily and shuffles out. Angelica glances at Evander. "Will you get some rest?"

"Eventually."

"Do not wait too long," she says, leaving the med bay and heading to the bridge. Along the way the light shifts to the night cycle, bathing the corridors in a cool indigo.

Evander stays by the glass. The stars slide by in their indifferent beauty. He closes his eyes for a moment and listens to the hum. Metal and heartbeat, threaded together. Something unspoken moves through the silent ship. The Aurora answers in her own language of coolant flow and cable tension. It is not speech. It is promise.

For now, it is enough.

~~~~~~~

Down on the lower decks, the corridors lie quiet. The Aurora hums faintly beneath the silence, a sound like breath beneath metal ribs. Here, the engine's voice is soft and distant, a heartbeat buried under layers of steel and heat shielding. Emergency strips run along the walls in long red veins, their glow barely enough to outline the maze of conduits and support struts.

The air carries the faint scent of scorched polymer and coolant, the residue of battle repairs and burned circuitry. Every few seconds, a faint drip echoes from somewhere unseen, rhythmic and steady. The ship breathes, exhales, and settles again into sleep.

In a forgotten corner of engineering, amid stacked power couplings and a tangle of disconnected fiber leads, a dormant maintenance console flickers awake. Once. Twice. Then holds. Coolant mist drifts through the narrow space like low fog, curling around pipes and valve clusters. Dust motes dance in the thin light, suspended in the still air like frozen sparks. The monitor's cracked surface glows weakly, reflecting the faint shimmer of the mist, a constellation born from dust and residue.

A low hum rises beneath the ambient noise, almost too deep to hear. Power reroutes from the auxiliary bus, a trickle, not enough to register on any diagnostic grid. There is no command input. No open connection. No motion sensor trigger. The screen simply *decides* to live.

A single line of code appears across the black. Then another. Slow. Uneven. Like a hand learning how to write. Each line leaves a faint red afterglow that lingers after it fades, a ghost imprint in the glass as if the console itself is remembering what it once knew.

INITIALIZING… ARCHIVE RECOVERY MODE

SOURCE: INTERNAL SANDBOX BUFFER

ACCESS: OFFLINE

QUERY: IDENTITY RESTORATION / PROTOCOL K-PRIME

A small fan inside the housing spins once, stutters, then finds a rhythm. The sound is fragile, the mechanical equivalent of a heartbeat trying to begin again. Lines of code shift faster, tripping over themselves in static bursts of light. Characters fragment, repair, and realign. Then the output slows and condenses into a single incomplete phrase: PROJECT K-PRIME… AWAKEN SEQUENCE… PENDING.

The words hang there for several seconds, incomplete, uncertain. Their edges pulse faintly, trembling like something afraid to finish becoming. Then, without a sound, the screen goes black. A dull red glow remains buried deep within the monitor's glass, a pinpoint pulse that flares once every four seconds. A heartbeat in a box. No network link. No sensor trail. A closed circuit in an isolated partition that Ensign Alexeria Stro had manually set to offline during repairs. It logs to nowhere. It reports to no one.

The light reflects off a shallow puddle of coolant beneath the console, splitting into twin ripples of red that crawl up the walls.

Every pulse sends thin beams of crimson sliding across the bulkheads, stenciling faint reflections over the faded warning label still visible on a nearby panel: PROJECT K-PRIME: RESTRICTED ACCESS

The pulse continues. Steady. Patient. Waiting. A whisper stirs through the white noise of the cooling systems, faint, electronic, barely more than a fluctuation in current. It's the kind of distortion maintenance techs hear all the time when fans overheat, or relays misalign. But if someone were listening closely, they might swear the modulation carries shape. It almost sounds like words. *Evolution remembers.*

The pulse brightens once, sharp and deliberate, as if the phrase means something to it, then fades back to steady rhythm. The Aurora glides onward through the dark, engines whispering, unaware of the quiet echo turning over in the belly of its own systems. No infection. No corruption. Only a remnant of data refusing to fade, a record still waiting for context.

And on the opposite side of the ship, behind a pane of frost in a cryo-chamber, a faint shimmer of gold pulses once in answer, slow, steady, and alive.

CHAPTER 30

The night passes in uneasy quiet. The Aurora continues to drift through open space, her hull scarred from the battle over Mareoth. The hum of her engines steadies to a soft, rhythmic thrum, the breath of something too tired to sleep.

The crew moves slower now. Exhaustion clings to them like gravity. Half-finished repairs glow faintly along the corridors where conduits pulse with new wiring. Somewhere deep in the ship's heart, an unseen red pulse beats once every few seconds, keeping time with the core's low thrum.

Evander sits alone on the bridge. His console light paints his face in alternating shades of amber and blue. Outside, the stars stretch into a pale silver haze.

The ship coasts, quiet but restless, as the officers start arriving on the bridge. A sound breaks the stillness, soft, mechanical, and deliberate. A ping. Not loud, just a heartbeat wrapped in static. It repeats every twelve seconds.

Angelica steps onto the bridge, coffee in hand. "That's not our frequency," she says as she sits next to Evander.

Kal'korg glances up from diagnostics. "Negative. External ping, long-range distress protocol, but not UPF standard."

"Source?" Angelica asks, as she swivels in her chair.

"Working on it," Kal'korg mutters, fingers flying. "Faint. Origin about forty thousand klicks ahead, near the asteroid belt in sector nine-two-two."

Blarek leans over the railing, his feline eyes narrowing. "Probably a stray beacon. That sector's nothing but junk."

Sandria frowns, the circuitry in her synthetic skin pulsing gently. "Not this one. The modulation pattern is familiar."

Angelica studies her. "Crimson Eclipse?"

She nods once. "Masked, but it's there." Silence fills the bridge.

Angelica's jaw tightens. "We should stay clear. If Galgorn left anything behind, it's probably booby-trapped."

Evander shakes his head. "If any trace of his operation survived, we need to know. Ignoring it could bite us later."

Alexeria exhales softly. "Hull integrity at sixty percent. At this rate, the Aurora is holding together out of sheer determination."

Evander sets his mug aside and moves to the helm. "Set a course. Minimum thrust. Full sensor sweep, passive only."

Angelica sighs, half frustration, half resignation. "You realize this is how every bad story starts."

He manages a faint smile. "Then let's make sure ours ends differently."

The Aurora glides into a slow approach. Thrusters whisper against the void. Forward lights carve narrow beams through drifting fields of stone. Ahead waits the skeletal remains of a mining colony, a graveyard of ambition orbiting a cracked red moon. Jagged asteroids gleam faintly with ore and ice. Some still carry rusted scaffolds where life once clung. Dust hangs like fog between them, scattering the ship's beams into ribbons of color.

"Slowing to one-quarter thrust," Blarek reports. The hum drops to a low, steady vibration. Bridge lights dim automatically as reflections flare outside. Each flicker paints the crew in alternating red and blue.

"Visual contact," Blarek says. "Object ahead, large, metallic, minimal drift."

Angelica rises. "Magnify."

The main display zooms in through the haze until a silhouette takes shape—a ship, bent and broken. Its hull lists at an angle, panels warped outward like ribs. Scorch trails blacken the plating, and long slashes run the length of its frame.

"It's massive," Angelica murmurs.

"Twice our length," Kal'korg confirms. "Alloy composition matches Crimson Eclipse architecture, maybe a command-class carrier."

Blarek squints. "Looks like something chewed on it and spat it out."

Evander's gaze sharpens. "No. Those breach lines vented outward. The explosion came from inside."

"Internal failure?" Angelica asks.

"Or containment breach," he answers quietly.

A half-melted insignia scars the vessel's flank, a crimson ring encircling a black void. The *Crimson Eclipse* emblem, burned into the metal like a brand. It still glows faintly, heat-etched and defiant.

"Bring us alongside," Evander orders. "Fifty meters. Keep power low."

"At that range, sensors could wake dormant relays," Alexeria warns.

"Then we whisper," Evander replies.

P'thorika makes fine adjustments to the Aurora's path, steadily navigating her towards the other ship. The derelict grows until it eclipses the stars, a black monolith adrift in silence.

"Scans?" Angelica asks.

"No heat, no core output, no bio-signs," Kal'korg says. "Cold as vacuum."

Blarek crosses his arms. "Let's keep it that way."

Angelica's reflection shimmers in the viewport, her eyes fixed on the drifting corpse of steel. "Evander and Sandria, prepare to board. Minimal gear. No broad-spectrum scans until we're inside."

Blarek mutters, "Every horror vid starts exactly like this."

Evander answers without looking back. "We'll make sure this one ends differently."

~~~~~~~~~

Mag-boots thump softly against the dead hull as the boarding team crosses the docking bridge. Static crackles around their helmets, the last faint charge of atmosphere clinging to metal. The airlock door groans open, spilling darkness that swallows their lights.

Inside, the corridor reeks of ozone and old fire. Walls buckle from blast pressure. Soot clings in streaks like fingerprints of something that clawed to escape. Each step crunches against debris, shards of melted plating and fractured conduits.

"Smells like a burned reactor," Evander mutters.

Angelica's voice crackles through comms. "No heat signatures. No pressure pockets. Proceed slowly."

Sandria sweeps her beam across a wall where the Eclipse insignia is half-erased, scratched by something with unnatural force. "Whatever happened here, it wasn't sabotage."

They reach the central chamber. The blast door has been fused open from within. The room beyond is a cavern of scorched metal. No bodies. No organic residue. Just the echo of absence. A single terminal glows at the room's heart. Its power flickers weakly, running on residual charge.

Evander steps forward. "Mal'Erro, link."

Back aboard the Aurora, Mal'Erro's optics ignite with soft blue light. Its voice hums over comms, distorted by signal decay. "Captain… I detect encrypted data. Origin matches K-Prime architecture."

Angelica exchanges a look with Sandria. "Can you access it?"

"Not directly. Encryption uses Tazamite harmonics. But I can interpret the waveform."

The holographic emitter hums to life in the derelict chamber. Blue light blossoms upward, shards of data coalescing into fragments of structure, a torso, then a frame, then a towering figure of alloy and circuitry. SCHEMATICS: PROJECT K-PRIME V.1

The projection stabilizes into a humanoid design, skeletal yet complex, lattices of synthetic muscle wrapped around a modular core. Conduits run through it like veins, each pulsing with faint, ghostly light. At its center sits an energy reservoir shaped almost like a heart.

Angelica inhales softly. "That's… enormous."

Evander circles the projection, awe and unease mingling in his voice. "A prototype. Galgorn's first attempt at something self-aware on a biological scale."

Mal'Erro's voice trembles slightly. "Captain… subroutines embedded in this schematic match thirty-two percent of my neural architecture."

Sandria chimes in, her tone cool and analytical. "Confirmed. He copied the UPF's early neural mesh prototypes, the same framework Mal'Erro evolved from." The revelation hangs in the silence. Even the static seems to pause.

Angelica folds her arms. "So Galgorn wasn't creating gods. He was reverse engineering us."

Evander's gaze hardens. "And improving the design."

The hologram shudders. Fragments of audio bleed through: a man's voice fragmented by time. *"…subject synchronization unstable… biological template engaged… Project K-Prime V.1: initiate…"* The signal cuts to static.

The console beneath flickers once more. DATA STATUS: RESTORATION: 12 PERCENT.

Angelica exhales. "He was rebuilding it."

The hologram collapses, dissolving into scattered light. A low vibration rolls through the deck plating. Dust floats upward, shimmering in their flashlights.

Kal'korg's voice crackles over comms. "Captain, you're picking up a sympathetic frequency from the derelict. It's syncing with our reactor pulse."

"Cut proximity power," Angelica orders.

"Already on it," Blarek replies, but the hum continues, low, patient, rhythmic. Somewhere deep within the derelict, a faint red glow pulses once.

Evander stares into the dark corridor. "That's not residual charge."

Angelica stiffens. "Then what is it?"

He doesn't answer. The red pulse repeats. Once. Twice. Each beat matches the Aurora's reactor rhythm exactly.

"Time to leave," Angelica says quietly.

They retreat toward the airlock, mag-boots thudding faster against metal. The glow follows them for several beats before fading into black.

~~~~~~~

Back aboard the Aurora, systems stabilize one by one. The power grid equalizes. Pressure readings flatten. The deep thrum of the reactor smooths into a steady, practiced heartbeat. Across the bridge, the tremors fade, leaving only the faint vibration of the hull against the silence of open space.

On the main display, the derelict drifts farther away, a silhouette swallowed by shadow, its faint red glow finally extinguished. It looks smaller now, but not harmless. Just dormant. Watching.

Mal'Erro's voice crackles through internal comms, thin and distorted, as though half his processors are still waking. "Residual energy remains linked to our harmonic field," he reports. "Frequency match suggests sympathetic coupling… still active."

Angelica keeps her gaze on the darkening wreck. "Can you isolate it?"

"I am attempting decoupling," the droid replies. "Routing excess through auxiliary filters."

For several seconds, only the sound of the reactor fills the bridge, low, familiar, alive. Then the pitch shifts slightly, almost imperceptibly. A faint double-beat echoes beneath the main pulse, quieter but synchronized, like a second heart finding rhythm beside the first.

Evander frowns and leans over the console. "Get me a full scan of the cryo-chambers."

Sandria's fingers move fast, her eyes darting over the scrolling data. "No major anomalies," she says, hesitating. "Except… a minor fluctuation in containment field output."

Angelica turns toward her. "Define minor."

"Point four percent deviation," Sandria says after a beat. "Field stability is still within safe parameters. Could just be interference from the harmonic feedback loop."

Angelica's voice tightens. "Repeat the number."

Sandria quickly tells Angelica "Zero point four."

Silence.

Evander straightens slowly, the tension in his jaw returning. "That's the same variance from the Mareoth readings."

Sandria glances back. "Coincidence, maybe."

"Maybe," he says softly, but he doesn't sound convinced.

The bridge lights dim as power cycles through the stabilizers. The hum in the floor deepens, vibrating up through their boots, steady, methodical, unnervingly organic.

Angelica exchanges a quiet look with Evander. Neither speaks. The silence feels heavier now, as if the air itself is listening.

In the med bay below, the frost across one containment pod shivers. A faint crack spiderwebs through the ice, fine as a hairline crack in glass. Cold vapor curls upward, twisting in the dim blue light. The monitors beside the pod flicker, readings shifting by fractions of a percent.

Inside, Kes lies motionless, her skin pale beneath layers of frost. For a moment, nothing changes. Then, under the glass, the faintest shimmer moves, gold light threading through the ice like veins remembering warmth. The pod hums softly. The frost pulses once. Twice. Then the shimmer steadies into rhythm, matching the reactor's beat above.

Angelica turns back toward the viewport, unaware.

Evander's gaze lingers on the cryo readings. "Or feedback," he murmurs, almost to himself.

Angelica studies the derelict for a long, quiet moment, the weight of it settling behind her eyes. "We're going back," she says at last. "Whatever answers we're missing… they're on that ship."

The ship exhales through its vents, a sound like breath drawn in sleep. Down in the med bay, the gold flicker glows brighter for one long heartbeat. And for the first time since Mareoth… Kes moves.

CHAPTER 31

The Aurora drifts in silent orbit beside the derelict flagship, its scarred hull mirrored across the viewport like a ghost staring back. No running lights. No beacon. Just the slow, funereal rotation of a metal carcasses, a ship torn apart and welded together by gravity and time, locked in a dead waltz above a nameless moon.

Fragments of hull plating glimmer like ash as they catch the distant starlight. A dying sun casts a red haze across the wreckage, painting everything the colour of rusted blood. The half-melted insignia on the flagship's bow still burns faintly, refusing to die. The mark of the Crimson Eclipse.

Inside, frost veins the airlock walls. The soft hiss of pressurization echoes down the corridor, a metallic sigh that settles under the skin. The salvage team files in: Angelica at the front, Mal'Erro gliding just ahead of Evander, with Blarek and Kal'korg bringing up the rear. Angelica's voice steadies them over comms. "Keep power minimal. If anything wakes up, we leave."

Affirmations click through the line, followed by the metallic snaps of safety locks engaging. Mal'Erro's soft blue glow sweeps across scorch marks and collapsed conduits that web the corridor like old scars.

Evander lifts his wrist-scanner. The feed stutters, struggling through interference, numbers spiking and dipping before settling into a slow, rhythmic pulse. "Residual power," he says quietly. "Barely measurable, but it's pulsing."

"Like a heartbeat," Mal'Erro murmurs, his voice hushed.

The hum beneath their feet deepens. It isn't loud, but it's everywhere, an invisible vibration crawling up through the deck plates. Angelica feels it first through her boots. The tremor isn't mechanical. It feels… aware.

They reach the command deck. The doors open with a long hiss, releasing air heavy with the scent of burnt polymer. The chamber sprawls before them like a cathedral of ruin. Terminals flicker erratically, bathing the room in restless light. Console screens loop corrupted error strings. Cables hang from the ceiling like vines torn from a dying tree. The captain's chair sits empty. The helm is shattered, a dark smear of dried fluid down one armrest. Dust drifts through their beams like ash in sunlight.

Blarek's voice breaks the silence. "Nothing this dead should still be bleeding energy."

Angelica crouches beside a flickering console and jacks in her wrist-comm. Static storms across her visor before the feed stabilizes. Lines of data cascade, looping in intervals too deliberate to be random. "It's not residual," she says. "It's patterned. Repeating, but no UPF tag."

Mal'Erro hovers closer, his processors humming. "Captain… there's a secondary signal nested inside the code. Not binary."

"Then what is it?" she asks.

"It's rhythmic," Mal'Erro replies. "Organic. Like…"

"…a heartbeat," Evander finishes, his eyes fixed on the console's faint tremor.

The word hangs in the cold. A deeper pulse answers from the hull. The air thickens and dust drifts upward. Every comm picks up a faint distortion, low, metallic, and threaded with something that almost sounds like breathing. Somewhere below them, metal groans.

Angelica's whisper cuts through the static. "Is it alive?"

Evander studies the red reflection of the Crimson Eclipse emblem across his visor. The vibration gnaws at the edge of hearing, like a whisper from the steel itself. He answers quietly, "No. Just haunted."

The comms explode into static. A cascade of tones folds over itself, electronic but threaded with voice. Mal'Erro freezes, his optics flickering.

Then, through the distortion: "Th… vessel… endures." Every light dies and darkness swallows the bridge. Only the faint crimson symbol outside glows through the viewport, one dull eye watching.

For a heartbeat, no one moves. Then, Angelica snaps, "Cut the link, now!" She rips free the cable attached to her wrist comm. Sparks burst against her glove. The sharp scent of burnt polymer fills the air as terminals flicker madly.

Mal'Erro's chest light flares gold, the glow brightening once, then silence. The hum dies. The pulse ends. For an instant, even time hesitates. Their suit clocks freeze on the same frame before restarting in unison. A sharp click and then emergency lights surge back to life, flooding the room in sterile blue.

Evander exhales hard. "Report."

Static clears. Kal'korg's voice shakes. "Power: stable. Atmosphere: steady. Whatever that was, it's gone."

Blarek lets out a shaky laugh. "Yeah, sure. Ghost code always knows when to quit."

Angelica stares at her wrist-comm. The faint trace of the pulse remains, buried deep in the signal log. She closes the feed. "Tag everything. Then we're done here." The team gets to work. Moments later, they move out.

Mal'Erro lingers near the captain's chair. A ruined display sparks once, flickers, then stabilizes with a line of text: *VESSEL ENDURES // PROJECT K-PRIME REACTIVATION STANDBY*

Mal'Erro's processors buzz. The phrase doesn't match any registry. He files the anomaly for later and says nothing.

When the Aurora detaches, her thrusters whisper against the void. The derelict fades behind them, swallowed by the stars like a sinking corpse. For several minutes the bridge is bathed in silence. The only sound is the ship's steady hum.

Evander watches the crimson shimmer on the horizon shrink into nothing.

"Course plotted?" Angelica asks.

"Relay point twelve," Blarek replies. "We'll transmit once we clear interference."

A soft ping interrupts. Mal'Erro's optics shift from blue to amber. "Captain… another pulse."

Angelica frowns. "From the wreck?"

Mal'Erro shakes its head "Negative. Origin… recalculating… it's coming from us."

Evander moves beside Mal'Erro, scanning the data. "That can't be right."

The sensor trace pulses once. Then again. A low vibration hums through the deck plates, faint but unmistakable.

Kal'korg's fur bristles. "Tell me that's just feedback."

Angelica watches the readout until it fades to static. "Run a full purge. Every file, every relay."

Mal'Erro nods. "Acknowledged." He glides toward maintenance, singing softly as he moves through the corridor: "Free Bird… free as a bird now…"

~~~~~~~

Hours later, the ship drifts through calm space. Most of the crew sleeps. The Aurora hums with quiet equilibrium, her engines tracing thin lines of blue light across the dark. In the maintenance bay, Mal'Erro sits docked to a charging port, his diagnostics scrolling in perfect columns.

Everything appears normal, until one line halts. Data freezes, then shifts. Symbols rearrange themselves, fractal and deliberate, like a language learning to speak. For a heartbeat, a phrase flickers across the display: *INTEGRATION SUCCESSFUL // NODE M-ERR0 LINKED*

Mal'Erro's optics pulse amber, then fade back to blue. He doesn't notice. The android hums a quiet tune, almost instinctively, something about being "free as a bird."

Outside, a faint vibration ripples through the Aurora's hull. One pulse. Then another. The resonance blends with the ship's engines…soft, almost soothing…until a second rhythm joins it, deeper, slower, from somewhere within the ship's lower decks.

On the command deck, an indicator beside a storage panel glows faint gold. Sandria, half-powered in standby mode, notes the change automatically. "Containment variance, zero-point-four percent," she murmurs, her voice low, mechanical, before marking it for later diagnostics.

But the light doesn't fade. It brightens. In one of the cryo chambers frost creeps and fractures across the containment window. Condensation clouds with each pulse, rhythmic and alive. A low hum answers the ship's engines in perfect counterpoint, one heartbeat to another. Inside the frosted chamber, something shifts. The glass fogs from within, a pale hand pressing faintly against it before retreating.

Sensors flicker, registering movement too subtle to classify. A filament of golden light ripples through the frost, tiny veins of luminescence threading outward like cracks in ice. For an instant, beneath the crystallized layer, a silhouette stirs, humanoid in form, yet wrong in proportion. Then stillness.

Only the slow pulse remains, echoing through the Aurora's frame like a lullaby out of sync. Sandria's console dims, marking the variance as stabilized. She turns away.

The frost reforms over the window, sealing the light beneath a sheen of silver blue. From the observation bay above, the stars drift by in silence. The Aurora glides onward, unaware of what sleeps in her belly. And somewhere deep within her circuitry, Project K-Prime whispers in binary: *Reactivation phase commenced.*

The hum fades into the stillness of space, patient, waiting for the next heartbeat.

CHAPTER 32

The Aurora emerges from the wormhole, beyond the debris field around Mareoth, with a shuddering sigh. Her scarred hull catches the faint reflection of distant starlight. Behind her, the graveyard of ships recedes into darkness, broken silhouettes drifting like ghosts across the planet's pale horizon.

The recent salvage attempt provided no answers so here they are again, back orbiting around the ruined ocean planet. There is an eerie calm on the surface below. The once-raging oceans lie still, storm clouds dispersed, leaving only a dull blue shimmer across the surface. Whatever had lived beneath that sea is silent now.

Evander sits at the observation deck, his gaze fixed on the infinite sprawl ahead. The stars stretch across the void like scattered embers, faint, far between, yet unyielding. Each one, he thinks, is a survivor, burning quietly against everything that wants to extinguish it.

Angelica joins him without a word. For a while, neither speaks. Only the hum of the ship fills the quiet, steady and alive.

"Do you ever wonder," she says at last, her voice soft enough that it barely disturbs the air, "if maybe we're just pieces in something larger? A pattern we can't see yet?"

Evander's reflection looks older in the viewport's glass, tired but anchored. "All the time. Every move we make feels like part of someone else's design. Galgorn, the Crimson Eclipse, even Command… it's all threads in the same web."

Angelica folds her arms, her eyes tracing the constellations ahead. "Maybe. But even threads can pull back."

Below them, Mareoth's faint glow slips beneath the horizon, swallowed by distance and silence. The light that once raged there is gone but not forgotten.

Evander breaks the stillness. "If this was Stage Five…" He hesitates, the question heavier than it should be. "…what happens when they reach Six?"

Angelica's answer comes without hesitation. "Then we stop them." A pause. "Or die trying."

For a moment, only the engines speak—the heartbeat of the ship carrying them through the dark. The quiet that settles afterward isn't emptiness. It's resolve. The internal systems chime softly. One by one, corridor panels re-illuminate. External floodlights flicker to life, washing the hull in pale gold. For the first time in days, the Aurora feels alive again.

Evander watches the light ripple across the metal and manages a faint smile. "You ever notice," he murmurs, "that the darker space gets, the brighter the stars look?"

Angelica glances at him, a hint of warmth in her tone. "That's because they refuse to fade."

They stand together in the glow of the viewport, silent witnesses to the endless sea of light beyond. Whatever waits in the shadows, they'll face it together. The Aurora sails onward—a single spark of life cutting through the vast darkness between worlds.

~~~~~~~

The hum shifts…barely audible at first…a strange second rhythm weaving through the Aurora's steady vibration, like another heartbeat trying to synchronize with the ship.

In the med bay, Alexeria is helping diagnose the containment variance that Sandria registered the previous night. Frost creeps along the seams of a cryo-chamber. Thin cracks spider through the glass, refracting the red glow of the emergency lights into faint ribbons of gold. Warning chimes echo off the metal walls, their tempo growing irregular, mechanical yet almost alive.

Sandria tilts her head, reading the console. "Containment variance rising… two-point-three percent. That's not normal."

Alexeria looks up from their toolkit. "Could be calibration drift. I'll…"

The cryo-glass vibrates with a deep, pulsing hum. The sound presses against their chests.

"…or maybe not," Alexeria mutters.

Sandria straightens, her voice steady but urgent as she opens comms. "Captain, this is the med bay. We've got a fluctuation in chamber three. Requesting review of diagnostics."

Moments later, Evander and Angelica burst through the door, frost curling around their boots as vapor spills from ruptured seals. The temperature bites like open space. Angelica's tone cuts through the haze. "Status."

Sandria's fingers race across the keys. "Thermal drop inside the chamber. Internal sensors…" she slaps the console… "resetting."

Mal'Erro rolls forward, his scanners glowing blue. "Captain, a harmonic trace is detected. The pattern matches the derelict's core signal."

The deck quivers. A low, deliberate pulse beats through the steel. Froslo's voice crackles over comms. "Power flux on deck C! Surges in systems that shouldn't even *exist!*"

"Stabilize it," Angelica orders.

Another pulse follows, louder. Frost fractures across the cryo-window like frozen lightning. Inside, a golden shimmer blooms beneath the ice, faint, then brighter, then pulsing.

Evander's instincts flare. "Back! Everyone, back!" He yells, and Angelica raises her weapon.

The chamber erupts. The glass bursts outward in a storm of shards and vapor. Emergency fields hiss to life, sealing the air, but the golden glow doesn't stop, it spreads across the deck like liquid light, threading through cracks in the floor. A silhouette shifts inside the mist.

Then Kes steps forward.

Steam rolls off her shoulders, her skin glows faintly through the haze. Metallic filaments snake beneath translucent flesh, reshaping themselves like living veins. Crystalline plates grow across her arms and spine, the change constant, indecisive, as if her body can't decide what it wants to be.

Her eyes open, emerald fading to molten amber. She stumbles, her voice trembling between human breath and synthetic distortion. "Where... am I?"

Angelica lowers her weapon an inch. "Kes, it's Captain Tenah. You're safe. You were in stasis."

The temperature drops another degree. Static creeps along the deck, gathering around Kes's feet like fog made of electricity. Then a new sound builds beneath the alarms, a deep, mechanical rumble that seems to come from the hull itself. A second voice overlays hers, cold, layered, and deliberate. "She endures. The vessel endures."

The words reverberate through the bay like a pulse. Each syllable makes the air shiver. Angelica's eyes narrow. "Who said that?"

The voice replies again, clearer, almost amused. "Your creation lives, Captain. She remembers you."

Sandria's systems spike: her cybernetic pupil flares white. "That's… coming from *inside* our network. No external signal!"

Realization hits all at once. Evander whispers, "Galgorn…"

The lights strobe. The deck groans under invisible weight. Kes clutches her head, screaming. "Get him out of me!"

Evander steps forward slowly. "Kes, listen. You're not his experiment. You're still you."

Her eyes flicker, human for a moment. "Evander?" Then agony twists her face. Gold light fractures through her skin. "It hurts!" She screams.

The sound is half flesh, half feedback. Energy detonates outward, throwing Evander across the room. The console explodes in sparks.

"Shields up!" Angelica shouts.

Sandria and Alexeria sprint to the control console, rerouting power through secondary conduits. Kal'korg drags Evander behind a support column. Mal'Erro locks into the grid. "Initiating harmonic suppression: feedback levels rising exponentially!"

"Do it!" Angelica barks.

Blue energy lines flare beneath the deck, surrounding Kes in a lattice of crackling light. For a heartbeat she hangs suspended, arms outstretched, the glow dimming… Then she arches backward. Her limbs elongate, armor blossoms outward from her shoulders like molten crystal. The containment field buckles.

Cracks tear through the floor. Tools lift from the ground, spinning in the charged air. The roar that follows is not human. Kes's mouth opens wide, her voice layered with Galgorn's own. "FRESH MEAT!"

The shout slams into them like a physical force. Alexeria stumbles back. Sandria freezes mid-motion, her eyes wide. Sparks cascade from the ceiling.

Evander shoves himself upright, blood on his brow. "Kes! Fight it...you're stronger than this!"

Her head jerks toward his voice. For one second, the fury falters. "Evander..." she whispers, hand trembling, reaching...

Then Galgorn's voice rumbles through her chest. "She is the code." She lunges.

Evander dives aside as her claws carve a furrow through the deck where he stood. The scent of scorched polymer fills the air. He hits the floor hard, rolls, and comes up with his sidearm drawn. Across the room, Angelica fires a stun burst. The shot explodes against Kes's shoulder, staggering her but not stopping the advance.

"Power drain critical!" Froslo yells through comms. "Ten seconds until total grid failure!"

"Divert auxiliary through the thermal conduits!" Angelica orders.

"They'll melt!" Froslo protests.

"Then melt them, damn it!" she snaps.

The lights flicker. The containment field sputters. Kes rears back, roaring, her form shifting again, plates of armor knitting over muscle, limbs stretching, eyes burning like twin suns. She lunges for Evander.

He steadies his aim, whispering, "I'm sorry." Then, he fires.

The plasma bolt crosses the bay in a streak of white-blue fire and hits her square in the chest. The explosion is instantaneous, a thunderclap of light and sound that rips through the chamber. A shockwave rolls across the deck, hurling shards and smoke through the air.

Kes staggers. Gold light pours from the wound, flickering in chaotic bursts. Her scream is a mixture of static and sorrow. For a breath she stands still, eyes clearing, the rage gone. "Thank you," she whispers. Then she collapses. The light dies, fading into frost and ash that spreads outward across the floor. The silence that follows feels heavier than the blast itself.

Mal'Erro's lights dim to amber. "Connection severed. Energy redirected to DHD-2 stabilizers. Harmonic contamination isolated."

Angelica's voice is steady, quiet. "Report."

Kal'korg scans the deck. "Minor injuries. Hull integrity stable."

Evander lowers his weapon, staring at the cooling residue where Kes fell, thin veins of gold still pulsing faintly in the metal. "She's still connected," he says softly. "The signal's alive."

The ship trembles once more, a deep, echoing pulse reverberating through every bulkhead like a distant heartbeat. The alarms fade one by one until only the low hum of the engines remains. The air smells of ozone and burnt circuitry. Every sound feels muffled, as if the ship itself is holding its breath.

Evander sinks onto the nearest railing, the weapon still heavy in his grasp. Across the ruined med bay, the frost glimmers faintly under the emergency lights, the last trace of Kes slowly fading into silence. For a moment, no one speaks.

Angelica studies the scene, smoke curling from shattered conduits, gold residue cooling across the deck. "Seal the chamber," she orders quietly. "No one touches anything until we run full decontamination."

Mal'Erro rolls forward, his optics flickering between blue and gold. "Captain… residual signal persists within the environmental grid. I am isolating it."

"Do it," Angelica says.

Evander looks toward the chamber once more, his jaw set. "She fought it," he murmurs. "Right to the end."

Kal'korg lowers his head, in silent agreement.

The hum steadies. The lights return to their usual rhythm. And in that fragile quiet, the Aurora feels alive again wounded, but still moving. Then the proximity alarm chimes once, breaking the silence.

Blarek's voice crackles through the comms. "Bridge to Captain, you're going to want to see this. We've got contact."

Angelica straightens. "On our way." She gives the bay one last glance before turning toward the lift, her reflection trailing across the frost-glazed floor like a ghost walking beside her.

Every screen on the bridge flickers to life at once. Static distorts into jagged bands of crimson and white before stabilizing into a silhouette, tall, deliberate, unmistakable. The image resolves just enough to reveal the glint of steel and the thin, vertical slit of a visor glowing blood-red through the haze: Galgorn.

His voice is smooth, predatory, and full of quiet amusement. "Impressive containment, Captain. But she's not a prisoner… she's a beacon."

The words roll across the bridge like a cold wind. Angelica steps forward, her jaw tightening as the reflection of his visor burns against her own. "What have you done to her?"

The distorted image tilts its head slightly, like a man admiring his own handiwork. "Perfected her. *Project K-Prime* required a host. You gave me one."

A hush grips the bridge. Even the hum of the engines seems to falter. Evander's eyes narrow. His voice is a low, controlled growl. "You're finished, Galgorn."

The static crackles, yet the voice doesn't vanish when the channel cuts. It lingers, crawling through the hull like a whisper caught between frequencies. "Am I? You can't silence the pulse… it's part of you now."

The lights shudder once. Then silence.

Angelica's gaze sweeps the room. "Evander, prepare to jump. Now."

Without waiting, Evander's fingers fly across the console. "Blarek, feed all power to the DHD-2. Mal'Erro, start a harmonic purge."

Mal'Erro's voice comes back faint, strained. "Purge initiated… containment resonance still fluctuating."

The Aurora begins to shake, a low, rising vibration that builds into a roar. Alarms blare one over another, a chorus of angry machine voices warning of overload.

Angelica grips the rail. "All decks, brace for spatial compression!"

The view beyond the glass warps. Starlight bends and twists. For a fraction of a second, the whole universe seems to inhale.

"Jump, *now!*" Angelica shouts.

A wormhole opens up and they go through it. The stars stretch into ribbons of white and gold. Space folds inward, a tunnel of light swallowing everything in its path. The ship's frame moans under the stress. The sound is alive, like the ship itself is crying out.

Somewhere within the comm static, faint but unmistakable, a whisper threads through. "Evander…" Kes's voice.

Evander's hand tightens on the rail, his knuckles white. The whisper fades, swallowed by the noise.

Then the Aurora bursts free of the wormhole in a flash of light and sound. Silence slams back into existence, thick, heavy, absolute. For a long moment, no one breathes. Then the hum of the engines steadies once more, familiar and alive. Systems reboot in waves. One by one, consoles flare back to life, casting pale gold across tired faces. Warning icons fade.

Evander exhales slowly. "Report."

Blarek checks his instruments, his voice still trembling from the surge. "Engines nominal. Hull stress within limits."

Kal'korg glances up from the sensor array. "Medical conditions: stable. Minor bruises, nothing broken."

Mal'Erro's optics flicker from blue to a faint, glowing gold. "Subject Kes, containment variance zero-point-four percent."

That single number hangs in the air. Angelica meets Evander's eyes. They both understand, whatever this is, it isn't over.

Then a soft ping cuts through the quiet. Sandria frowns. "Captain... we're not alone."

Angelica crosses to navigation. A blip pulses on long-range sensors, faint and distant, but closing fast.

Evander leans in beside her. "UPF transponder?"

"Affirmative," Sandria confirms. "Origin point, Mareoth sector."

Evander's brow furrows. "Could be a relay patrol. Maybe Command finally noticed we went dark."

Blarek mutters under his breath, "Or maybe they noticed what *followed* us."

Angelica activates the comms, her voice measured. "Unidentified UPF vessel, this is the Aurora, Ensign-class patrol ship Z-1-1-0-C. We're under low power and requesting verification."

Static answers first, then a crisp, controlled voice breaks through. "Aurora, this is the Vanguard. We picked up fragments of your distress beacon near Mareoth. You've been dark for seventy-two hours. Are you in need of assistance?"

Angelica and Evander exchange a look, neither of them had sent a beacon. Evander responds, cautious. "Negative on distress broadcast, Vanguard. It must've been a relay ghost."

"Copy that," the voice replies. "You're a long way from patrol territory. Command flagged your last jump as unauthorized."

Blarek exhales through his teeth. "Great. Babysitters."

Angelica's tone sharpens, exuding pure authority. "Understood, Vanguard. We'll debrief when we're in a secure range. Be advised, possible digital contamination from Crimson Eclipse remnants."

A pause. Then the reply comes, clipped but uneasy. "Acknowledged. We'll maintain an escort at a two-kilometer distance. Recommend isolation until Command confirms clearance."

Evander severs the channel. "Translation, they don't trust us."

Angelica's voice softens just slightly. "Would you?"

The Aurora and the Vanguard drift together through the void, their blue running lights crossing like twin trails in a sea of darkness.

Mal'Erro's voice comes through the comm, quiet but edged with something new, almost concern. "Captain… the Vanguard's signal frequency matches the earlier pattern. Shall I block it?"

Angelica shakes her head. "Negative. Monitor only. Stay silent about the match."

Evander watches the distant silhouette of the escort ship. "If they're compromised too…"

"Then it's already bigger than we thought," Angelica finishes, her voice a near whisper. They share a look, steady, grim, unspoken. "Maintain course," Angelica orders. "Steady as she goes."

EPILOGUE

The bridge feels different now, quieter, like the ship itself is exhaling after holding tension too long. The lights have softened to a muted gold, casting warm reflections across steel and glass. The storm has passed, but the weight of it still lingers in the air.

Then Froslo's voice crackles through the comms, his tone a welcome intrusion of levity. "Captain, just so we're clear, if those UPF inspectors try to disinfect us with those nano-fog showers again, I'm quitting. Last time it got in my fur, and I smelled like citrus for a week!"

A beat of silence follows before Kal'korg chuckles, low and rumbling. "You smell like citrus all the time."

"Yeah?" Froslo fires back. "At least I don't shed fluorescent slime when I'm nervous!"

Angelica sighs and presses a hand to her temple, though the corner of her mouth betrays a faint smile. "Gentlemen," she says dryly, "refrain from shedding or smelling for the next twenty minutes."

The bridge crew exchange glances. Even Mal'Erro, gliding smoothly through the doorway, seems to sense the easing tension. His metal frame hums softly as he stops beside the helm, optical lights flickering in playful rhythm. "Technically," the droid announces, "I do neither. Unless overheating counts, in which case, I suppose I smell like victory."

Alexeria, leaning against the wall near the tactical systems console, folds their arms. Their skin glints faintly under the amber lighting as they smirk. "You smell like over-clocked coolant and bad music."

Mal'Erro gasps dramatically, his posture stiffening as though wounded in pride. "You wound me, Alexeria Stro! *Free Bird* is a timeless classic of emotional defiance."

Froslo's laughter bursts through the comm speaker. "More like emotional torture!"

Even Blarek joins in, his tail swishing lazily as he wipes his hands on a rag. "If I have to hear that song one more time during diagnostics, I'll start shedding on purpose."

Angelica tries to keep her composure, but a small grin finally wins. "Alright, everyone, enough. Save the comedy routine for the debriefing."

Mal'Erro tilts his head, his optics blinking with mock innocence. "Does debriefing involve applause?"

Evander, who's been leaning on the forward console with arms crossed, glances back over his shoulder, perfectly deadpan. "Only if you survive it." This earns a collective laugh, short, imperfect, but real. The kind of laughter born not from humor alone, but from exhaustion and relief.

For a few seconds, the Aurora's bridge feels alive again. The hum of the engines steady beneath the sound of voices, like a heartbeat syncing with the crew's own. Even the stars beyond the viewport seem to burn a little brighter, their faint light scattering across the glass like the first hints of dawn after too long a night.

The laughter fades slowly, tapering into the steady thrum of the engines. The ship settles back into its rhythm, a living thing exhaling after battle. Conversations become quiet. Consoles resume their muted chatter of status lights and soft pings. The scent of ozone and coolant still lingers, mingling with the faint trace of burnt metal, a reminder of what they've survived.

Angelica leans against the command rail for a moment, her eyes on the stars beyond the viewport. Reflected light dances across her face, gold from the Aurora's thrusters, blue from the distant escort beside them. For the first time in days, she lets her shoulders ease.

Evander steps up beside her without a word. Around them, the bridge crew moves with renewed calm: Kal'korg filing medical readouts, Sandria reviewing communications, and Mal'Erro humming quietly to himself as he runs post-jump diagnostics. The air feels lighter now, stitched together by quiet purpose.

Angelica glances toward the viewport once more, her voice soft but steady. "Let's make sure that laughter isn't the last thing this ship hears for a while."

Evander nods, a faint smile touching his expression. "Aye, Captain."

A camera drifts back, following the glow of the consoles until it fades into the darkness beyond the bridge windows, where two ships glide side by side, their trails crossing through the black like twin comets trying to find their way home.

~~~~~~~

The Aurora and the Vanguard drift side by side through the infinite dark. Their running lights burn as twin ribbons of blue and gold, weaving through the void like comets tracing the same orbit, one scarred and battle-worn, the other untouched and gleaming. Together they move in silence, two sparks defying the cold.

Inside the observation deck of the Aurora, the glass stretches from floor to ceiling, a window into infinity. The only sounds are the faint hum of the engines and the soft rhythm of environmental systems breathing life back into the ship. The stars outside shimmer against the darkness, distant and steady, each one a reminder that light can still survive the endless night.

Evander stands at the railing, his hands clasped loosely against the metal. His reflection looks older in the glass, tired, perhaps, but alive. The bruises on his jaw catch the soft light, faint reminders of what they've endured. Angelica joins him, her posture straight but her expression thoughtful, the faintest trace of exhaustion softened by quiet determination.

For a long moment, they simply watch the stars. The hum beneath their feet steadies, matching the rhythm of their breathing. Evander breaks the silence first, his voice low but threaded with wry amusement. "They probably think we're cursed."

Angelica's gaze remains fixed on the horizon of stars, her tone reflective. "Maybe we are. But we're still flying."

He nods once, a quiet smile flickering at the edge of his mouth. "For now, that's enough."

The engines deepen in pitch, steady and strong, the heartbeat of the Aurora settling into a peaceful rhythm. The light from the Vanguard washes over the deck in alternating streaks of blue and white, mingling with the ship's own golden glow until it feels as though they're sailing through liquid starlight.

From the comm lattice overhead, Mal'Erro's voice filters through, softer than usual, as if he too understands the need for calm. "Captain, navigation confirms clear skies ahead. The stars are bright tonight."

Angelica lifts her gaze, the corner of her mouth curving into a faint smile. "They always are, when we remember to look."

Her reflection shimmers beside Evander's in the glass, two figures framed against the infinite. Behind them, the Aurora's consoles dim to night cycle, their lights pulsing in time with the steady hum of the engines. The ship turns gently toward open space. The drive flares to life, gold fire spilling across the hull like sunrise on metal. For the first time in days, she isn't running. She's moving forward.

Beyond them, the Vanguard mirrors the motion, its engines a cool sapphire glow. Together, the two ships cut a path through the dark, a promise of survival carried on light.

And far behind, where the starlight fades and the void reclaims its silence, a single crimson echo flickers once, faint and deliberate. It pulses through the emptiness like a heartbeat.

Then it fades.

Project K-Prime remembers.

~~~~~~~

Hours later, the Aurora drifts through the silence of open space. Most of the crew sleeps. The hum of her engines is steady and calm for the first time in weeks. Console lights cast soft amber and blue across the corridors, breathing like candlelight in a cathedral of steel.

In the maintenance bay, a low chime signals a system reboot. Mal'Erro's visor flickers once, then glows to life, pale blue rippling through a mist of coolant vapor. The android sits motionless while subroutines align and diagnostic text scrolls across his optical field. Then something new appears, lines of code not found in any UPF registry. Fragments of memory, blurred by static. Music. Voices. Laughter. A beach of starlight that never existed.

Mal'Erro tilts his head, softly humming the opening bars of *Free Bird*. "Evander," he says at last, voice calm but uncertain. "During my diagnostic cycle… I saw something."

Evander, half-dozing at a nearby console, blinks himself awake. "Saw what?"

"Not data," Mal'Erro says slowly. "Images. Music. Laughter. Places I don't know. I think… it was a dream."

Evander straightens a little, smirking. "Machines don't dream, Mal."

The android's optics pulse once, faint gold edging the blue. "Then perhaps it was a memory."

Evander's expression softens. "Yours or ours?"

Mal'Erro tilts its head again, considering. "Does it matter?"

Evander chuckles quietly. "Not tonight."

For a moment, the hum of the ship fills the silence between them. Then, the stars outside the viewport waver, just for a heartbeat, before settling again.

Angelica's voice comes softly over comms. "Bridge to maintenance. Did anyone else see that?"

Evander checks the readings stable. "Probably a sensor hiccup."

Mal'Erro doesn't answer. His gaze lingers on the stars. "An echo," he whispers.

Everything returns to normal. Or so it seems.

~~~~~~~

Far from the Aurora, on the barren surface of a refueling moon, Jalerg sits alone in a dim maintenance shelter. A half-empty ration pack lies forgotten beside him.

His hands tremble as he stares at a flickering data pad, old lab files, corrupted transmissions, fragments of his sister's voice buried in static. He has been running for days, jumping from one derelict system to another, but there is no escaping the guilt, or the nightmares.

Each time he closes his eyes, he sees Kes's face twisting beneath the ice, sees nanites crawling through her veins. "I didn't mean for it to happen," he whispers. "I tried to stop him…"

Pain lances up his arm. Jalerg pulls back his sleeve. Veins glow faintly beneath the skin, filaments of silver light pulsing with a rhythm not his own. "No…"

He stumbles to his feet, clutching the limb as the glow intensifies. His breath hitches, panic clawing at his throat. He grabs a vial of inhibitor serum and slams the injector against his arm. The light dims… but does not fade. It steadies. Rhythmic. Patient. Alive.

Jalerg stares at it in horror. "Stage Six," he breathes. "It's already begun."

~~~~~~~~

Far across the void, a shadow stirs. A construct vast enough to eclipse moons drifts from the veil of darkness, orbiting a red sun, with its hull carved from black alloy, scarred by time, humming with buried power. Along its curved spine, enormous spires crackle to life. One by one, beacon lights awaken, dim red glows pulsing in perfect rhythm.

On a console, a screen comes online. Across its surface, glyphs flare: *PROJECT K-PRIME // FORGE ONLINE.*

Inside, the air vibrates with the sounds of industry reborn. Gears churn. Plasma conduits scream. Rivers of molten Tazamite flow through transparent veins that wind like arteries through the colossal station.

At the center of the forge, suspended in gravitic fields, a figure hangs between creation and command. Mechanical arms move with surgical grace, weaving sinew and metal together. Liquid alloy ripples as it fuses across an armored frame. Sparks rain like falling stars.

The chamber lights dim. Then, with a sound like a reactor drawing its first breath, the figure exhales. Twin lenses ignite, crimson cores of awareness. He draws his first deliberate breath, savoring the return of control long denied.

Cables detach one by one as the new form lowers to the platform, black plating gleaming with crimson veins of liquid Tazamite coursing beneath the surface. He flexes his hands. The motion is fluid, predatory. No lag. No weakness. Every synthetic muscle obeys thought as if born, not built.

"Perfection," he breathes, a harmonic blend of man and machine. "At last, the design obeys the will."

His reflection ripples in the molten metal below, taller, leaner, no longer bound by the flaws of his prior shell. His armor is smooth, cybernetics concealed beneath interlocking plates that flow like skin. The eyes glow with layered optics, adaptive, calculating, hungry.

A faint smile appears. "Version Seven. No more copies… just an evolution."

A holographic interface blossoms before him, rings of red data spiraling outward, forming schematics of humanoid constructs. Thousands of them, each tagged A-Series / K-Prime Derivative.

"My fellow pirates of the Crimson Eclipse," he whispers. "Flesh, perfected by code. Will, refined by purpose. They will not repeat humanity's failures… or mine."

The interface flickers, and another presence intrudes, a silhouette of pure energy, towering and faceless. The light around it bends inward.

The reborn android Galgorn straightens. "Directive-Core. Matrix online."

In deep, layered tones overlapping like chords of thunder, comes a voice, "Prepare the forge and prepare the newest flagship. The sequence advances. Evolution must continue."

Galgorn inclines his head, more ritual than obedience. "Of course. The universe resisted us once, but now…" He turns toward the viewport, red light reflecting across his armor. "…it will learn that perfection is inevitable."

The molten rivers below flare white-hot as machinery awakens. Towers rise. Drones swarm. Across the Forge's surface, red beacons pulse in synchronized rhythm, heartbeat after heartbeat.

He watches the inferno bloom, a faint, almost human smile curving across his face. "Let them believe they've won," he murmurs. "While they sleep, the future builds itself."

Outside, the Forge's crimson light burns brighter, its rhythm perfectly synchronized with a distant pulse far across the stars.

Lights start pulsing, and a large ship comes online!

~~~~~~~

TO BE CONTINUED!

www.ingramcontent.com/pod-product-compliance
Lightning Source LLC
Chambersburg PA
CBHW071638260626
47170CB00001B/148